"We bookhounds owe an immeasurable debt of gratitude to Max Allan Collins for writing *The Legend of Caleb York*. The story is based upon an unproduced screenplay that Mickey Spillane wrote for his friend John Wayne. Collins has added some meat and bones to what was obviously a potential customized story for Wayne. The result is a lot of fun . . . Collins is respectful of his source material, and he honors the western genre with an old-fashioned Oater that might have once made a pretty damn good film. Collins has not only given us another Mickey Spillane story but he pays tribute to John Wayne with his characterization of Caleb York. Max Allan Collins is one of the great pros writing adventure novels. Collins deserves the lion's share of the credit here for taking a screenplay that's over fifty years old and turning it into a solid prose entertainment. The plot is a stylized variation of 'a stranger rode into town one day . . .'—a tad traditional, but exciting nonetheless. The book is easy to read and fairly short, and that works in its favor. Saddle up, pilgrims."
—**Thomas McNulty, Dispatches from the Last Outlaw**

"A complete story by Mickey Spillane, with Max Allan Collins putting his considerable skills into turning it into a novel . . . Recommended for western lovers."
—**Randy Johnson, Not the Baseball Pitcher**

MICKEY SPILLANE
AND
MAX ALLAN COLLINS

The LEGEND OF CALEB YORK

PINNACLE BOOKS
Kensington Publishing Corp.
www.kensingtonbooks.com

PINNACLE BOOKS are published by

Kensington Publishing Corp.
119 West 40th Street
New York, NY 10018

Copyright © 2015 Mickey Spillane Publishing LLC

All Kensington titles, imprints, and distributed lines are available at special quantity discounts for bulk purchases for sales promotions, premiums, fund-raising, educational, or institutional use. Special book excerpts or customized printings can also be created to fit specific needs. For details, write or phone the office of the Kensington sales manager: Kensington Publishing Corp., 119 West 40th Street, New York, NY 10018, attn: Sales Department; phone 1-800-221-2647.

PINNACLE BOOKS and the Pinnacle logo are Reg. U.S. Pat. & TM Off.

ISBN-13: 978-0-7860-3614-1
ISBN-10: 0-7860-3614-1

First mass market paperback printing: May 2016

10 9 8 7 6 5 4 3 2 1

Printed in the United States of America

First electronic edition: May 2016

ISBN-13: 978-0-7860-3615-8
ISBN-10: 0-7860-3615-X

For Bill Crider—
best of the West

"Heroes never die.
John Wayne isn't dead.
You can't kill a hero."

—Mickey Spillane

HOW THE LEGEND OF
CALEB YORK BEGAN

An introductory note from the co-author

It's been my honor and pleasure, over the past several years, to complete a number of suspense novels begun by Mickey Spillane, the most famous and popular American mystery novelist of the twentieth century.

I began, as so many did, as Mickey's fan. Over the years, as I became a professional fiction writer myself, we became friends and at times collaborators. Shortly before his death in 2006, Mickey asked me to complete the Mike Hammer novel he was working on (*The Goliath Bone*, 2008), should he not be able to. Around the same time, he instructed his wife Jane to conduct "a treasure hunt" after his passing, and to gather any other unpublished material of his and turn it over to me—"Max will know what to do." I can imagine no greater honor.

After completing *The Goliath Bone*, my first order of business was five novels featuring Mickey's signature character, tough detective Mike Hammer, that Mickey had set aside, as well as two other non-Hammer suspense novels. These were substantial manuscripts of one hundred pages or more, often with plot and character notes. Currently I am developing Hammer novels from shorter but still significant unfinished works in Mickey's files.

In addition to these stories-in-progress were several unproduced screenplays by Mickey, with the potential to become novels. One of these was of particular interest—*The Saga of Caleb York*, a Western that he developed for John Wayne.

Mickey and the Duke (and Mickey knew him well enough to call him that) were great friends. Wayne cast Mickey as a detective version of his superstar mystery-writer self in the 1954 film *Ring of Fear*. Backing Mickey up in *Ring of Fear* were legendary character actor Pat O'Brien, John Ford stock-company player Sean McClory, lion tamer Clyde Beatty (whose circus provided the setting), and lovely Marian Carr, who would go on to co-star in director Robert Aldrich's celebrated Mike Hammer adaptation, *Kiss Me Deadly* (1955).

Wayne himself did not appear in *Ring of Fear*, producing it (with Robert Fellows) for his Batjac company, which was responsible for such Wayne-starring classics as *Island in the Sky* (1953) and *The High and the Mighty* (1954).

Problems during the filming of *Ring of Fear* led Wayne to ask Mickey to do a rewrite on a screenplay by other hands (Paul Fix, Philip MacDonald, and director James Edward Grant). The Duke, fearful that the Cinema-Scope picture was turning into a circus documentary, wanted Mike Hammer's daddy to tighten the story and provide new, more suspenseful scenes. Mickey did, but refused payment (and co-writer screen credit). By way of thanks, Wayne had a brand-new Jaguar dropped off in front of Spillane's home in Newburgh, New York, the white convertible tied in a big ribbon with a card reading, *Thanks—Duke.*

Now and then, Wayne would bring Mickey in to view rough cuts of films to provide notes. Mick recalled sitting with famed director William Wellman in one such Hollywood screening, specifically of Wayne's money-pit pet project, *The Alamo* (1960). When the lights came up, Mickey's suggestion to Duke was "change the ending." Astonished, Wayne—who played Davy Crockett in the picture—said, "Mickey, we can't change the ending! It's the Alamo." Mickey's response was: "Nobody wants to pay two dollars to watch a bunch of Mexicans kill John Wayne."

However un-PC Mickey's critique might be, he had a point. The disappointing returns on the Wayne-directed *Alamo* were the downfall of the actor's Batjac production company. Wayne embarked on a succession of highly successful pictures (starting with *North to Alaska* that same year), but for producers other than himself.

Which is why the screenplay Mickey wrote for Wayne and Batjac was never produced (apparently, no money ever changed hands). Written around 1959, the screenplay finds the famous mystery writer drawing upon the "Print the legend" West of John Ford and Howard Hawks (set in fictional Trinidad, New Mexico, in the early 1880s). It's easy to imagine rolling into a movie theater in the late fifties or early sixties and seeing Caleb York's saga unfold.

You are free to picture John Wayne as the stranger who rides into town, though that's hardly a requirement—at Batjac, Wayne produced films starring Glenn Ford, Robert Mitchum, and, of course, Mickey Spillane. The great Batjac production *Seven Men From Now* (1956) represented a Burt Kennedy script Wayne sent to Randolph Scott, initiating the much-admired series of Scott Westerns directed by Budd Boetticher (several others of which were also written by Kennedy).

Cast the hero here as you like, in the movie theater of your mind. Both Wayne and Scott would work fine. But who knows? Maybe Batjac would have hired Ford or Mitchum, or perhaps Joel McCrea or Audie Murphy. Remember, there are no budgetary concerns for the reader. Nor does the passage of time prevent you from casting this as you like—Maverick-era James Garner? No problem. Sam Elliott? Good choice. Gary Cooper? You can afford him, too. Both Clint Eastwood and Lee Van Cleef are available in the Bijou of the brain. So is an idealized version of yourself, which was how Mickey always wanted readers to envision Mike Hammer.

So I'll leave you with Mickey's words, which he often inscribed in books he signed to fans he described as his "customers": Have fun!

—Max Allan Collins

CHAPTER ONE

Everybody called it Boot Hill, but there was no hill about it—not even a rise on the flat, dusty ground just off the rutted road half a mile out of Trinidad, New Mexico.

The spot had been chosen because of a resilient mesquite tree that provided some color and shade, but this scrubby patch of earth otherwise had nothing to recommend it. For serving a town of less than three hundred, this was a well-populated cemetery, wooden crosses clustered with the occasional flat tombstones popping up like road markers. On this April morning, a breeze flapped hat brims and bandanas into flags and stirred dust into foot-hugging ghosts. Like diffident mourners, distant buttes lurked, turned a light rust color by a sun still on the rise, faces of their steep cliffs sorrowful with the dark shadows of erosion.

Willa Cullen, her father's only daughter—only

offspring—by rights should have worn a Sunday dress, its hem weighted down with sewn-in buckshot to fight the wind. But she was in a red-plaid shirt and denim trousers and boots with stirrup-friendly heels, the kind of work clothes worn by the handful of her papa's ranch hands that could be spared to attend the small, sad graveside service for Bud Meadow.

Reverend Caldwell from Trinidad's church, Missionary Baptist, presided over this congregation of half-a-dozen cowhands, their boss, his daughter, and a dead boy in a pine box in its fresh hole. No townsfolk were present.

No surprise, really. Nobody knew Bud very well. He'd drifted in looking for work, Papa had given it to him, and come first pay, end of the month, Bud had gotten himself shot outside the Victory Saloon.

Trinidad had a reputation for looking the other way when cowhands came in on those particular Friday nights. It became routine for any business—save the Victory, the two restaurants, and the barbershop—to board up their windows till the boys got it out of their systems. In front, the affected businesses just stacked the lumber up under the windows along the boardwalks.

But Bud had mouthed off to the sheriff, and the sheriff had shot him down in the street. Funny how only the Cullen cowhands seemed to wind up that way—half a dozen were already buried here on Boot Hill. Now among them was a Meadow, planted but never to blossom.

Who were his parents? Willa wondered. *Did he have brothers or sisters? Friends forged on trail drives?*

They would never know. No date of birth, no full name. Just a white wooden cross, freshly painted but soon to be windblown and blistered.

Willa was a pretty thing but not delicate, near tall as her father but with her late Swede mother's hourglass figure and also the same straw-yellow hair worn up and braided back. She had been called a tomboy in her youth, but was too much of a woman for that now, though she often wore ranching-style riding apparel like today.

She meant no disrespect to the late Bud Meadow. She just knew she needed to be dressed to ride, though her father—in his black Sunday suit and string tie and felt hat—had brought the big buggy, drawn by a pair of horses, with plenty of room for her to sit beside.

Really, this was about Papa's stubbornness. In buggy or wagon, he refused to let his daughter take the reins, leaving her to ride alongside on Daisy, her calico, and surreptitiously guide the hitched-up horses, should Papa need the help he refused. Leaving the hard-packed, rutted road to take the turn into Boot Hill was an example of that.

But for a blind man, George Cullen got around well.

Her papa's blindness had come on gradual over these five years past, until now his unseeing stare had a disturbing milkiness. He would wince and narrow his eyes and widen them, as if that would somehow summon vision that was only a memory now. Still, their world was small enough—ranch, road, town—that Papa could manage. Mostly.

When the service was over, and the grave diggers gone to shoveling, Papa sent Whit Murphy, his foreman, back with the boys, and—with Willa's subtle help—steered the buggy back onto the road and headed into town. Whit had offered to come along and several others chimed in their willingness, too.

It had been Willa who discouraged them.

"If just Pa and me ride in," she said firmly, "there'll be no trouble. You boys chaperone us, we could be back out here at another service tomorrow. Maybe more than one."

Whit, lanky and weathered with a Texas-style Stetson and droopy, dark mustache, only nodded, touched his brim, and rode off, the rest following.

It didn't have to be said: a blind man and a girl could ride in and, no matter what transpired, ride back out again. Even Sheriff Harry Gauge had to respect *some* things.

The buggy and its calico escort took it easy down Main Street's row of facing frame buildings. At this end of Main, the white wooden church seemed to stare all the way down at its bookend, the barewood livery stable whose high-peaked hayloft mirrored Missionary Baptist's steeple. The street itself wore a layer of sand, carted in from the nearby Purgatory River, to hold down the dust. Wooden awnings shaded the boardwalks, a few women in gingham out shopping, encouraged by the cool breeze, always welcome in this hot dry climate.

All very civilized, Willa thought.

Hardware store, apothecary shop, barber, hotel with restaurant, mercantile store, bank, telegraph office, saloon. From Main's stem several streets shot off and modest houses hid back behind the tall false-fronted clapboard stores and the occasional brick building. Trinidad existed to serve the ranchers, large and small, who lived and worked in the surrounding area. The population here was merchants and their employees. Nicely dressed, genteel folk who depended on the rough men and frontier women who made making a living in this hard country possible for those softer than themselves.

Down toward the livery stable, with its blacksmith forge out front, was a scarred adobe building that had once been a Mexican army outpost and still sat apart from the rest of the town, across from a scattering of adobes, the homes and businesses of the town's modest Mexican contingent.

Seated under an awning that had been added onto the tile roof, watching the world go by, were two big rough-looking men in their thirties, one leaning back in his wooden chair with his boot heels catching the railing.

Willa and her father were only halfway down Main when her father asked her, "You see him?"

Papa meant Sheriff Harry Gauge.

"I see him, Papa."

"Where is he, child?"

"Where he always is, when he's not in that saloon."

"In front of his office."

"In front of his office."

"Anyone with him?"

"Just that nasty deputy. Rhomer."

"Let's go on down, then."

She frowned at the unseeing face as they kept up their leisurely pace. "Papa, you said the telegraph office. We're almost there. Let's do your errand and go about our business."

"Willa, make sure I stop right beside him."

"Papa, please . . . let it be."

"You heard me, girl."

When they got to the sheriff's office, Willa cleared her throat just a little and her father brought the buggy to a stop.

Sheriff Harry Gauge took his feet off the rail and let the chair and his boots hit the plank porch, purposely loud. Gunshot loud.

Her papa flinched. "You there, Gauge?"

Gauge was a big blond man with ice-blue eyes, six-two, broad-shouldered, rugged but clean-shaven, with a cleft chin and a propensity for smiling at jokes he never shared. He wore a wide-brimmed middle-creased Stetson, a spotted cowhide vest, and a dark blue shirt with a badge, his dark duck trousers tucked into his finely tooled boots. The Colt .44 hung loosely at his side, its tie-down strap dangling.

Seated near him was Deputy Vint Rhomer, a redheaded, red-bearded man even bigger than Gauge. Eyes so dark blue they almost looked black, Rhomer was in a store-bought gray shirt with sleeve garters and badge and a buckskin vest, denims tucked in his boots. His .44 was tied down with a holster strap keeping the weapon in place.

"Right here, Cullen," the sheriff said, his voice low and mellow, and a little thick—he was chewing tobacco. "Mornin', Miss Cullen."

Willa gave the sheriff the smallest nod she could muster.

Her father's face was stony with rage, but his voice didn't show it. "Thought you might make it out to the burial, Sheriff. Seems the least you might do."

"I didn't know Mr. Meadow that well."

"Knew him well enough to kill him."

Gauge said nothing.

His tone still casual, her father nonetheless pressed: "There was no need to shoot that boy down in the street. Like a rabid dog. None at all."

"He *was* a rabid dog, Cullen. Wild kid, liquored up. Threatened me when I asked for his gun."

"Bud was no gunfighter. Just a kid I give a job."

An edge came into her father's voice. "But that was enough for you to cut him down, wasn't it? That he worked for *me*."

Gauge turned his head and spat a black tobacco stream. "Nothing to do with it, Cullen. He just had a big smart mouth. Big enough to get him killed."

Now the rage in her father's voice was a storm rattling at windows. "You're no sheriff! You don't even *sound* like a sheriff."

Gauge spat again, put his shrug into his voice: "Well, the good folks of Trinidad elected me one, just the same."

"Because they're scared as hell!" Her father's anger unsettled the horses some. "Scared of you, scared to death of you and your badge and your whole damn bunch!"

"Cullen . . . a lady's present."

Willa said, "Don't either of you hold back on my account."

Gauge grinned. "A sheriff needs deputies, Mr. Cullen. I rounded up some reliable men, hard men for a hard job. No 'bunch.' " He shrugged again, and his eyes went to Willa. "I seem to do all right by this town."

Her father snorted a laugh. "Like hell."

The sheriff shifted in his wooden chair, scraping the wooden porch. "Cullen, you're riled because that kid worked for you. I can understand that. But you didn't see the shooting, did you? You wasn't even in town. And if you was, well . . .

you wouldn'ta seen it, anyway. You don't see *anything*, do you, old man?"

The insult—however true, it *was* an insult—hung in the air like a sour smell.

Finally her father said, "I *can* see that you're trying to take over all the good grazing land around here. And so do the 'good folks of Trinidad.'"

Gauge was grinning again. "And what if they do? What would any of *them* do about it? Storekeepers. Bankers. Cooks and barkeeps. Children all, who need a strong hand."

Her father was trembling with anger now. "One day it *will* happen."

"What will, Cullen?"

Papa's smile had something terrible in it. "You'll run into a real one. A *man*. The kind who built this country."

"Like *you*, you mean?"

"Like I *was*. Yes, I'm an old man. A blind old man. And you are damn lucky I am, because could I see, I would find no greater pleasure than cutting you down like you did that boy."

Gauge laughed and so did his deputy.

The sheriff spat another black stream, then said, "Old man, even with eyes, you'd be out of luck. I am just too damn fast for you or any man. You haven't *seen*, but you've surely heard."

"I've heard," her father said. His smile remained. "That's why I wouldn't bother tryin' to face you down. Wouldn't be worth it. Why, I'd just get you from a dark alley with a blast of buckshot."

Gauge's expression seemed to drip delight. "In the *back*, old man? Bushwhack me like that? Where's your pride?"

"No pride or shame in killing a snake. You just kill the damn things. Blow their evil heads off."

Gauge and his deputy laughed some more.

Then the sheriff said, "Those were the days, right, Cullen? Back before law and order came west, and men like me were around to keep the peace. But, old man—them days are over."

"Not for you they're not." Now her father's smile was gone and the cold-rage mask was back. "Not for you. For *you*, Sheriff? 'Those days' are just about to start."

With confidence belying his sightlessness, her father shook the reins and guided the two horses around and rode back up Main. Willa smiled back at Gauge as they left, giving him a bigger nod now.

"This is good right here, Papa," she said. "Right here is fine."

They had stopped outside the telegraph office.

Deputy Vint Rhomer had not been a lawman long, and he might have seen the irony in having shot and killed two deputies himself, in his outlaw days, had he understood the meaning of the word.

The redheaded deputy, looking down the street where Willa Cullen was hitching her calico, said,

"What the hell's he *talkin'* about, Gauge? *What's* about to start?"

The sheriff spat black liquid. "No idea, Rhomer. Old coots like that never make no sense. Goin' blind turned him loco, maybe."

Rhomer shook his head. "He had *somethin'* on his mind. You saw his face. He must've been a tough one, in his day."

"Only this ain't his day."

Willa was helping her father down from the buggy.

"Pretty girl," Rhomer commented. "Looks like a good time to be had."

Gauge gave his deputy a smile with a sneer in it. "Watch what you say, son."

Rhomer scratched his bearded cheek. "Huh?"

The sheriff put his feet back up on the railing, rocked back. "You're talkin' about the woman I love."

Rhomer snorted. "You don't love nothin' but money, Gauge. Money and land. And if you need *lovin'*, there's always Lola."

"Maybe. But one day soon, I am going to own that Cullen filly."

The deputy studied the sheriff. "Own her like you will the *Bar-O* . . . someday?"

The Bar-O was Old Man Cullen's spread.

The sheriff gave a slow couple of nods. "Just like that, Rhomer. Like that and every piece of land worth havin' around these parts."

Horses clopped. A wagon rolled by. A fly buzzed

them. Willa Cullen and her father were talking out-side the telegraph office. Maybe arguing. Maybe not.

"How will you manage that, Gauge? You can't *buy* that kind of female. Not like you buy an hour with a saloon gal you can't."

Gauge had a distant look, like he was gazing into the future. "There's where you're wrong, Vint. I'll buy her and she'll welcome it."

"Come on, Gauge. . . ."

"Willa Cullen was born on that ranch and she wants to stay on that ranch, and her old man can't run it forever. He'll just get older and sicker and pretty soon she'll have to look after him. Day will come, she'll be happy for me to buy the Bar-O . . . and her."

The Cullen girl and her father were going into the telegraph office.

Looking that direction, Rhomer said, "Tell you, that old boy is up to something."

Gauge spat a tobacco stream. "Maybe you're right."

"I know I'm right."

"Okay, then. You're a lawman. You're suspicious. Do what a lawman does. Go see what he's up to."

Rhomer nodded, got to his feet and headed down there, leaving the man he worked for to laze in the morning sun, hat over his eyes, boots on the rail.

When the deputy stepped into the small telegraph office, Ralph Parsons, the scrawny, bespectacled operator behind the counter, was looking at a slip of paper as if it were his own death warrant. More likely, it was a form for a wire that the old man's daughter must have written out for her father.

Nervously looking up from the paper slip, the operator said, "Mr. Cullen . . . this is nothing I can do, in good conscience. . . ."

"I said *send* it," the old man said, his daughter at his side. "Never mind your damn conscience."

"Please, Mr. Cullen! There are regulations. . . ."

Rhomer strode over and snatched the slip from the operator's hands. "Let's see that," he said.

The deputy had book learning enough to decipher the wire Old Man Cullen intended to send, though he read slowly and moved his lips.

To Raymond L. Parker, it read, *Kansas City, Kansas. Use the ten thousand you hold for me to hire Caleb York or other top shootist to kill Harry Gauge this city. George Cullen.*

Rhomer shoved his face in the old man's. "Are you plumb *crazy,* Cullen? Who's this Parker, anyway?"

"Old business partner of mine," Cullen said coolly. "Not that it's any of *your* business."

Rhomer was almost nose to nose with the coot now. "You wantin' to kill the *sheriff* ain't my *business*? I really oughta let you send this damn thing! You'd find out soon enough there ain't any top gun who can take down Harry Gauge! The fastest around have faced him and died before a gun cleared a holster."

The old man's upper lip curled back over a smile. "Not Caleb York."

Staring into the milky eyes, Rhomer said, "That's *another* reason why I oughta let you send this cockeyed thing."

"What is?"

"Caleb York is dead." Rhomer laughed in the old man's face. "Wes Banion *killed* him two years ago in Silver City! You are way behind the times, old man."

Cullen swallowed, then shrugged. "Then we'll send for Wes Banion."

Rhomer gave the old boy another horselaugh. "Gauge has taken down faster guns than Banion!"

"That right?"

The deputy pointed toward the front windows. "Jack Reno stood down Banion, winged him and walked away. Two months ago, Reno died right out on that street there, bullet in the heart, courtesy of our sheriff. You could've said hello to Reno out at Boot Hill."

Cullen appeared unimpressed. "Then let me send my wire. Willa, take that form from the deputy here, and revise it—cross out 'Caleb York' and make it 'Wesley Banion.' "

Rhomer sputtered, "Just because Banion wouldn't bother Gauge none don't mean I'm lettin' you *send* this thing! No, sir. You and your pretty daughter need to go back out to the Bar-O and milk a damn cow or somethin'."

Cullen leaned even closer and now the two men's noses did indeed touch. "Give that to my daughter."

"Old man, you best—"

Then Rhomer felt something nudge him in the belly.

"Look down, Deputy," the old man said, teeth bared in an awful grin.

Rhomer glanced down at the derringer shoved in his gut.

"Even a blind man can't miss at this range," Cullen said casually. "Daughter, revise that wire! Deputy Rhomer, if you don't mind . . . ?"

Shaken, Rhomer handed the piece of paper to the girl, who seemed half-terrified, half-amused. At the counter, she found a pencil and did as her father bade.

Rhomer and the blind man stared at each other.

"Done, Papa!"

"Ralph—send that."

The operator said, "Mr. Cullen, really . . ."

Willa said, "You heard the man, Ralph. That derringer has two barrels, you know."

Ralph sighed. "Yes, ma'am."

They stood while the operator keyed in the message.

Cullen said, "I don't think we'll be needing your assistance any longer, Deputy. Thanks for being such a fine servant of the public."

Face red under his red beard, Rhomer backed away.

As the deputy opened the door, jangling its bell, the old man said, "Maybe you'd better tell Sheriff Gauge that Wes Banion is coming to town. Or . . . someone like him."

From the doorway, Rhomer said, "Oh, I'll tell him, all right, Cullen."

The blind man swung the small deadly gun toward right where Rhomer stood. "Make that *Mister* Cullen. My taxes help pay your salary, Deputy. Something to keep in mind. You will tell Gauge?"

"I'll tell him, Mr. Cullen," Rhomer said.

Outside, heart pounding, the deputy considered going back in, .44 in hand, and arresting that old buzzard and maybe that roll-in-the-hay daughter of his, too.

But the wire had been sent, the damage done, and the sheriff needed to be told.

And anyway, Rhomer rarely killed anybody without the sheriff's say-so.

CHAPTER TWO

Just before noon, Willa and her father made it back home without further incident, riding in under the log arch from which hung a chain-hung plaque bearing a bold line above a big *O*—the carved brand of the Bar-O.

Their spread was no empire, though the largest of those remaining ranches not yet swallowed up in Sheriff Gauge's landgrab. Washed in bright sunshine were corrals left and right, two barns, a rat-proof grain crib, a log bunkhouse, and a cookhouse with hand pump out front, a long wooden bench lined with tin washbasins on its awning-shaded porch. The main building was a sprawling log-and-stone affair, added onto several times, the only really impressive structure among the scattering of ranch buildings. The cowhands were off working the beeves, giving the place a deserted look, with only the plume of smoke from the cookhouse chimney indicating otherwise.

Willa twirled Daisy's reins around the hitch rail in front of the house, and when she turned, lanky Whit Murphy was there, helping her father down from the buggy. She was not surprised that their foreman stayed behind to help them in and see if there had been trouble in town.

"I'll tend to this," Whit said, indicating he'd drive the rig over to the barn and get the horses into their stalls.

"Come inside, Whit," Papa said, "when you're done. Something you need to know about."

Whit nodded, and began walking the horses and buggy toward the barn. He glanced back at Willa with a searching look and she responded with one that told the foreman, *He's gone and done it now.*

Papa needed no help up the broad wooden steps to cross the plank porch to the elaborate cutglass and carved-wood front door that her mother had bought in Mexico a decade or more ago. They entered a living room, where only occasional touches of the late Kate Cullen lingered, finely carved Spanish-style furniture sharing space with rustic carpentry by her father's hand. This chamber remained overwhelmingly a male domain—beamceilinged with hides on the floor and mounted deer heads on the walls. A formidable stone fireplace had a Sharps rifle on one side and a Winchester on the other, each cradled in mortar-mounted upturned deer hooves turned gun racks.

Her father had come west with a horse and that Sharps rifle, and buffalo hunting had made him the seed money from which the Bar-O grew.

Soon Papa and Whit, sipping at china cups of coffee she'd gotten them, sat in the twin Indian-blanket cushioned rough-wood chairs that faced the fireplace as if it were roaring and not unlit since February. This, of course, allowed Willa to sit on the hearth between the two men, able to face either.

She knew very well that they did not consider her their equal. But she also knew they would tolerate her presence, and even give consideration to any opinion of hers, as the sole heir to this ranch. That she still wore the morning's riding apparel somehow strengthened her position.

And she knew, though she did not encourage it, that Whit had notions of his own about Willa and the ranch—not the gross ambitions of a Harry Gauge, but the dreams of a ranch hand who had risen to foreman.

Whit said nothing as her father described sending his telegram, the old man in funereal black relishing relating the confrontation with Deputy Vint Rhomer. But the foreman's long expression spoke volumes, as he sat there in knotted neck bandana, work shirt and Levi's, bowed legs akimbo, turning his tan high-beamed Carlsbad hat in his hands like a wheel.

When Papa stopped speaking, Whit said, "All due respect, Mr. Cullen, but you don't know what you're gettin' yourself into."

Papa was bareheaded, too, his white hair as thin as grass that cattle had finished with. He frowned at his foreman, and you would swear he could see the man.

"I paid you the respect of sharing this with you, Whit. Now you do *me* the service of sparing me any disapprovin' comments. You can just stay out of it. It's done."

Whit shook his head, hat turning in his hands more quickly now. "You're beggin' for a wide-open range war, Mr. Cullen . . . and that puts me in it already. You know how outnumbered we are? Gauge has all them deputies—outlaws to the man—and his ranch hands look like he emptied out a hoosegow to hire 'em."

Her father snorted a laugh. "You think you're telling me something new? Ever since Gauge shouldered his way into that town, we've *been* at war. For how long? Near two years now!"

Whit nodded, then remembered his boss couldn't see and added, "Two years, more or less, yes, sir."

Papa shook his head. "Bud Meadow makes seven of our men buried out there in that excuse for a cemetery. Seven dead in this war, and who knows how many head rustled."

Hands on her knees, Willa said, "That's a good reason to appeal to the authorities again, Papa."

"Is it girl?" her father said, turning his milky gaze her way. "And what will the 'authorities' say after I tell them my sad tale? What they *always* do! That under territorial law, Gauge *is* the duly constituted authority in these parts."

"That just can't be possible, Papa."

"It's very damn possible, daughter. So far, everything Gauge has done—taking over the other spreads, buying out businesses in town—is *legal* in the eyes of the law."

Whit was nodding. "Any . . . what's the word I hear you use for Gauge's tactics, Mr. Cullen? 'Intimation'?"

"It's called 'intimidation,' Whit."

"Well, *I* call it 'muscle and murder,' but Gauge and his crowd have a way of doin' it on the sly. Strikin' under cover of night like the damn bandits they are. . . . Excuse the language, Miss Gauge."

Willa just smiled a little, sadly. "Language, I can excuse."

Papa said, "Whit is right, girl. Gauge is an animal, but he's a smart one. So if he's going to operate outside the law, even while he poses at representing it, we'll play this game *his* dirty way."

She was shaking her head, rolling her eyes. "Papa, that makes us no better than him."

"We're better than that buzzard on our worst day."

She spread her hands, her words for her father but her eyes on Whit. "Go down to his level, and what will happen to us? Look what happened to Peterson, Reese, and the rest of the ranchers!"

Papa said, "They just rolled over for Gauge. Not one stood up to him. And if *we* don't stand up, it'll happen to us."

Straightening, Whit said, "Every one of the boys will be right there with you, Mr. Cullen. With you all the way. But . . . we only number fifteen, and we ain't gunhands."

Papa swung his gaze toward the foreman. "And that is why I sent for one."

Then the spooky eyes were on Willa again.

His voice softened, but there was nothing gentle about his tone. "Daughter . . . must I remind you what Harry Gauge wants the most out here at the Bar-O?"

That hung in the air like acrid smoke.

Then she said, "I know that all too well, Papa. He's *told* me. And I gave him my answer, too."

Color had come into Whit's tanned face. "Somebody oughta *kill* that filthy son of a—"

"That," her father said, "is the idea."

Willa said to Whit, "He's a filthy animal, all right. But for all his men and land, he's *still* not big enough to touch the Bar-O. And, sure as sin, he isn't big enough to touch me."

Her father said, "He'll only get bigger, girl. He'll

own all the land around us and we'll be choked off by what he's managed to do."

The old man shifted in the rustic chair he'd built so long ago; it creaked as if it were his own aging bones. But the hard young man he'd been was somehow still in that face and the set of his shoulders.

"But before our good sheriff can do that," Papa said, "my old pard Parker will find the right man and send him to us." He sighed, shook his head. "I only wish it could be Caleb York. . . ."

Whit said, "You're lucky it *ain't* Caleb York . . . if you'll forgive me sayin', sir."

Papa frowned at his foreman. "Fool talk, Whit! York was the fastest gun alive, best of 'em all! He'd be *perfect* for the job."

"No. All due respect, sir, but no. Caleb York was no hired gun. Oh, he was a killer, all right . . . but in his own way." Whit shrugged. "Not that it matters. Surprised you hadn't heard he was dead, Mr. Cullen. Common knowledge."

"Is that right?"

"It's right, sir. They say Banion killed Caleb York near Silver City. A good two year ago."

Papa's jaw muscles worked. "That's exactly why I told Parker to send Banion."

Willa scooted forward on the stone hearth. "But that man *is* a murderer!"

"So is Harry Gauge, girl. So is Harry Gauge."

Her father almost snapped at her: "You think I wouldn't *rather* have a man like Caleb York?"

She sighed wearily. "A man, Papa . . . or a legend? Who *was* he, really?"

". . . A man."

"A killer, too, remember," Whit put in, his eyes as gentle on her as his words were harsh.

She said to the foreman, "You said . . . a killer 'in his own way.' "

Whit nodded. He wasn't turning the hat in his hands now. "York was a Wells Fargo agent—a detective. The shoot-first-investigate-after breed. Known for returning with the money and the men who stole it—slung dead over their horses."

She laughed a little. "That sounds like the stories little boys tell."

"Then they better tell their story to the Monte Pierson gang—every one of them shot dead, and Caleb York? Not a graze. He faced down both Nub Butler and Wild Angie Hopper and both lay dead in the dust in an eye blink." Whit chuckled deep. "They say York had enough notches on that gun butt of his to make it look like a saw blade."

"More little-boy talk," she said.

"Maybe, Miss Cullen. But I will tell you one story I *don't* believe."

She cocked her head. "Oh?"

Whit's thin lips formed a smile that might have been a gash in his face. "Ten to one, Banion never faced him down."

Her Papa stirred.

Whit finished: "The only way Wes Banion could take down Caleb York was with a bullet in the back."

Eyes wide, Willa said, "Father! Is *that* the kind of man you sent for?"

"It's the kind of man we need," Papa said defensively. "The kind of man it takes to deal with the likes of Harry Gauge."

She covered her mouth with a trembling hand. "Oh, Papa . . . I can't be hearing this."

His expression was cold. "This ranch was built on ground soaked in the blood of Indians and white men alike, who all thought it should be theirs. Never forget that, daughter."

She swallowed. "I know who you are, Papa. I know the things you've done. But they were necessary and right, in their way, in those days. You met adversaries face-to-face, and protected what you worked for. You didn't kill anybody for . . . for *money*."

"Land is money."

She felt the tears welling and fought it. "This is not *you*, Papa."

The unseeing eyes stared into something known only to him. Then he said, "I'd face Gauge down if I could. But a blind man has to seek other ways."

"There are different kinds of blindness, Papa."

His head swung toward her. "You wouldn't fight for the Bar-O, daughter? You wouldn't scratch that devil's eyes out if he came near you?"

"Of course, I would. But we can fight our own battles. We still have fifteen men, Papa."

"You *heard* Whit, girl! They're cowboys, not gunfighters. I pay them enough to make a living, but not enough to die." His eyes squeezed shut. "Gauge must have thirty top gunhands at his beck and call."

Whit sat forward. "Your men *will* fight, sir."

Papa batted that away. "Why make that sacrifice? No, it won't be necessary. Not when . . . the man comes here who Parker sends."

Whit's eyes were wide again. "And you don't think Gauge will be waiting for him?"

Her father had no answer for that.

And Willa, with no more questions, left them there.

The office of the jail was a modest plank-floored space with two windows onto the street, open to let the breeze in, and four cells in back. No prisoners today.

Seated behind his big dark wooden desk, Sheriff Harry Gauge had his feet up and crossed on its scarred top. His boots wore no spurs, not in town—he didn't care to announce himself. Across the way was a wood-burning stove, and a table with a few chairs by a wall with WANTED posters haphazardly nailed there. In front of him, seated in a high-back chair, was his redheaded deputy, Vint Rhomer, frowning so hard as he worked at thinking that the man looked as if he might cry.

Rhomer, arms folded, said, "Well, at least we *know* who's comin'."

The big blond sheriff said, "Banion, you mean."

"Yeah. Who else?" Then a thought made it through to the front of his head and the deputy leaned forward. "But suppose it *ain't* Banion? Old Man Cullen sent word asking his buddy to send Banion or some *other* shootist!"

"Most likely be Banion." Gauge poured tobacco from his pouch into a waiting curve of paper. "Not that it makes much never-mind. I'll know him when I see him."

"So you've *seen* Banion, then?"

Gauge licked the paper's edge. "Nope."

Rhomer got some more thoughts going. "Remember Jake?"

"I remember Jake."

"*Jake* knew Banion. They pulled some jobs together."

"This would be more helpful," Gauge said lazily, rolling the cigarette, "if Jake wasn't dead."

Jake Farrow had been killed on a bank job Gauge and his boys had pulled about six months before taking over Trinidad and—the thought making Gauge smile—going straight.

"Talked about him enough, Jake did," Rhomer said, still on his thinking jag. "Said Banion's meaner than an Apache and fights twice as dirty. They say, in Tombstone? Even the Earps steered clear of him. And in Ellis, Reg Toomey turned his badge in, second he saw Banion ride into town."

Gauge lit a match off a boot heel. "That right."

"Jake saw him burn out the Casaway bunch. Set fire to their house with their *women* in it, too. Banion and his crew left half of that town dead, and all they got for their trouble was a few hundred greenbacks."

Gauge had his cigarette going now. "Do tell."

"Anybody who wasn't part of his gang got shot dead. By Banion hisself. Didn't like havin' his face seen."

"That ugly, huh?"

"No! Didn't want to be identified. . . . You yankin' my leg, Gauge?"

"Mebbe. You say Jake saw him face-to-face. Well, *Banion* didn't kill Jake. What, was Jake lucky? Makes him a lucky dead man, don't it?"

"Well, Jake was part of his gang. Banion's a bad egg, but he don't kill his friends without good reason."

"Ah. That would explain it. Say, Vint—who was it again, outdrew Banion? Remind me."

"Gill Peterson."

"Whatever happened to Peterson, anyway?"

Rhomer smiled. Chuckled. "He pulled on you and you gunned him down. Last month it was."

"Where was it I got him? Remind me."

"Front of the Victory."

"No, I mean *where?*"

"Oh. 'Tween the eyes. Dead center." Rhomer grinned. "He *did* have kinda wide-set eyes, though."

"Still in all," the sheriff said, with a shrug.

"Still in all," Rhomer allowed.

Gauge tamped cigarette ash on the floor. "And who was it shot Jack Reno through the heart?"

"That was you, Gauge."

Gauge took in smoke, held it, let it out. "So tell me—why is it again, I should worry about Banion?"

Rhomer leaned in. "Because we got dark alleys in this town, Harry. And you got a *big* ol' back 'tween them shoulders."

Gauge nodded, unconcerned. "And that's what I got *you* fellas for. So's nobody gets the chance to back-shoot me."

"You mean, 'cause we walk behind you."

"Well, that's part of it. But what else do I mean?"

Rhomer frowned. "Not sure I follow, Harry."

"There's more than one way to watch a man's back."

"Is there?"

"You can keep track of anybody new in town. Somebody don't smell right . . . well, there's plenty more room in that bone orchard outside town. And lots of range out there to bury strangers in."

Rhomer thought about that. "But what about the Bar-O boys? We already planted our share of them. Even in *this* town, there's only so far we can go, nippin' trouble in the bud."

"They ain't gonna be a problem much longer."

"That right?"

Gauge nodded. "I hear pretty soon it's going to get real warm out there. Hotter days're comin', you know. And that long grass burns *real* damn hot. And fast."

Rhomer grinned. "Takin' a page out of Banion's book?"

"Now you *are* thinking, Vint. We kill Banion and let him take the blame."

"How does that stack up?"

Gauge shrugged, let out more smoke. "It's got all around town by now, that wire Old Man Cullen sent. Banion comes to Trinidad, things get warm out at the Bar-O, Banion shows up dead."

"Okay. . . ."

"How's it look, Vint? Like a fallin'-out between employer and employee, windin' up bad for all concerned. Anybody left still breathin' out at the Bar-O, that's what we got these cells for."

Rhomer squinted at his boss. "What about the pretty filly?"

"We make sure she don't get burned. I'll sweet-talk her how Banion was responsible for the bad things that happened at the ranch—pity. And then she'll need a man to help her rebuild that spread, won't she?"

The deputy had been smiling through that, but now was staring out the window, distracted by movement and sounds out there. "Harry—somethin' goin' on out there."

Both men got up and went out into the dry, warm afternoon. The sheriff and deputy stood on the porch and watched. Men and women were on

the opposing boardwalks, but weren't going anywhere, just clustered talking, often in an animated
fashion, some pointing toward the sheriff's office.

"What are all them people doin' on the street?"
Rhomer wondered aloud. "I don't like it. It's like
they's waitin' for a parade to go by or somethin'."

"They're waiting for something to happen."

"*What* to happen?"

"For me to react to that telegram Cullen sent.
Only I ain't gonna react just yet." Gauge nodded
toward the gossiping citizens. "But get used to that,
Vint, over the next week or so. You'll see the good
folks of Trinidad out watchin', talkin', every damn
time they hear a horse ride in or a stage roll up."

"Yeah?"

"Oh yeah. They want to get a good, long look at
this bad man Banion."

"*If* it's Banion."

Gauge pitched his cigarette sparking into the
street. "I hope it is. Killing him will make me look
pretty damn good. Show this town just what kind
of sheriff they got for themselves."

The two men went back in the office, smiling.

Beneath their porch, in one of his favorite hiding places, a white-bearded, skinny old desert rat
known only as Tulley was smiling, too. Grinning to
himself as if the sheriff and his deputy had been
telling jokes. A fairly new addition to the Trinidad
populace, Tulley was well on his way to becoming
the town drunk.

Sipping at his latest bottle, then grinning stupidly to no one in particular, he cackled out loud. *"Banion! That's* a good one. Banion . . ."

Then he took another sip, curled up, and went back to sleep.

CHAPTER THREE

W hen Sheriff Harry Gauge pushed open the telegraph office door, he hadn't intended to startle operator Ralph Parsons. But the skinny, four-eyed Parsons was always on the skittish side, and plainly the wire Old Man Cullen had sent earlier today—now the talk of Trinidad—had the pip-squeak well and truly spooked.

Faintly amused, Gauge leaned an elbow at the counter and gave Parsons a small, calm smile in exchange for the operator's big, nervous one.

The sheriff asked, "Any message for Cullen come in yet, Ralph?"

The nervous smile disappeared and a rush of words squawked out: "Oh, uh, oh no, sir, Sheriff." The man's expression was gravely serious now. "And, uh, look . . . about the wire Mr. Cullen sent this morning? I didn't want to do it. No, sir, I didn't. But that old man had a gun, and—"

Still amused, Gauge said, "Why, do you want to press charges, Ralph?"

"No!" Eyes behind glasses went so wide that white showed all around. "I mean . . . did you *want* me to?"

Gauge shook his head. "Forget it, Ralph. The old boy's in a tizzy 'cause of the man he lost. Grievin' and all. We'll cut him some slack."

"That's real white of you, Sheriff."

Gauge curled a finger to draw Parsons closer. "But I want you to let me know the minute an answer to that wire of his comes in."

The operator swallowed thickly. "I'm all alone here, Sheriff. But I can come over right after closing."

"Well, you just *close* the second something comes in. That sign in the window has two sides, don't it?"

"It does, Sheriff. I'll be glad to do that, Sheriff. Is there . . . anything else I can do for you, Sheriff?"

Gauge thought if the man said "Sheriff" one more time, he might slap him. But he forced a smile and kept his tone friendly.

"Yes. Take this down for me, would you?"

"Surely." The operator reached for a form and a pencil.

" 'To all territorial sheriffs,' " Gauge dictated. "You do have that list, right, Ralph?"

"I do indeed."

" 'To all territorial sheriffs. Send photograph and general information regarding Wesley C. Banion immediately.' Sign it, 'Harry Gauge, Sheriff, Trinidad, New Mexico.' "

The operator had blanched upon hearing the name. Parsons let out enough air to blow up a balloon and said, "You think . . . you think maybe this Banion character is around these parts, Sheriff?"

"I surely hope so."

Parsons didn't know what to make of that. "Well, from what I hear, he's . . ."

"He's what, Ralph?"

Now it was the operator who forced a smile. With the filled-out form in one hand, he made a dismissive gesture with the other. "Nothing, Sheriff. Not my business. I'll get this right out for you."

"Thank you, Ralph. In case you're wondering, I'm well aware this Banion is the gunfighter Old Man Cullen sent for. And it doesn't bother me a lick. I just like to keep . . . on top of things."

Parsons nodded, said, "You bet, Sheriff, you bet," and went to his telegraph key to send the wire.

That evening, back in his office by himself, Gauge sat with his feet on the floor, hunkered over a WANTED poster he'd plucked off the wall. His request for a picture was likely a long shot. This poster had no photograph or drawing, just the following information:

WANTED
WESLEY CHARLES BANION

FOR MURDER, ARMED ROBBERY, ARSON.
Known to carry two Colt Peacemaker .45's,
Sleeve Derringer, skilled knife fighter.
Last seen Abilene, Kansas.
BELIEVED TRAVELING SOUTHWEST TO MEXICO.
DEAD OR ALIVE
$5,000 REWARD

The bell over the door jangled as if announcing a customer in a general store—Gauge was a careful man in practice, if reckless in ambition—and a beautiful woman familiar to everyone in town entered.

If Lola had a last name, no one in Trinidad, not even Harry Gauge, knew it. Not that it came up much in conversation. Darkly beautiful, her black curly hair worn up, tall and slender but for a full bosom, Lola was Gauge's partner in several ways, among them co-owner of the Victory Saloon, where she ran the girls, though she herself was available only to the sheriff.

She wore a long gray mannish coat over her blue-and-gray satin gown. She wore the coat in part due to it getting chilly here after dark, but also because she rarely traversed the boardwalk in her low-cut dance-hall-queen working clothes.

Entering as if she owned the place, Lola removed her coat in a swirl, folded it like a blanket, and dropped it on the sheriff's desk like a present. Her satin gown had black lace that caressed and lifted her bosom, and the dress parted in front at the knees to reveal fishnet silk stockings and high-laced high-heeled shoes.

She sat on the chair opposite him, shoulders back, chin high, folding her lacy-gloved hands in her lap. Her eyes were big and dark brown and wide-set in her oval face; her nose small and tip-tilted; her lips wide and sensual and red-rouged. The dark beauty mark near the lush lips was nature's work.

Her voice was a throaty purr as she said, "Working a little late, aren't you, Harry?"

"Shouldn't you be over at the Victory? Your 'day' is just starting, ain't it? Cowhands get paid today, remember."

She shrugged and the half-exposed bosom did a little shimmy. "They won't be in for another hour or so yet. I thought maybe you and me could kill a little time, Sheriff. Don't you have a bottle that isn't swill, down in one of those desk drawers?"

"I do."

"And don't those shades draw?"

"Ain't in the mood, Lola."

She got out of the chair and sat on the edge of the desk, leaning in to show off the breasts even more. "Since when are you 'not in the mood'?"

"Since I said I wasn't. I got work to do."

"Where's that dumb deputy that follows you around? Not that I care."

"Doin' my bidding. What else?"

Smiling at that, she glanced at the WANTED poster

on the desk, turned the sheet toward her. Then she nodded. "I heard about this, Harry. That's why I came over."

"Is that right."

She leaned in even more. "I figured you might like to take your mind off your troubles, Harry."

He gave her something halfway between a smile and a sneer. "Sit it down. I ain't buyin'."

Hurt flashed in the dark eyes. He'd meant to give her the needle—she hadn't sold herself for a very long time, so the insult surely stung. But she did as she was told, sitting back down, folding her arms, hiding the exposed flesh as if to punish him.

"There was a time," she said, voice still throaty but the purr gone, "when there was nothing in your life that meant more to you than me."

"You're wrong. You've always come in second to *my* life, Lola."

She frowned. "You're *that* worried? When I first brought you here, nothing used to bother you."

"Bigger a man gets," Gauge said quietly, "bigger his troubles."

She smiled. She had nice teeth, a rarity among her breed. "Well, you're a big man, all right. County sheriff, land owner, co-owner of damn near every business in town."

"I told you not to curse, Lola. Ain't ladylike."

She ignored that. "How much can you own, Harry? How much land can one man handle? How damn big do you expect to *get?*"

"Bigger than the biggest. I came up hard, you

know that. Now nobody runs Harry Gauge any-more. Now *I* run things."

"I guess when you're *that* big, nobody can say no to you."

"That's right."

Her wet red smile was faintly teasing. "What about the Bar-O? They aren't like these other little spreads you forced out and swallowed up. They'll *fight* you."

"Let them try. There were people in this town that tried to fight me before. What happened to them? All I had to do was look at them hard and they fell apart. Sometimes I sweetened it with a lit-tle dough. But they're all of them soft. They can't handle the idea of maybe dying on their own front steps."

"Suppose they get together. It's happened in other towns."

"I'll see that they don't." He shook his head. "Nothing in Trinidad gets by Harry Gauge."

She frowned and worry lines touched her fore-head. Sitting forward, to reveal not her charms but her concern, she said, "Harry, the talk around town . . . it's like everybody's just *waiting* for some-thing to happen."

He shrugged, nodded toward the WANTED poster. "Cullen's wire to his old partner got 'em all stirred up."

She was shaking her head, just a little, dark gyp-syish curls flouncing. "Ten thousand dollars is a hell of a bounty, my friend. And you can *bet* Cullen isn't paying this Banion character or anybody else up front."

"What's your point?"

She shrugged. "You figure you can take Banion."

He returned the shrug. "I already took down two men who outdrew him."

"Sure . . . but Banion lived through both tries. So fine, so you come out on top of a showdown with big, bad Wes Banion. Do I have to tell you what happens next?"

"Can I stop you?"

Her expression was grave. "You have a reputation, Harry. How many men have come looking for you, these past few years, to build a rep of his own?"

"Enough."

"Well, Harry honey, it's gonna be an *army* of 'em with Old Man Cullen's ten thousand in the game."

"Plenty of room on Boot Hill."

"Not really. You've filled most of it already. That mesquite tree can only shade so much. Of course, they'd make room for *you*."

What he grunted was almost a laugh. "Banion will go down just like Caleb York went down."

"They say York was back-shot."

"If that's what it takes. Dead is dead."

"Yes, and if a legend like Caleb York can die, so can the biggest man in Trinidad, if he isn't careful."

"What are you sayin', Lola?"

She flew to her feet and leaned her hands on the desk. "I'm saying maybe it's time to cash out. How rich do you have to be? Do you know how well we could live over the border on gringo dollars? I don't want to be a damn madam the rest of my life, helping soiled doves duck babies and disease. And do you want to spend your days looking back over your shoulder, jumping at shadows?"

"I don't jump at nothing or nobody."

She gestured around them. "Harry, you're sitting in your office in the dark, reading a poster over and over about a man that's coming to kill you. Face it—the great Harry Gauge is scared."

He slapped her.

The sound rang out like a gunshot, and she clenched one hand into a hard, little quivering fist as her other fingers went to a mouth where the red now wasn't just rouge.

Her voice trembled not with fear but rage. "Someday, Harry. Someday you'll do that once too often. . . ."

"Shut up. Go do your job. Get your girls to find out from these payday-rich cowhands if anybody new has signed on lately. Could even be on one of my own spreads and I wouldn't know it. A smart man might hide in plain sight like that. Now . . . get out."

She'd found a handkerchief somewhere and was rubbing the blood off her mouth. That made him feel a little bad and he got her coat and helped her into it.

Her voice trembled again, but it wasn't rage and it wasn't hurt. More like hurt feelings.

"I won't have you hitting me," she said, sounding like a kid.

"Won't happen again, sugar," he said, making himself smile as he held the door open for her.

She paused, glancing back. "A gentleman would walk me down there."

He grinned. "You're a big girl, and I'm no gentleman. Sheriff don't need to make an entrance just yet. I'll be down there. I'll be down."

She nodded and went out onto the porch and down the steps into the street, where a full moon was climbing to paint the dusty town ivory. He watched her go, admiring the sway of her hips, until she got to where the boardwalk started.

Then he went back in his office and got the bottle out of the bottom desk drawer. That had been one good idea she had.

Under that same moon but a little higher now, on the porch of the Bar-O ranch house, Willa Cullen stood with her father as foreman Whit Murphy, already on horseback at the head of a party of ten mounted cowhands, waited for his final instructions.

Both father and daughter remained in the attire they'd worn to Boot Hill this morning, and Papa was back in his wide-brimmed black hat.

Willa, almost whispering, said, "Papa . . . are you *sure* . . . ?"

"That I know what I'm doing?" The old man laughed hollowly. "Do you think Harry Gauge is going to wait for Banion to show up? I know our sheriff's kind too well. He'll try hitting us from every angle he can think of. Soften us up."

"You said it yourself," she said, still very quiet, "our men aren't gunfighters."

"No, but they don't have to be. Most fought for one side or the other, not so long ago, in a conflict bigger than this. And this is war, too."

Then Papa strode down the steps with the confidence of a sighted man and positioned himself just in front of the mounted foreman.

"Whit, my boy," he said. "You straight on what to do?"

"We're set," he said. His hat was off in respect to Willa and her father. "Bulk of the cattle are on the north end, have been since dark, and the trenches are dug. Carmen took the crew out with the water wagons two hours ago."

"Good." Papa took off his hat and lifted his unseeing eyes to the sky, turning his face toward the breeze, which was not considerable. "Long as this wind doesn't pick up, we should make out fine."

Whit leaned down and spoke directly to Papa, soft enough that Willa barely heard: "You think it's wise to just leave five men here, Mr. Cullen?"

"Gauge's first move won't be against the house."

"Can we be sure of that, sir?"

"Nothing's sure in this life but death. Just do it my way, son, and we'll see how we come out."

"Yes, sir." Whit put his hat back on, turned to his men and said, *"Okay—let's move on out!"*

The other cowhands waited for Whit to bring his horse around and take the head position. Then they went out, two by two, in an even gait that built into pounding hooves when the riders had disappeared into the night.

Willa came down and joined her father, slipping an arm in his. "How can you be so sure, Papa, that Gauge will do what you think he will?"

"Because when I was his age," her father said, "and not such a nice fella myself . . . it's exactly what *I* would have done." He sighed. "Anyway, we can't pin all our hopes on this Banion."

Frowning, she said, "Well, you're putting all your money on him."

The old man sighed. "Would have been a better bet," he admitted, "if it was Caleb York coming."

"If you're pinning our hopes on a dead man, Papa, we really are in a bad way."

He didn't seem to be listening to her. To himself he said, "It would have been so easy for that man. As easy as it would have been for me. Back when these sorry eyes could see."

Her arm still in his, she tugged at him. "Come inside, Papa. Come inside. Coffee's on the stove."

"I'll be in, girl. Leave me be."

She left him there in the moonlight, staring out at the dissipating dust cloud his men had left, as if he could see it.

Moonlight lent a rugged beauty to the three open wagons loaded down with barrels of water, positioned a dozen yards apart, with the cowhands' horses tied up behind them. Blankets had already been soaked down and tied onto the backs of the saddled and ready steeds. One cowhand was back there with the animals, tending them, steadying them.

Another dozen yards down the gentle slope were three four-foot-deep trenches, each with room enough for three men with rifles. For a short while, Whit moved from one trench to another, keeping low, passing along instructions, until completing the armed trio in the center. Beyond the trenches in high grass, a scattering of underfed cows stood stupidly under the moon, as if contemplating jumping over it.

"We're ready," Whit told the two other middle-trench cowboys.

Stubby Jerry Morris, not as dumb as his close-set eyes made him look, said, "You see anything out there, Whit?"

"Not yet. It'll come."

Roughneck Rafe Connor, black handlebar mustache falling below his face, said, "I sure as hell hope Old Man Cullen knows what the hell he's doin'."

Two utterances of "hell" in one outburst seemed disrespectful to Whit, but he let it go.

Jerry said, "I ain't known ol' Cullen to be wrong yet."

"Me neither," Rafe admitted with a sigh. "But there just ain't enough of us."

Jerry shook his head. "We can't know how many men Gauge'll send."

All three men were peering over their Winchesters into the nearby tall grass, which riffled in the breeze, tickling the legs of the handful of cows.

Calmly, Whit said, "Don't matter how many there are. Not if we're ready and they ain't."

Rafe, always something of a complainer, said, "But how do we know we're in the right spot? They could come in over there, or over yonder, and we'd never get wise till it was too late to do a damn thing about it."

Whit placed a patient hand on Rafe's shoulder. "We're right where we need to be. Out there is where the high grass is. Gauge knows our line shack is just over the ridge behind us, and figures to run them cows right on through it. Losin' Mr. Cullen some steers and maybe a man or two and cost him considerable."

Jerry said, "Sure glad we moved them beeves out. You think we left enough of them scrawny ones to sucker 'em?"

"Should be just what they want to see," Whit said. "They'll just figure the rest of the herd's bedded down. Anyway, they wouldn't risk a fire right by the main herd."

"Why not?"

"Think about it, boyo. A fire would stampede 'em right onto Gauge's range. All his cows would join in and there'd be hell to pay."

Rafe said, "Would that be so bad? Maybe that'd be the last of Gauge, then."

Whit shook his head. "Too high a cost. Steady your rifle, boy, and don't think about nothin' but what's out there and about to come at you."

"Okay," Rafe said, and shivered, though it wasn't all that cold. "I just hope we ain't the Alamo and they's Santa Anna."

The men with rifles watched in quiet silence for five minutes. Ten. Twenty. Then a few along the line began to chat in their boredom.

"You know," Rafe said, "those dumb cows'll get caught in the cross fire."

"That just means," Jerry said, "we'll have a hell of a barbecue tomorrow."

Whit whispered harshly, "*Hold it down.* I heard something. . . ."

Silence took over again.

Then: *snorting horses and metal clanking.*

Whit pointed.

Shadowy figures on horseback were moving toward the edge of the high grass. Somewhere a steer bawled, and horses were brought to an abrupt whinnying halt.

Silhouetted men climbed down from their saddles. Across the grass, orange flashes, chest-high, lit the night like plump fireflies. Then lower, bigger pops of yellow-orange-blue seemed to float toward the watchers while half-a-dozen intruders with torches dropped blossoms of flame onto the grass. For now, the cattle ignored them.

Whit said, "They've made their move. *Now!*"

The Bar-O cowhands down in their trenches let go with a fusillade of rifle fire over the heads of the scrawny beeves.

One man howled and dropped. Another man fell without a sound, disappearing into a fire he'd just set. Dead already, or he'd be screaming.

"It's a trap!" somebody yelled on the other side of the grass.

Deputy Vint Rhomer's voice! Whit thought.

The remaining intruders—*four? five?*—tossed their torches and ran to their horses, mounted them, and tried to head across the burning grass, but their horses protested, neighing, rearing, damn near throwing them. Bullets falling around them like deadly rain, Rhomer and his raiders retreated, the deputy's voice rising above the crackle of flames: *"Clear out! Clear out!"*

Then the intruders were swallowed back into the night, leaving a field whose fiery edge was spreading, the cattle starting to bray in fear, stirring but too far apart from each other to stampede in any meaningful way.

Whit raised up in the trench and held his rifle high in one hand like an attacking Apache. *"Bring those horses and blankets up!"*

The men scrambled from the trenches and circled behind the water-barrel-loaded wagons to get the horses. The cowhands climbed up into their saddles and rode across the high grass to where it was burning, then cut across the edges of the burning patch of range, never exposing the horses so directly to the flames that they, too, would protest, cutting in, cutting out, expertly dragging those soaked blankets across the burning grass, making it smaller and smaller, until in minutes the fire was doused and only gray wisps of smoke remained. That, and a scorched smell to the air and a strip of blackened prairie.

Most of the cows had just stood there through all this; a few had wandered off, but two had been drilled by one side of the fracas or the other. Jerry had been right—there *would* be good eating tomorrow.

The men gathered between the trenches and the wagons. Everybody was breathing hard and grinning, some laughing. Whit remained somber.

He said, "Anybody hurt?"

Holding on to his arm, some red seeping between his fingers, Jerry said, "I got grazed. Nothin' some alcohol won't cure."

Whit knew the cowhand probably meant alcohol poured down his gullet, not onto the wound.

Rafe said, "We got two of them."

"Yeah," Whit said, nodding, letting out air. "I saw them go down and nobody of theirs bothered pickin' 'em up. Let's check 'em out—pretty sure one's dead, but the other may just be wounded. So six-guns ready, gents."

Whit was on his way to one of the fallen when, from over to his left, he heard Jerry call out: *"This here's Stringer!"*

The foreman went over for a look. Bending for a closer view, he said, "Stringer, all right. Part of the first batch Gauge brought to town. Dead as hell—head shot."

Whit went over to the second fallen man, found him also deceased, bullet in the chest. The foreman said, loud enough for all to hear, *"This one's Bradley! One of Gauge's men, all right."*

They removed one empty water barrel to make room in one of the wagons for the two bodies. Whit figured Mr. Cullen would want a look at them. They loaded up the two dead steers, too, in another wagon.

Cocky and confident now, Rafe ambled up to Whit and asked, "Think they'll be back again?"

"Not tonight, they won't," Whit said, allowing himself a grin, finally. "We won this battle."

But all of them knew one battle wasn't a war.

CHAPTER FOUR

Sheriff Harry Gauge sat quietly in his darkened office and enjoyed a few fingers—well, maybe more than a few—of the whiskey from his bottom desk-drawer bottle. Then the big blond man rolled and smoked a cigarette as he mulled his situation, and barely noticed when, around nine, arriving in groups from the various ranches, cowhands started roaring into town, whooping and hollering and firing off rounds. Similarly, he'd barely noticed when the more timid storekeepers boarded up their windows in anticipation of the monthly hooraw. He hadn't stuck his nose out of his office in either case.

Just past ten, feeling loose but in no way drunk— at least from where he sat—the sheriff gave his sidearm, a .44 Colt, a cursory check (he'd cleaned and oiled it earlier) before locking up the office and heading down to the Victory Saloon, Trinidad's only watering hole.

But with a watering hole like the Victory, who needed another option?

The sheriff pushed through the batwing doors into the impressive saloon with its ornately decorated tin ceiling and gas lamp chandeliers, its long, well-polished carved oak bar at left with mirrors and bottles of rye and bourbon behind, towels hanging down for brushing beer out of mustaches, and gleaming brass foot rail with an array of spittoons. The contrast was sharp between the high-class bar's bow-tied, white-shirt-sporting bartenders and the dusty cowboys in frayed bandanas, faded work shirts, and seat-patched Levi's who leaned there.

Though there were tables for drinking men at right as you came in, most of the big space was a casino, filled to capacity tonight with already liquored-up cowhands freely losing their money at dice, faro, red dog, twenty-one, and poker. Busy, too, were the roulette, chuck-a-luck, and wheel-of-fortune stations. At the far end of the saloon—whose walls bore such rustic decorative touches as saddles, spurs, and steer horns, riding the fancy gold-and-black wallpaper—rose a small stage with a piano and a fiddle player, near which a modest dance floor was crowded with cowboys doing awkward steps with the patient silk-and-satin saloon gals who were plying their own trade.

Gauge and Lola owned the joint, fifty-fifty, and

it was a sweet damn moneymaker. Imagine running half-a-dozen spreads, on which several hundred men worked for you, only to fleece them out of their wages month in, month out. But this was chickenfeed compared to where Gauge was heading.

Once he'd taken over all the surrounding ranches, and could establish one big spread, he would stick a badge on somebody else's shirt, Rhomer maybe or some other fool he could control, and become the land baron he was born to be.

Despite the music and raucous laughter, maybe half of the patrons had noticed Gauge come in. They would squint at him, frown a little, and look away. These were better men than the lily-livered townspeople, but they feared him, too. A badge with a fast gun to back it remained the ideal way to keep the peace . . . and people in their place.

Among those who'd spotted Gauge was Lola, who threaded around tables and wheels toward him, nodding and speaking and smiling to cowboys as she went. She approached Gauge with a smile—he knew she wouldn't stay mad at him long—and they found a table in the corner, away from the merriment.

"Looks like a decent night," Gauge said, "considering."

"Not bad," she admitted. "We've been busier. What do you mean, 'considering'?"

"That Meadow kid gettin' planted this morning," he said with a shrug. "Might put a damper on any Bar-O boys stoppin' by for fun and games."

She frowned and glanced around. "I don't see any Bar-O boys, at that." Then her dark eyes were on him. "But that kind usually *likes* a good time after one of their own gets a send-off. A little drink, a little lovin', can make death seem far away."

"You got a point."

She was studying him now. "Why aren't they here, *really*?"

A bartender delivered Gauge a beer that the sheriff hadn't needed to order.

"Could be," Gauge said, after a sip that required sleeving foam off his upper lip, "they got their hands full out at the Bar-O this evening."

Lola glanced around again. "Some of your bunch aren't here, either. No Rhomer. None of your other . . . deputies."

"Could be they was busy tonight."

She lifted an eyebrow. "Something you want to share with me, Harry?"

"It's nothing to do with the Victory, other than maybe we're short a few patrons. Don't worry your sweet, little head."

"I'll try not to strain myself."

He leaned in, put a hand on a lace-gloved one of hers. "You put your girls onto that matter of mine?"

"Yes."

"You check back with them yet?"

"I have. The girls say no new faces to speak of."

He frowned. " 'To speak of'?"

"The Larson spread's been hiring on hands. For roundup, I guess." She nodded toward the bar. "Those three down at this end are takin' in the Victory for the first time."

"Do tell."

"Of course, there's only one that might pique your interest."

Which cowboy she meant was obvious—he stood out for a couple of reasons. He was a good six feet, and most cowboys, like the two bookending him, were smaller men. Ranchers tended to hire smaller hands to make it easier on the horses. The bigger cowboy didn't look familiar, and yet he did. He was a type Harry Gauge knew very well.

The man had a hard edge to him while lacking the dark, leathery look of those who worked under the sun on horseback day upon day. About thirty, with barbered brown hair, he had a rugged, scarred face and a well-tended mustache that belied his cowboy apparel. And the smile he was giving Pearl, one of Lola's girls, had a confident nastiness to it.

Gauge said, "Get her over here."

Lola turned toward the girl, quickly caught her eye and waved her over. She came right over and sat with them, rightly nervous to be honored with an audience with the sheriff.

Gauge said to her, "Enlighten me."

Pearl, a skinny brunette whose prettiness was getting blurred by too much laudanum, said, "He's working for Ben Larson."

"That much I know."

"Says he's from Cheyenne. I already talked to some of the other Bar-L fellas, and nobody knows anything about him but his name."

"And what would that be?"

"Smith."

Funny as that was, he neither smiled nor laughed. "How long has Smith been working for Larson?"

"Oh, just signed on today."

"Just today?"

"Late afternoon. Rode in looking for work, Larson took him on. The boys say Smith told them he's never worked as a cowhand before, but he's lookin' to 'turn over a new leaf.' "

"What kind of 'new leaf'?"

Pearl narrowed her eyes; they were the same dark blue as her satin gown. "One feller said he asked Smith what his trade had been, you know, before? And Smith just said, 'Workin' one side of the law or the other.' "

"Pearl honey," Gauge said, "go back to the cowboy who told you that and send him over here. No fuss. On the quiet."

Pearl nodded and was getting up, but the sheriff stopped her by the elbow.

He added, "Then go back and keep that Smith cowboy company."

"Take him upstairs?"

"No. Stay there at the bar. If he wants to go upstairs, tell him you have to wait for a room. Lay on the charm."

Pearl smiled slyly and nodded. Then she went off to find the Bar-L hand who had told her about Smith.

Vaguely suspicious, Lola said, "Okay, your wheels are turning. I can hear 'em, Harry, and they could use some grease."

"Why? You think you know what I'm thinkin'?"

She gave him a slow nod. "You think that big, tall cowboy is Banion, or somebody like him."

Gauge said nothing.

She leaned in. "Maybe you been hanging around that dope Rhomer too long. How could Banion get here today?"

"Might not be Banion. Like you said, might be somebody like him."

She smirked. "Old Man Cullen sends a wire this morning, and Banion is getting a job at Larson's by late afternoon?"

He looked at her hard. "Maybe Cullen's partner in Denver knew somebody in the area. You can send a wire damn near anywhere these days. We're only thirty miles from Ellis. A man on a good mount, leaving late morning, could make that. And the Swenson spread is on the northeast, on the way to Ellis."

She was shaking her head, dark curls bouncing. "And you think Banion or some other top gun-hand was just sittin' in some saloon in Ellis, waiting for a wire to come in, requesting his services?"

"What I think," Gauge said, "is that a man should be careful. And a woman should watch her mouth."

Lola said nothing, just leaned back and sat there, burning.

Gauge watched the rugged-looking character at the bar, working on a beer. Pearl sashayed up and began flirting again with the man calling himself Smith. He seemed to like the attention.

The cowhand who came over, having been sent by Pearl, had his hat in hands as he stood before the sheriff.

"You want to talk to me, Sheriff Gauge?"

Gauge knew the man a little, Frank Harper, a typical cowboy of medium size with a droopy, untrimmed mustache, long, unkempt hair, and leathery skin. His face was narrow, his eyes wary under a shelf of shaggy brows.

"Sit down, Frank," Gauge said, friendly but not overdoing it. "Can I buy you a drink? Beer? Shot of rye?"

"Kind of you, Sheriff," he said, "but I'm in the middle of a game. Just lost my"—he glanced at Lola, who was sitting listening, her arms folded—"*shirt* trying to draw to an inside straight. How can I be of help?"

"This Smith," Gauge said, barely nodding toward the bar, "just rode in this afternoon, I understand. You make him for a gunhand? Don't have a cowboy look."

"Funny you should say. There's . . ." But something caught in Frank's throat.

"What is it, Frank?"

"Sir, I don't want to speak out of turn. I know things between you and my boss can sometimes get . . . a tad tense. But you can understand, a body has to be loyal to the man that pays him."

"There's no bad blood between me and your boss. Ben Larson and me just been wrangling over price. No secret I been tryin' to buy him out for over a year."

"No secret at all. And I'm just a cowpoke earnin' his monthly wages, and I don't want to be smack-dab in the middle of *anything*."

"Frank, you're not in the middle of a damn thing. Just tell me about Smith."

He sighed and the droopy mustache shuddered. "Well, Mr. Larson is takin' on hands for roundup. But he's keepin' an eye on men who would make good drovers, for when we head the herd to Las Vegas."

"Makes sense," Gauge allowed. Las Vegas, New Mexico, with its railroad, was a two-day cattle drive away.

"Well, uh, there's, uh, rustlers and bad men of various stripe out there on the trail that you can run into."

"So I hear."

"So Mr. Larson has been particular about who he hires on. There's certain, uh . . . *skills* he'd prefer they have."

"Skills such as?"

Frank lifted two palms. "Now, don't get the idea

that Mr. Larson is takin' on gunhands. No, sir. He just wants men that can handle themselfs in a tough sitch-i-ation."

"Right. Just good business, Frank. Are you saying Smith is good with a gun?"

Very quietly, holding his hat to his chest like a shield, Frank said, "I'm just sayin' that Mr. Larson tries to see what kinda skills any hands he takes on has."

"Did he ask Mr. Smith to demonstrate *his* skills?"

Frank nodded. "The boss lined up some bottles on these fence posts and had Smith show how he could shoot. And, Sheriff, let me tell you—the man *can* shoot! Knocked every bottle off their darn perch."

"Taking his time?"

"No, sir! Blasting away!"

"Fast, is he?"

"Greased lightning. Faster than almost anybody I ever seen."

Gauge smiled a little. "Just out of curiosity, Frank . . . who *is* the fastest you've ever seen?"

Frank's grin was a sly yellow thing. "Why, do you even have to ask, Sheriff? You are, without a darn doubt."

"You flatter me."

Frank's eyebrows went up and his eyes widened. "Is that all, Sheriff? Can I get back to my game? They'll only hold my chair so long."

"You surely can."

With a relieved smile, Frank got to his feet; though just as he was leaving, the sheriff called out to him.

"Oh, and Frank?"

"Yes, Sheriff?"

"You *do* know how bad the odds are, drawing to an inside straight?"

Frank grinned. "I know it, Sheriff. Not that the knowledge ever done me a lick of good."

The cowboy ambled back to his game.

"Well," Gauge said quietly to Lola, "maybe the odds that Smith is Banion *are* about the same as filling an inside straight."

"Worse, I'd say," Lola said.

"Even so," Gauge said, smiling pleasantly, taking off his badge and slipping it in a pocket, "we can't have these ranchers hiring on gunhands. Not a good policy."

He rose and was moving past her when she gripped his arm, probably to beg him to be careful.

But what she said was "Gauge, if you start something, take it outside. We don't need a mess to clean up or any broken furniture or mirrors to replace."

"Your concern is touching, honey," he said with a sneer, and headed over to the bar, putting some drunken swagger into his gait.

There were no spaces at the bar, which gave Gauge his play. The rugged cowboy and a bowlegged buddy were standing sideways, leaning against the counter, talking, beers in hand. Gauge shoved in between them, pushing each aside hard, making them lose their balance and spill the glasses a bit.

Some of the big man's beer got on Gauge's shirtsleeve, and the sheriff—who without a badge seemed just a surly drunk—snarled, "Look what you done, you clod! Get the hell out of my way!"

The scar-faced gunman glared at the drunk.

And gunman was what he was—no cowboy, not with that single-loop holster home to a Colt double-action Army revolver tied down low on his right thigh.

The shootist was sizing up the obnoxious drunk standing before him. The long oak bar was clearing of customers as whispered warnings were exchanged.

Finally, Smith, with a near smile, said, "No need for trouble, friend. Plenty of room here, now."

Gauge kept his speech slurry. "Why don't you go straight to hell and find your own damn room?"

The gunman raised his hands, waist-high, palms out. "You spilled my beer. Why don't you buy me another? And I'll take the next round."

"You deaf? I said, *go to hell!*"

Smith's hard features hardened further. His hand drifted toward the holstered Colt, but he stopped short. "You've had too much to drink, friend. Why don't you just back off and stop asking for trouble."

Weaving, Gauge slurred, "Trouble? Who's gonna give it to me . . . a mangy dog like you?"

By now, the hard face had turned to stone, and a powerful-looking hand hovered above the butt of the holstered Colt.

Smith said, "Time you shut that big mouth, mister. Or I am going to shut it for you."

Still playing drunk, Gauge said, "Try it, why don't you? Or maybe you ain't got the *guts*?"

Slowly, Smith moved away from the bar about two feet. Gauge, still loose-limbed, mirrored him. They faced each other, three feet apart.

Smith said, "Buddy, you just had one too many. That ain't worth dyin' over."

"So you're talk. All *talk*. Just another lily-livered talker!"

Smith went for his gun and Gauge pulled his .44 and blasted three times, shots placed so close they tore a hole in his opponent's belly from which bloody intestines spilled like snakes fleeing a disturbed nest. The gunman had his gun in hand, but it had only just made it out of the holster, and he wouldn't be firing it now or ever. Smith, or whatever the hell his name was, was too busy dying a terrible death, setting an example for any other gunhands playing at cowboy who might be looking on.

Somebody grabbed Gauge from behind, by the upper arms, and shouted, "Get the sheriff!"

Gauge glanced back—it was the smaller cowboy

who Smith had been talking to at the bar—and
shoved his left elbow back into the little man's
ribs. The cowboy yowled and fell back, and the
grip on Gauge's arms popped open into fingers.

Gauge took a step away, facing the bar and the
stunned cowboy, with the gasping, bleeding Smith
on the floor nearby, curled up as if to guard the
gory mess that had poured out of him. Gauge
kicked the revolver from the dying man's hand
and got his badge out of his pocket and pinned it
back on.

"I *am* the sheriff," Gauge said, not shouting it
but loud, directing it to the smaller cowboy but
wanting everyone to hear.

Gauge sent a bartender to fetch Doc Miller,
though Smith would obviously soon be the undertaker's purview.

Then the sheriff turned to the shocked faces of
his patrons—frozen in mid-game or mid-dance, the
music having stopped when the gunfire began—
and his voice was a preacher's on Sunday morning.

*"This is an example for any shootists who think they
can come to Trinidad and pretend to be honest cowhands!
Spread the word, gentlemen. I will keep this town . . .
and this saloon . . . safe!"*

There was a rumble of murmured conversation.

Gauge spoke again, just as loud: *"The show is over.
The house is buying one round, and then get back to
your cards and what-have-you!"*

A free drink forgave many sins, and the place
was soon raucous again, with no pall whatever cast

by the dead man with his guts hanging out on the floor near the bar.

Lola appeared at Gauge's side.

"Well," she said, "I'm glad we didn't invest in that Oriental carpet."

"I detect a tone of disapproval."

"I asked you to please take it outside."

"Would not have got my point across as well."

"You didn't have to do that at all. That man was creating no disturbance, and I don't see what threat he gave you."

"He might be Banion, for all we know."

"And he might not," she said, shaking her head. "And without finding that out first, what good did you do?"

"I'll find out who he was, don't worry about that."

She was studying him again, and something strange was in her expression.

"What is it, honey?"

"You just killed a man, Harry. Doesn't that mean anything to you?"

"No. Should it?"

Lola sighed, rolled her eyes, and began moving through the casino, smiling, friendly with her customers, getting the free-spending mood going again.

Gauge sat at a corner table with a bottle and his back to the wall, keeping an eye on things. Maybe Smith had a friend among the other new cowhands at the Bar-L. Always paid to be careful.

He watched dispassionately as Doc Miller pronounced Smith dead—*you needed a doctor's degree to do* that?—and had a couple cowhands dump the corpse in a basket, cover it with a sheet before directing them out with it.

Sawed-off and plump, in a dark gray suit that looked slept in, the white-haired doc trundled over, black bag in hand, though he hadn't opened it. The operation here required a mop, not a scalpel.

"Doin' quite a business tonight," the doc said in his dry, folksy manner.

"Are we? I only remember killing one fool."

"Well, there's a *live* fool who dropped off two of your men at my office. Last half hour, I been tendin' 'em."

Gauge sat up. "*What* live fool?"

"Take a wild guess."

"Rhomer."

The doc nodded. "He said to ask you to get over to your office, quick. I'm going to guess it's not good news."

Gauge collected Lola and walked her down the chilly moon-swept street to the office, where Rhomer was milling outside, looking like a naughty child awaiting Papa's punishment.

"What happened?" Gauge asked as he unlocked the door.

They all went in. Nervous, Rhomer sat across from Gauge. Lola stood in back of the desk, looming just behind the sheriff.

The red-bearded hangdog deputy shook his head

and said, "They was *waitin'* for us, Gauge. They was down in these damn trenches with rifles and they just shot the hell out of us."

". . . We lose any men?"

"Stringer and Bradley."

"Hell. What about the two at Doc Miller's?"

"Flesh wounds."

"Give it to me in detail."

Rhomer did.

Lola was pacing a small area behind Gauge. She said to Rhomer, "Who knew about this?"

The deputy said, "Just the eight of us in it."

Gauge glanced back at Lola. "Were any of my bunch at the Victory this afternoon?"

She nodded, and shared the names.

Rhomer frowned. "That's them. Musta stopped by for some liquid courage."

Gauge gave her a long, hard look. "Did you hear them talking, Lola?"

Her face reddened. "Don't you *dare* say it to me, Harry. I would *never* . . . ! Don't even *think* it."

Rhomer asked her, "How much drinking did they do?"

She sighed, shrugged, thought. "Not much. A beer or two. A shot. No, they weren't soused when they left. Like you said, Vint. Liquid courage."

Gauge was flexing his fists. "Somebody talked. We're going to find out who. And we're going to kill them. Just like that shootist tonight, only worse."

Lola leaned in. "Harry, come on. You don't

know *anybody* talked. Cullen's a cunning old coot. Maybe he just outthunk you."

Teeth bared, he slapped her. Hard.

"Nobody outthinks me, get it? Nobody!"

She reared back against the adobe wall, agape, trembling, with a curled hand against one cheek. "Harry . . . I *told* you . . ."

Gauge, still seated, swung his gaze to Rhomer. "Go back to Doc Miller's and see about getting our boys back in their bunks."

Rhomer, obviously glad to be going, almost jumped out of the chair and left quickly without a word.

Gauge sat with his back to Lola. But he could feel her there, trembling, seething. Hear her breathing heavily.

Finally she said, in almost a whisper, "Don't ever hit me again, Harry. Not . . . *ever.*"

He almost leapt from the chair and he pressed her against the wall. He kissed her roughly on the mouth, then on the neck, and on the mouth again.

Then, his face in hers, he said, "I'll do anything I want to you, Lola. Understand? *Anything.*"

Breath heavy again, she clutched him to her and whispered into his ear, "Yes . . . yes, you can, Harry. *Anything.* Just . . . just never *hit* me."

He took her by the hand and led her to the nearest jail cell.

CHAPTER FIVE

From the size of him, you would think the stranger was nobody to mess with.

He was big and broad-shouldered, firm-jawed and raw-boned, saddle-tall and long-legged, his pleasant features lent an edge by prominent cheekbones and washed-out blue eyes in a permanent squint. His rifle scabbard was home to a double-barreled twelve-gauge shotgun, and a Colt Single Action Army .44 dangled off on his right hip, holster tie-down loose. The horse he rode was a dappled gray gelding with a black mane, an animal that had some prance in its step as it started lightly down Main Street, as confident as its rider.

Yet, overall the stranger who rode into Trinidad that morning brought one word to mind: *dude.*

The man's face showed some age—he might be as old as forty—and was tanned and had seen its share of weather. But those duds were dude all the way, a city feller trying to fit in out west and missing the mark wide.

His black shirt had gray trim on its collars, cuffs, and twin breast pockets, with pearl buttons down the front and on those pockets and cuffs, too. His trousers were new-looking black cotton tucked into black boots with an elaborate hand-tooled design. The stranger was clean-shaven and bareheaded, his hair reddish brown and barbered short, a gray kerchief neck-knotted, his curl-brimmed black hat with cavalry pinch riding his saddle pommel.

Tulley—stretching and groaning as he emerged from the livery stable where he'd spent the night in a stall—saw the stranger ride in. He'd never laid eyes on anything like this creature, and blinked at him like the man on horseback was a drunken dream or a hangover hallucination.

Pockets on the front of a shirt! Buttons all the way down the front?

To this bowlegged desert rat in his torn BVD shirt, ancient suspenders, and scroungy old canvas trousers, the dude looked like something out of Ned Buntline or maybe a Wild West show.

Tulley wasn't the only one who noted the stranger's arrival. Two of Gauge's bunch, Riley and Jackson, were sitting on the porch in front of the sheriff's office, minding the store.

No sight of Gauge himself or Deputy Rhomer, neither, Tulley noted. *Musta been a late night for the sheriff. Scrapin' the bottom of the barrel to leave* them *two in charge. . . .*

Riley was mustached, brawny, and mean, whereas Jackson was bearded, brawny, and meaner. The former stood near six foot, the latter several inches shy. Otherwise, Tulley saw little difference between the gunnies. Neither man had seen a barber in some time, and their dark blue threadbare army shirts and brown duck trousers showed considerable dirt and wear. The only thing either man seemed proud of was the pistol slung low on their respective hips—.45 Colt Army revolvers for either man.

When the stranger rode lazily by, Riley was sitting, leaned back, with his chair resting against the time- and bullet-scarred adobe wall of the sheriff's office-jailhouse, his Carlsbad Stetson down over his eyes. When Jackson elbowed him, Riley damn near fell off his chair.

Tulley, who had sneaked up alongside the building, stifled a laugh.

"Riley, wake the hell up," Jackson said in a rough whisper. "Feast your eyes on this!"

Riley righted his chair, frowned toward the street, saw the stranger going by at an easy pace, and gaped. "What the hell . . . ?"

"That is one crazy dude," Jackson said through snorting laughs. "*Look* at him! Where's the rest of the circus?"

Riley seemed considerably less amused than his pard. "Better check him out. Sheriff's orders."

"Come *on*, Riley boy. That tenderfoot ain't Banion!"

"Why, you ever see the man?"

"Hell, that *can't* be him."

"Best check, just the same."

They came down the steps and into the street, where Riley yelled, "Hold 'er up there, mister!"

The stranger brought the gelding to a halt and looked back blandly at the two hard cases coming his way.

Tulley, grinning to himself, sneaked up onto the porch and helped himself to Riley's chair.

This might be good, he thought, then immediately felt a little guilty. Hell, seeing an innocent feller like that dude get cut down by prairie trash like Riley and Jackson would be a damn shame.

Still, a front-row seat on a shooting was always worth having. . . .

Riley came around on the mounted dude's right side and Jackson on his left, each man with the heel of a hand resting on the butt of a holstered Colt. The gelding was standing statue still. And the stranger was sitting that way, too.

"Help you, boys?" the dude said, his voice mid-range and mellow. He wasn't looking at either man.

Riley, staring up at the rider, said, "Goin' somewhere, mister?"

A slight smile traced the stranger's wide, narrow lips as he turned his head slightly in Riley's direction. "The nearest restaurant for some breakfast."

Jackson said, "Why aren't you wearin' your hat?"

The stranger glanced over his shoulder the other way. "I like the sun."

Jackson grinned up nastily at the newcomer. "Maybe you been *out* in it too long."

"Well, the sun wasn't up when I started out. I had it on then, took it off come dawn, since you seem interested in what I do with my hat."

Riley said, "Keep a civil damn tongue in your head, dude. What's your name?"

The stranger gave his attention to Riley again. "Well, I'm pretty sure that's my business."

"We're making it ours."

"Any special reason why?"

Jackson said, "We're deputies."

His eyes still on Riley, the stranger said, "I don't see badges on your shirts."

Riley said, "We work for the sheriff. Take our word."

"Tell you what. I'll be down at the restaurant . . . at the hotel there?" He nodded in that direction. "Why don't you just send the sheriff around, when he comes in? Glad to talk to him."

Riley started to draw his gun and the stranger kicked him in the throat, boot heel first. Riley tumbled to the dirt and his hands went to his neck as if strangling himself, rolling around gurgling, raising dust.

Tulley blinked and almost missed it, but now the desert rat's eyes were wide and not about to blink and miss the next slice of action—the stranger kicking out with his left boot and catching Jackson, whose gun was halfway out of its holster, high and hard in the chest, sending him windmilling backward, landing him on his ass, .45 leaping from the fallen man's grasp as if trying to escape its owner.

The dude dropped down from his saddle with an unhurried grace, the gelding keeping its place and making only the faintest movement, its rider coming around to where Riley was on his back like a wriggling bug trying to right itself. The stranger plucked the .45 from Riley's holster and pitched it away like he was playing horseshoes.

Jackson was crawling after his .45 like a baby for his rattle, and the big man in black came over and kicked the gun well out of reach, then kicked Jackson in the belly with the square toe of a boot, hard enough to double the fallen man, who puked with a retching cry and then puked some more, till he was bawling like the baby he'd seemed.

The stranger stood over the man, as if deciding whether anything else needed to be done, then turned quickly to see Tulley at his side.

Grinning, Tulley nodded down at the steaming vomit soaking up the dust like an awful spilled pie and asked, "You *still* want breakfast, mister?"

The stranger gave up a nice, wide narrow-lipped grin. "Takes more than a welcoming committee to make me lose my appetite."

A few townspeople on the nearby facing boardwalks had heard the commotion and had taken in at least some of the fuss, and were pointing at the fallen would-be deputies and magpie-chattering to each other. The stranger smiled at them and nodded. Waved a bit.

"Nice, friendly town you got here," he said.

He got his hat from the saddle pommel, put it on, snapping the brim in place, and began to walk his horse down the street, heading to the nearby Hotel Trinidad. Tulley fell in at his side, having to work to keep up with the stranger's easy but long-legged stride.

Tulley grinned, shaking his head. "That was somethin' to see, mister. Somethin' to see."

"Was it?"

"Gen-you-wine pleasure to see them buzzards get more than they dished out for once. But doin' that wasn't the wisest move a man might make."

"There a law against defending yourself in this town?"

"In this town? Hell, there's a law against *breathin'*, if the sheriff and his mob don't like the way you're goin' about it. And right now, you're breakin' that law mighty hard."

"That so."

"That's so, all right. Good thing for you you're a city dude."

A small smile tickled the stranger's lips. "Why's that?"

"'Cause them two won't likely admit to Sheriff

Gauge that some pavement pounder knocked 'em around like that. So you should have no trouble with our sheriff. Of course, that in itself presents another problem entirely."

"Does it?"

Tulley nodded. "That scurvy pair'll figure a way to take care of you later, if you're still around."

"I'm sure things will work out."

Still working to keep up, Tulley said, "Their names is Riley and Jackson. Riley, he's the one with the mustache, and Jack—"

"Don't care who they are, Pop."

"Name's Tulley."

"All right, Tulley. But I don't."

They were at the hotel. The stranger hitched the gelding to the rail. Stroked its face. The animal nodded in approval at the attention.

Tulley said, "Don't know that you should be stoppin', mister. Even if you *are* hungry for breakfast."

"Because?"

"Because you want to keep on movin'—goin' to wherever it was you was headed. Leave Trinidad and them two snakes behind you, and good riddance."

"Suppose," the stranger said, "I decide to stay around awhile."

"Well, then," Tulley said, grinning, "I'd buy me a drink and let me tell you more about friendly, little Trinidad, and the big, bad lawman those two scoundrels work for."

The stranger shook his head. "No drink. Not right now. Settle for breakfast?"

"I ain't et a thing since day before yesterday. Maybe I *should* et some today."

"Why not?" He grinned. "You might get to like it."

The hotel restaurant wasn't fancy, but it was clean and even had white linen tablecloths. The waiter seemed confused by the pairing of dude and desert rat, but he seated them without comment.

Soon they'd been served steak and eggs and coffee. They chowed down without conversation, then sat back and had more coffee as Tulley began to tell the stranger about Sheriff Harry Gauge and his bunch of outlaw deputies, the landgrab that was well under way, and how the Bar-O was one of the last holdouts.

The stranger listened with seeming interest but asked no questions, just occasionally nodding.

"So I guess you can see this is no kind of town," Tulley said, "for the likes of you."

"You're right," the stranger said. "After all, I'm just passing through."

"What's your name, anyway?"

"When you're passing through, why leave that behind?"

Tulley had no answer for that. "So where you headed?"

The stranger was not at all reluctant to share that information: "California."

"Where's about in California?"

"Haven't narrowed it down just yet."

That seemed reasonable to Tulley.

The stranger had a question. "How does it pay?"

"How does what pay?"

"Being the town character."

That made Tulley guffaw. "I only been the resident eccentric here since, oh, February, I guess. Got run out of Ellis. Sheriff give me a dollar, stuck me on top of a stagecoach, and said fare-thee-well. But any information you get from me, mister, it'll be well worth a drink or a meal. Didn't take me long to get the gist of Trinidad."

"How do you get by?"

"I sweep out at the livery and a few other places. I do odd jobs, it's called."

The stranger dug out a quarter-eagle gold piece and gave it to him. "This is for that drink. Try to have something left for a meal or two."

"Much appreciated, mister. So you're leavin' then?"

He shrugged. "I had my breakfast, didn't I?"

The stranger got up, left a ten-cent tip, and Tulley followed him out onto the boardwalk in front of the hotel. The sound of horses coming up the street from the church end caught the attention of both men.

Tulley and the stranger watched as Old Man Cullen, saddled up like a sighted man, rode in with his pretty daughter riding along near his side. Their foreman, Whit Murphy, was just behind them, leading a pair of packhorses with a body slung over each like sacks of grain.

Willa's eyes swept over the stranger, but didn't linger.

Shaking his head, Tulley said, "That's the kinda town it is, mister. Shootin's every whip stitch."

"Who are those people?"

"That's George Cullen and his daughter, Willa. Cullen's foreman leadin' the packhorses. Don't recognize the dead men from just their backsides."

The Cullen party stopped outside the sheriff's office.

Even from well down the street, the old man's shout could be plainly heard: *"Sheriff Gauge! I have something for you!"*

Gauge came out, in no hurry, followed by his deputy. The sheriff took it all in, hands on hips, spat tobacco, then spoke loudly himself, perhaps aware of how many townsfolk were listening from the boardwalk or windows.

"What's on your mind, Cullen?"

"Clean-shaven one is the sheriff," Tulley told the stranger. "Harry Gauge. The fire-bearded fella is his deputy, Vint Rhomer. Only Gauge is smart. But they's both mean as rattlers."

The narrow eyes narrowed further. "I've heard of Gauge. Never heard him to be on the right side of a badge, though."

"Well, mister, you know how it is out here. Seems

like men good with guns are always on one side of a badge or the other, but it ain't always the same side."

The stranger nodded at Tulley's wisdom.

Old man Cullen was saying, "I'm returning some things you mislaid, Sheriff. I believe these two belong to you. Last night they tried to set fire to my range."

"By damn," Tulley said, "the old man is really standin' up to Gauge! This is that big trouble I was tellin' you about. And now it's gonna get even bigger."

The stranger shrugged. "Well, let's walk down there and see the show. Get a good seat."

"Are you loco, mister? Not me! The bullets could start flyin' at any time now."

"Not loco, Tulley. Just curious. Your colorful stories got me interested in this town."

The stranger started down the boardwalk.

"Well, *I* call it loco," Tulley insisted, but found himself tagging along again. "And I can't let you go wanderin' off around town this dangerous without *somebody* to hold that citified hand of yours."

They paused at the end of the boardwalk, which provided a good catercorner view of the sheriff's office and the five horses stopped in front of it.

Deputy Rhomer was over having a look at the two corpses slung over the pack animals. He turned toward the sheriff, who stood at the edge of the porch above the steps.

"It's Stringer and Bradley!" Rhomer said.

Gauge ambled down and positioned himself in front of the old man and his daughter, both still on horseback. "I suppose you have witnesses to what happened?"

"We have plenty, Sheriff," Cullen said.

"All on the Bar-O payroll, of course."

"Right. Like these two here were on *your* payroll."

"You mean, these two men of mine who your men shot down in cold blood."

The girl, who was in a red-and-black plaid shirt and denim pants, yellow hair braided up, said, "In self-defense, Sheriff Gauge. They sneaked in at night and were setting fire to our high grass where cattle were grazing."

"And your boys were *waiting*? Big range to know just the right spot."

Cullen said, "I had a good idea where you'd hit. Do you deny these are your men?"

The sheriff shook his head. "No. Not at all. Good loyal employees. They wear deputy badges when we go out on posse. And that's why I'm afraid you took yourself too big a bite this time, Mr. Cullen. Really boxed yourself in."

"Oh?"

Gauge still had his hands on his hips, which put one hand near the butt of his .44. He was smiling up into a face that couldn't see, but no doubt the old man could make out the nastiness in that unseen smile by the tone of the sheriff's voice.

"You knew I was sending my men out to see you, old man, with a proposal to buy out your land. Wouldn't be any trouble at all for you to lay an ambush for them, then start a fire that you could put out quick . . . but point to as something the dead men done."

As they watched from the end of the boardwalk, Tulley and the stranger were aware that other onlookers, who'd filled in behind them, were now backing away.

As Tulley said earlier, bullets might fly. . . .

Maybe that was why the stranger was knotting that tie-down strap, securing the holstered .44 to his right thigh.

Old Man Cullen was saying, a snarl in his voice, "You know damn well that it didn't happen that way."

Gauge shook his head. "I don't know any such thing, Mr. Cullen. But I *do* know this. Those men were deputized by me before I sent them out, in anticipation of what you might pull."

The stranger stepped down from the boardwalk and started across the street. Tulley reached out to stop him, but the man was already on his way. And that stride of his was a long one.

Gauge was saying, "And you don't just kill lawmen and get away with it, old man. Not in *my* town."

Rhomer gripped Gauge's arm and pointed to where the stranger was over, having a look at the two bodies, turning the head of one to look at a dead face, doing the same with the other.

Then the stranger called, "Mr. Cullen!"

The old man's face turned toward the voice, his expression quizzical. "Yes? Who is that?"

"Sir, are you responsible for these deaths?"

Cullen's chin rose. "I am. Not personally, but men who work for me did, protecting my property. I take full responsibility."

Gauge, frowning, whispered harshly to his deputy, "Who the hell is this?"

"Damn if I know," Rhomer said. "Just some dude. Never seen him before."

The stranger walked around to look up at the mounted Cullen, giving a respectful nod to the man's daughter as he did. "Then don't worry about it, sir."

"Don't . . . don't *worry* about it?"

"No. You've done the law a service. These are wanted men. Dead or alive in four states that I know of. The posters are up all over the territory." He turned and gave the sheriff a pleasant smile. "I'd be willing to bet you have them up in your office, Sheriff."

"Who are you?" Gauge demanded.

The smile left the stranger's face. "Or maybe you don't. Maybe you took those circulars down, or never put them up."

Gauge reddened. "What are you *talking* about?"

"I'm talking about the company you keep. Not very good."

Gauge's upper lip curled back in a terrible smile. "Listen to me, stranger . . . this is *not* your business. Back off and back away or we're going to have a problem that I'm going to solve."

The stranger ignored the threat. "In fact," he said, loud enough for any onlookers or eavesdroppers to hear, "Mr. Cullen has a reward coming. About five hundred U.S. dollars for the pair of them."

Stunned, a slack-jawed Cullen said, "Five hundred . . . ?"

The stranger grinned. "Yeah, I know. Two of a kind usually doesn't pay off that well."

Tulley didn't see them till it was too late—Riley and Jackson, coming around the near side of the sheriff's office-jailhouse. They'd been inside there all this time, and were coming up behind the stranger, who was facing the sheriff.

"Mister!" Tulley called.

Willa Cullen had seen them, too, and she pulled her horse between the two bushwhackers and the dude, who immediately came around the back of the animal to find the two supposed deputies, already with guns in hand.

"Time to die," Riley said, "you lousy, slicked-up—"

The stranger drew and fired, and neither man, despite the guns already in their hands, could do a damn thing about it except look down at the red blossoming over their hearts before dropping onto their backs to sprawl in the dusty street.

So close had the shots been together, they might have been one big blast. Tulley had never seen anything like it—drawing on two men whose guns were at the ready, taking them down like target-practice tin cans.

To himself the desert rat muttered, "And I was gonna hold *his* hand. . . ."

CHAPTER SIX

A wide-eyed Willa Cullen had seen the shooting,
too, leaving her stunned but admiring. Her father shouted her name, but Willa calmed him, saying, "It's *fine*, Papa! I'm fine."

She and the rest of her party settled their horses,
riled by the gunshots, Whit filling her father in, as
Gauge and Rhomer ran to their fallen comrades.
Neither man had seen the gunfight itself, Willa on
her horse blocking their view.

Gauge knelt over the men, who both stared
back at him as sightless as George Cullen. Rhomer
knelt there, too, and he and Gauge both looked
up at the stranger, who was striding over, holster-
ing his .44.

"Do me a favor, Sheriff?" the stranger asked pleasantly. "Check for posters on them, too? Maybe *I* got
some reward money coming."

Then he tipped his hat to the local law and

started toward Willa, who was looking on, still on horseback. The scent of gunsmoke hung heavy.

Rhomer was glaring at the stranger's back, his hand heading for his own holstered .44. Willa drew in a breath, ready to give warning.

But the sheriff grabbed his deputy's arm, stopping him, shaking his head, mouthing what she thought were the words, *Not now.* Or maybe: *Not yet.*

The stranger swept off his hat in a gentlemanly manner and gave her a nod that was almost a half-bow. "Thanks for trying to protect me, miss."

"You looked like you might need it," she said. She dropped her head closer to him and spoke in a near whisper. "And you might want to take care, turning your back on those two."

He glanced over his shoulder at Gauge and Rhomer, who were getting to their feet. Returning his attention to her, the stranger looked up at her with an expression that was both friendly and serious.

"A man could ask for no better guardian angel than yourself," he said. "But I assure you it isn't necessary. I can handle myself."

These quiet words were somehow like a slap. *"Really?"*

Now he smiled and there was a twinkle in the washed-out blue eyes squinting in the mid-morning sun. "I wouldn't want to be responsible for anything unfortunate that might befall such a fine young lady."

"Well, let me assure you I can handle *myself*."
She looked past him. Whispering again, she said,
"The sheriff's coming. . . ."

The stranger turned as a stony-faced Gauge approached, ignoring the man who'd just shot two of
his people and glancing up to address Willa.

"What did you see, Miss Cullen?"

She pointed toward the bodies in the dust.
"Those two over there had their guns out and were
coming up on this man from behind. He shot in
self-defense."

"You'd testify to that?"

"I would."

The sheriff turned to the stranger and said,
"What's your business here?"

"Just passing through."

"Any idea why Jackson and Riley attacked you?"

"Is that their names?"

"That's their names."

"Sheriff, you had a look at the bodies. You may
have noticed that Mr. Jackson and Mr. Riley were
already in sad shape before they died."

Gauge studied the stranger's impassive face.
"Yeah. It looks like somebody gave them a beating."

"Somebody did. Me."

"Why?"

"They gave me cause."

The sheriff thought that over. On the boardwalks, and in the street, townspeople continued to

gather. Some had likely seen the shooting—the smiles they were sharing, and the excitement in their faces, the fevered murmur of their conversation, indicated as much. Like Willa, at least some citizens had seen the stranger draw his weapon and fire so fast the human eye could barely register it.

Gauge said, "Just passing through, huh?"

"Just passing through."

"*Keep* passing through."

The stranger grinned. "If you're suggesting there's a stage out of town at noon and you want me on it, Sheriff—you mind if I ride out on my horse, instead?"

"I don't care if you leave on foot. Just leave."

He gave Gauge an easygoing smile. "Like I said, I'm passing through. But I might stay a day or two. I rode most of the night and I need to rest some. Maybe find a game of cards. Have a drink. Spend a little money in your fine town. Any objection?"

Gauge glanced around. So many witnesses.

"No objection. I can't fault a man for defending himself," the sheriff said, louder now. "But I'll be watchin' you, mister. We don't tolerate reckless violence in Trinidad."

Willa almost laughed out loud at that. But mirth didn't come easy with so much death nearby—two men in the street, those two others on packhorses, the latter getting taken down now by the undertaker and an assistant.

"I'll keep that in mind, Sheriff," the stranger said.

Gauge's eyes tightened. "You got a name, mister?"

"Everybody's got a name, Sheriff. But I won't be around long enough for mine to matter."

The sheriff frowned, thought about that a second, nodded, then went off to join his deputy. Doc Miller had come onto the scene and the late Riley and Jackson were getting a final examination.

The stranger was taking that in, but still standing near Willa on horseback.

She said to him, "Just who *are* you, anyway?"

He looked back at her. "Like I said, miss. Just a traveler passing through."

"Headed where?"

"California. Taking my time about it. No hurry."

"That man you were bandying with? That's Sheriff Harry Gauge, and he's dangerous."

"I know who he is, miss. And I just killed two men, so some might say the same of me."

She reared back so much at the cocky remark, her horse almost did the same. "Are you *proud* of that?"

"No. But I don't feel guilty, either. They chose how they died."

She frowned down at him. He was an irritating sort. "You *have* a name, don't you?"

He grinned at her. "I sure do."

Then he nodded and put on his curl-brimmed

black hat, said, "Pleasure to meet you, Miss Cullen," and headed off. That ragged deadbeat—*what was his name? Tulley?*—fell in alongside the stranger, chattering and cackling. Drunken old fool.

As the Cullen party headed out of Trinidad on their way back to the Bar-O, Willa's father asked, "Who was he, girl? That stranger."

"He wouldn't say, Papa. But he's an arrogant one."

"That so?"

"He wouldn't give me his name, but then he calls me by *mine*. What nerve. How rude."

Her father was smiling. They were riding along easily.

He said, "Maybe so, but it appears he's quite handy with a shootin' iron."

Willa had to smile at her father's old-fashioned frontier language. They didn't converse for a while; then Papa chimed in again.

"That's just how Caleb York would have done it," he said with a big smile.

Whit, clearly tired of all the York talk, said grumpily, "He would have, except that he's dead."

"So they say," the old man granted. "Anyway, York would likely have taken the sheriff out, and Rhomer, too. Taken down every single one of them. Still . . . who do you suppose he is?"

Whit said dismissively, "Just some dude who got off a couple of lucky shots. He was dressed like a city slicker tryin' to *look* cowboy."

"Describe them clothes," her father said.

Whit did.

"Well," the old man said, "*Caleb York* dressed in black. Or so the stories go."

"But not like a damn *dude,*" Whit said, then added, "Pardon, Miss Willa."

"I don't know who or what he is," she said, not giving a damn about Whit cursing, "but he's no dude. You didn't see what *I* saw, Whit."

"And what did you see, Miss Willa?"

"I saw a man outdraw two men with their guns *already* drawn. *That's* what I saw."

For a while they rode on in silence.

Then not far from the fork that to the right took them into the ranch, her father said, "I know somebody else, besides Caleb York, they say wears black."

She said, "Who is that, Papa?"

"Banion," he said. "Wes Banion."

From the crowd of onlookers, Lola emerged twirling a parasol over her shoulder, looking a fine lady in a two-piece dark blue satin dress with fitted bodice and white lace trim at collar and cuffs.

Gauge gave her a glance and a nod. He and Rhomer were dealing with Perkins, the undertaker, who was about to take charge of the remains of Riley and Jackson, as well as the slightly scorched bodies of Stringer and Bradley. Small, skinny, bald, the twitchy-mustached Perkins was having trouble keeping somber, with business booming like this.

"No services," Gauge told the undertaker. "Just four holes and plant them. Nothing read over 'em. Send the bill to my office."

Perkins was clutching his top hat by its brim, as if it might fly away. "And the gentleman last night?"

"Same."

"Separate bills?"

"One bill. Charge the city as usual."

The undertaker nodded and went about his task.

Gauge went to Lola. "What did you see?"

She slowly spun the parasol on her shoulder, her manner casual, as if out on a weekend stroll. "Nothing. But everybody is saying this newcomer is the fastest gun *ever.* And most of them have seen you in action, Harry. Of course, you know how fickle people are. And how easily impressed."

He studied her, looking for smugness. "You think this is funny?"

"Not a little bit." The twirling stopped, her expression turning grave. "Could it . . . could it be *Banion,* Harry?"

He sighed. Shook his head. "Doesn't seem likely, but . . ." He gave her a sly smile ". . . how would you like to find out for me?"

Her smile in return was as confident as it was pretty. "That doesn't sound like a terribly difficult chore."

"Not with *your* special talents it isn't."

She smiled just a little. "I'm going to choose to take that as a compliment."

And she turned and walked toward the Victory, twirling the little shoulder-slung umbrella again.

Rhomer came up to Gauge, frowning. "You should have let me cut that buzzard in half."

"Not the time or place."

"You catch any of the action?"

"No. That girl's horse was in the way."

Frowning, Rhomer shook his head. "Well, he must have been pretty damn fast to take 'em both like that."

"Maybe. Or maybe Jackson and Riley were just clumsy oafs."

Rhomer nodded, acknowledging that possibility. "I heard you send Lola down, to scope out who and what that stranger is."

"Did you?"

Rhomer nodded. "Think she can get anything out of him?"

"If he's breathing, she can." He let out a nasty chuckle. "And then, pretty soon? Maybe he won't be."

Tulley and the stranger walked the black-maned dappled gelding down to the livery stable, where a stall and feed were arranged for the animal.

That taken care of, the pair walked back down the street as various Trinidad citizens gawked and pointed at the dude who had shot down two of the sheriff's toughs.

Still having to work at keeping up, Tulley asked, "Where to next, stranger?"

"Well, now that my horse can get some rest," he said, "maybe I better find myself a room. Fairly tuckered."

"You crazy? You can't get a room now."

"Oh?"

"Yesterday was payday! Hotel's chock-full of cowpokes sleepin' it off."

"Shame. Should've taken a stall next to my horse."

"You know what *you* need, stranger?"

"Tell me."

"A drink."

"It isn't even noon yet."

"But you already beat up two men today and shot 'em down to boot. I figure that oughter work up a *hell* of a thirst. Anyways, I reckon you owe me another drink for savin' your hide."

"I do at that."

Tulley jabbed a finger at the stranger without touching him. "In addition to which, it's about time you and me had a man-to-man talk, my friend."

He half-smiled, raised one eyebrow. "Like I used to have with my daddy?"

"Mebbe. Mebbe do you some good."

"What's to talk about? I already know about the birds and the bees."

"I *bet* you do! I just bet you do. But what you *don't* know is what's gonna happen to you right soon, and it won't be near as fun as the birds and the bees."

"Oh?"

"No, sir. A man don't pull what you did on Harry Gauge and live long around here."

The stranger shrugged. "Well, let's give the sheriff time to figure out what to do about me. Here we are."

They were at the Victory.

He gave Tulley a warm smile. "Ready for that drink, old-timer?"

"Well, now." Tulley licked dry lips. "I guess we can continue our little talk in there as well as anywheres."

The stranger pushed through the batwing doors with Tulley right on his heels. This time of day at the Victory, things were quiet—no music, very little gambling, just a row of cowboys lined up along the brass rail, seeking the hair of the dog. Faces exchanged wary glances in the mirror as the stranger found a place midway for himself and Tulley.

A handlebar-mustached bartender in white shirt and bow tie attended them immediately, or anyway did the stranger. "Yes, sir. What'll it be, sir?"

The stranger glanced at Tulley. "How about you, pal?"

"Beer's fine, mister."

"Two beers, bartender."

But when the foaming mugs arrived, and the stranger went to digging out a coin, the bartender held up a palm and said, "No charge."

"Right friendly," the stranger said, with a nod of thanks.

A cowhand called down from the far end of the bar: "Mister, that true what you told the sheriff, 'bout Stringer and Bradley? *Was* they wanted men?"

The stranger took a sip, nodded, said, "You can write the territorial governor for copies of the circulars if you want."

"That's okay, mister. Take your word for it."

From down the other way, a voice called out, "Four of them 'deputies' headed to Boot Hill! Sure puts the squeeze on the sheriff."

Somebody else said, "Couldn't happen to nicer fellers."

Glancing down the bar both ways, the stranger said, "If the sheriff and his bunch are all that bad, why don't you folks clean them out?"

As if in answer, two men pushed through the swinging doors, big, burly, unshaven, battered hats snugged down, six-guns low on their hips, their expressions daring you to look them in the eye. A dare no one was taking.

Tulley whispered, "*That's* why."

"Pretty playmates the sheriff has," the stranger said, speaking over the rim of his glass.

The two gunhands took a table. One of the bartenders automatically brought them beers. The taller of the two rolled a cigarette while the other lit up a stogie. Their eyes remained on the bar.

In particular, on the stranger.

"Now, don't you go *startin'* nothin'," Tulley advised his new friend. "You had enough fun for one mornin'."

"Is that possible, really?"

"What?"

"Can a man *ever* have enough fun?"

The doors opened again, but it wasn't a gunhand who breezed through: it was a beautiful, dark-haired female in a figure-outlining satin dress, a parasol over her shoulder.

The stranger, seeing this in the mirror, said, "You get my point, old-timer?"

Tulley said, "You might want to steer clear of that one."

"I can see a lot of reasons not to take that advice."

"That's Lola."

"It would be."

"She belongs to the sheriff."

The stranger gave him a mock frown. "Tulley, didn't this country get in a ruckus a while back that settled this whole business of folks belonging to other folks?"

They watched in the mirror as she hip-swayed up to them. Then the stranger turned toward her, Tulley keeping his back to her, but watching in the glass.

She looked the stranger up and down like a dress on display she was considering buying for herself. Then she smirked at him, eyes hooded, and purred, "You're quite a topic of conversation around this town, handsome."

"Am I? What topic would that be?"

"Whether you're a brave man or a fool."

"What's your preference?"

She shrugged one shoulder. "I'll buy either one a drink."

He grinned at her. "Everybody is just so darn friendly around here. Bartender already set me up, thanks. Anyway, I don't consider it gentlemanly to allow a lady to buy me a drink. But I'd gladly buy *you* one."

Shaking her head a little, still smirking, she said, "Maybe you're a brave man *and* a fool."

"Wouldn't be the first time in history."

She tilted her head, as if trying to get a different, better angle on him. "How about you buy the first round? Then the second is on me."

"I don't know. . . ."

"Come on! Lady's prerogative. Shall we sit?"

Tulley looked back over his shoulder at her.

"Not *you*, Tulley," she said in a scolding tone.

"Well, now," the stranger said, "*that's* not very friendly."

She frowned. "That barfly would drink the juice out of a thermometer. Why waste anything on him?"

"He's my friend."

She sighed. "All right, Mr. Tulley. Would you do us the honor of joining us?"

The desert rat chugged down his beer, then turned to them and raised his hands, as if in the process of being held up. "No, Miss Lola, thank you kindly, but I was just shoving off, anyway. Gettin' a little too old for all this excitement."

And he went out, leaving the stranger to his own devices.

After all, hadn't the dude said he already knew about the birds and the bees?

Lola went to the nearest table, but the stranger nodded toward the corner one, where the two Gauge gunmen sat, nursing their beers.

"How about over there?" he asked.

She smiled at him. There were half-a-dozen empty tables around. But she clearly liked his choice. She went over, tossed her parasol on the table and the beer mugs jumped. So did the two hard cases.

"Find somewhere else to sit," she said.

The bigger of the two said, "Now, look here, Lola. . . ."

"Sorry. I meant, find somewhere else to drink."

The other one said, "There *is* no other place in town to drink."

"I don't believe that's my problem."

They looked at her. She looked at them. They got up, shot her dirty glances that were kind of pathetic, and headed back out the batwing doors.

The stranger came to her side and said, "Brave woman or fool?"

"Neither," she said, and gave him a sideways smile. "I own the place." She gestured to the nearest chair. "Have a seat."

He did, but taking the chair that put the corner walls to his back.

"So that's why you wanted this table," she said, sitting.

"That was one reason," the stranger said.

"Always this careful?"

"Why learn the hard way?"

"That's what I like," she said with a chuckle. "A man who knows his mind. Now, why don't you tell me about yourself?"

He'd brought his beer along and he sipped it. "Not much to tell. Just drifting my way to California."

A bartender delivered her a mixed drink that she hadn't needed to request.

She asked the stranger, "What's a hard man like you doin' wearing such soft threads?"

He shrugged. "I like to look good."

And he did look good to her, but the clothes had little if anything to do with it. Such a big rock-jawed man with those hard Indian angles in his face, but such beautiful eyes peering from those cautious slits, a blue the color of faded denim. This was a man. But she somehow knew that this was not a man who would raise a hand to a woman, like some she knew.

"Anyway," he said, "if I look like a mail-order cowboy, I figure nobody will see me as a threat."

"And just leave you alone."

"That's right."

"How's that workin' out for ya?"

Her deadpan expression finally made him burst out laughing.

He seemed genuine as he said: "I like you, Lola."

She raised an eyebrow. "You know *my* name, but I don't know yours."

He waved that gently away. "Not worth knowing. Just passing through. Why make attachments?" He yawned. "Sorry."

"Am I boring you, cowboy?"

"Anything but. I just been up a long, long time."

"And killing dunderheads wears you out?"

He chuckled deep. "Something like that. But there's not a room available in the hotel, I'm told."

"Probably not. Payday hangovers gettin' slept off." She lifted a satin shoulder and set it down. "But I can arrange a room for you upstairs."

He half-grinned. "Well, uh . . . aren't those usually used for other than sleeping?"

"There's neither sleeping nor the other in most of them right now. I can fix you up so you can nap awhile. And come wake you up around supper."

"That would be very kind."

She walked him to the rear of the saloon and up the stairs to the landing along which half-a-dozen doors waited. She unlocked one at the end and showed him into the small functional area where there wasn't much but a brass bed and porcelain basin, though the red-and-black San Francisco-style wallpaper lent a certain mood.

"Thank you for this," the stranger said. He sat on a chair and started taking off his boots.

She got the kerosene hurricane lamp on a small bedside table going. "I'd sleep on top of those covers, if I were you."

"I already made that deduction, thanks." He was in his stockinged feet now. He stood.

She came over to him. "I just want to make sure you knew you were right in what you said."

"What did I say?"

"That this is a friendly town."

Which called for a friendly kiss, which she got on her tiptoes and gave him.

Then he put his arm around her waist and drew her close and returned the kiss with interest.

Her breathing was heavy and halting when he finally let go of her.

He gave her a boyish grin that lit up the rawboned face. "Just my way of saying 'you're welcome,' ma'am."

Her upper lip curled back over her teeth in an insolent smile. "My name isn't 'ma'am.' It's Lola."

And she kissed him again, the way he had her.

Then the kerosene lamp got turned down, and in the darkness came a rustle of satin and the clunk of a belt buckle hitting the floor.

Later, at the door, she stopped to look back and asked, "Your name wouldn't be *Banion*, would it?"

"Sounds like maybe you already know the answer to that." He climbed back onto the bed and the mattress springs sang. "You mind leavin' that key, ma'am?"

She grinned and threw it at him and left.

CHAPTER SEVEN

At her father's request, Willa put on a navy-and-white calico dress and played hostess for the meeting of the Trinidad Citizen's Committee at the Cullen ranch. Dutifully, she delivered smiles, gathered hats, and guided each man into the dining room, where Papa waited.

This impromptu gathering, on the afternoon after the morning of the gunfight outside the sheriff's office, was not being held in the usual space at the rear of Harris Mercantile. That was too public—anybody might wander in and overhear the discussion.

Including the sheriff. Or any of his men, for that matter.

And what the Citizens Committee had to discuss was about as private as town business got.

Before leaving Trinidad this morning, Cullen had told Thomas Carter, the president of Trinidad

Bank and Trust, to spread the word for a two o'clock get-together. And now the six men, including her father and foreman Whit Murphy, were seated around the big dining-room table, a heavy dark-wood, decoratively carved Spanish piece with matching chairs that her late mother had brought back from one of her buying trips across the border.

Willa served coffee, refilling cups, staying on the periphery as was expected of a female . . . but missing nothing.

Mayor Jasper Hardy, also the town barber and as such a well-groomed individual with slicked back hair and trimmed mustache, was saying, "My understanding is that this . . . this drifter is reluctant to give out his name. Could be he's a wanted man."

"Or a bounty hunter," said slender, bug-eyed Clem Davis, who ran the apothecary, Adam's apple making his bow tie bobble. "He knew those two, Stringer and Bradley, were wanted men, didn't he?"

Clarence Mathers, fleshy and in his fifties, bald on top with compensating muttonchops, was a reluctant partner of the sheriff's in the town hardware store. He said, "Could be anybody. Bounty hunter? Maybe. Former lawman? Possibly. Gunfighter? Surely. But just passing through."

Her father was shaking his head, his hands flat on the table. "He isn't just 'anybody,' Clarence. I'm telling you, my friend Parker sent him."

"You have confirmation of this, George?"

"No."

"Yet you're saying this man is Banion?"

"Or someone as good or better than Banion."

Mathers threw his hands up. "Then why in hell hasn't he *identified* himself to you, George? Excuse the French, Miss Cullen."

She smiled a little, but said nothing. She was making a round of filling coffee cups.

Her father was saying, "If he's Banion—or some other professional gun that Parker sent in response to my instructions—he came to do a job. That didn't require checking in with us. In fact, he could be protecting us by putting distance between himself and those who hired him."

"*You're* who hired him, George," the mayor reminded her father. "We didn't approve this enterprise. And if you'd brought it to us, I'd venture to say we would have voted it down."

The old man shrugged. "Well, it was my decision, my choice . . . and my money."

Wearing a humorless smile, banker Carter was shaking his head. "In any event, it's a moot point. This *couldn't* be Banion, or anyone else your friend might have sent."

"And just why is that, Tom?"

The banker flipped over a hand. "Simple reality. Very unlikely that any man could have made it here so fast."

The sightless host seemed to return his friend's gaze. "Is that so? Railroad at Las Vegas is only twenty-five miles from here. Parker could have reached Banion by wire and the man could have made it here from, hell, as far away as five hundred miles."

"What about those last twenty-five miles?"

"He'd been riding all night!"

Whit, smirking in doubt, said, "Mr. Cullen, what about his *horse*?"

Her father remained unfazed. "Maybe he bought it over at Las Vegas. Maybe he arranged to have a mount waitin' for him. Could be he shipped it with him by train. Just like they ship cattle."

The men around the table exchanged glances, weighing these possibilities.

No matter—her father had convinced himself. "By damn," he said, "that *must* be it. He *must* be Banion."

Hardware man Mathers said, "I still say, had that been the case, your man would contact you right away. He wouldn't leave you in the dark."

That remark, made to the blind man seated at the head of the table, had been unintentionally tactless enough to create a momentary lull in the conversation, though her father didn't appear to have taken any offense. Instead, his face was taut with thought.

"Perhaps you have a point, Clarence," her father said.

Willa set the coffeepot down with a small clunk that got everyone's attention. She sat at the other end of the table and joined the meeting, weary of her servile role.

"Maybe," she said, "he'd rather earn his money first."

Perhaps faintly irritated that she'd joined the male confabulation, Cullen said, "He's doing pretty well so far without any down payment, daughter."

"Well, he didn't take Gauge out or Rhomer, either," Whit observed, vaguely disgusted. "And they was standin' right there for the takin'."

Willa's eyes and nostrils flared, words exploding from her: "I'm beginning to think you good members of the Citizens Committee are all as bad as Harry Gauge! Hiring somebody to *kill* a man."

There were protests to that remark, flustered reminders that only her *father* had done the hiring, but she spoke over them, saying, "You're happy to have *George Cullen* take the lead *and* the blame, aren't you?"

The hardware man said, "Miss Cullen, we're between the proverbial rock and a hard place. When the sheriff took office, he bought interests in many of our businesses. You must know that. And maybe you know that it seemed a wise business move at the time. Gauge shared our tax burden, he provided new capital for expansion. Some of the newer businesses in Trinidad couldn't have opened up at all without the sheriff's backing and blessing."

"And now," she said, "he's returned all the tax burden over to you, and is calling these investments 'loans' and demanding repayment while retaining his interest in your businesses."

The Trinidad merchants wore glum expressions, several hanging their heads.

She went on: "Harry Gauge allows the cowboys from his spread, and for that matter ours and all the others, to come to town and shoot the place up every payday . . . because it's good for business. Especially the Victory."

Her father said, "What do you suggest we do, girl?"

Her voice was firm and clear. "Stand together. Stand up to Gauge and his men. You say you're a concerned citizens group. *Do* something about it!"

That prompted hollow laughter and head shaking among their guests.

The mayor said, "Harry Gauge has a small army of gunhands, Miss Cullen. You know that."

"He's lost four of them in two days," she reminded him. "The Bar-O boys took down Stringer and Bradley themselves. Papa, you came out on top because you outfought Gauge."

"No, daughter. It was because I out*thought* them. But superior tactics can't overcome strength of numbers."

All around Willa were the faces of men tolerating her, not really taking her words into account. "Gentlemen . . . Papa . . . there *has* to be a better way to stop Harry Gauge than calling upon hired killers."

Her father said nothing for several long seconds. Finally he said, "Best you stay out of it, Willa.

This ain't the kind of thing for a woman to decide."

Flushed, she stood and left the table, but she didn't leave the room. She went back to quietly refilling coffee cups. She wanted to hear anything these oh-so-wise city fathers had to say. So much in her life was riding on the decisions her father and his too-timid friends were making.

The mayor, smoothing his perfect, perfectly waxed mustache, said, "I think we should find out if this is indeed Wes Banion. I mean, none of us knows the man by sight, just reputation."

The banker said, "Well, you're the mayor, Jasper. Why don't you approach him?"

"And if Sheriff Gauge sees me? Mr. Cullen . . . George . . . you sent for him. Isn't it more appropriate that you make contact?"

The druggist said, "If George is seen talking to that gunfighter, by Gauge or any of his men, the only person to profit will be undertaker Perkins."

"*I'll* do it," Willa said.

Everyone looked at her. She was at her father's shoulder now, having just refilled his cup.

Looking toward her voice, Papa said, "Daughter . . . what are you—"

"The stranger and I chatted briefly. He seemed friendly enough. He seemed . . . to like me well enough. I could approach him, easily, and if Harry Gauge or any of his outlaw deputies notice, they won't do anything about it. They won't *like* it, but . . . they won't do anything."

Her father's milky eyes were on her, and he was frowning.

Then a shrewd expression came over the weathered features and he said, "There are things a woman can manage that a man can't. Yes, daughter, I think you're the one to have word with Banion."

"Or whoever he is."

"Or whoever he is. *But* whoever he is, he knows his way around a gun, and that's what we need right now."

Her frown got into her voice. "Papa, I won't hire your killers for you."

He reached for her hand and found it. "Not asking you to, girl. Just see if you can get a name out of him. And, whatever it might be, ask him if he knows Raymond Parker of Denver . . . who happens to be an old friend of your father's."

A meeting of a related nature, but of an entirely different sort, was under way in Sheriff Harry Gauge's office. No coffee here—just a bottle of whiskey and some scattered glasses. Nobody had been at the door to take their hats for them and, with the exception of the sheriff himself whose Stetson was on a hook behind him, the attendees kept their lids on.

Seated across from Gauge at his desk were Deputy Vint Rhomer and two rough-looking gunnies with deputy badges pinned on their shirts. After what happened this morning to Riley and Jackson, the sheriff had handed out deputy badges to all his bunch.

Lanky, dark-haired, dark-eyed Jake Britt wore a gray shirt, black vest, fairly new Levi's, and a low-slung Colt .44. His face was narrow, his mustache and eyebrows thick, smudgy dark stubble on cheeks and chin. He had killed half-a-dozen men that Gauge knew of.

Short, burly Lars Manning was blue-eyed and blond, like the sheriff; they might have been brothers but weren't. Manning wore a dark blue twill army shirt and knee- and seat-patched denims with a .45 fairly high on his hip. Manning was responsible for at least four killings, plus the occasional Mexican.

Both men were veterans of holdups and robberies from Gauge's pre–law enforcement days.

Britt, who had a languid way about him, seemed to taste his words as he uttered them. "Any shootist who can gun down two men at one time is nobody I care to face down."

Manning, more excitable, said, "Word around town is both Jackson and Riley already had their damn *guns* out when he pulled on 'em!"

Gauge stared at them in disgust. "Who the hell said anything about facing him down? *Ambush* the son of a bitch!"

Britt glanced at Manning, and the two men

shrugged at each other, as if such duties were no big deal to either.

"Townspeople are pretty edgy, though," Britt said. "We had five shootings around here in two days."

Manning said, "I got a feelin' some of them townsfolk *liked* seein' two of our boys go down hard like that. And wouldn't mind seein' more of the same."

Britt raised four fingers, tucking back his thumb. "Need to tally in Stringer and Bradley, too. Even if that *was* out on the range."

Gauge said harshly, "What these lily livers would *like* to see happen, and what they're *gonna* see happen, are two different things entirely."

Sitting forward tentatively, Manning said, "Maybe we should just wait and see."

Gauge almost spit the words: "Wait and see *what*, Lars?"

"Wait and see if the dude *does* move on. I mean, I don't mind gettin' rid of him, but if he's already leavin' of his own accord, why waste the ammunition?"

"You really think we can afford to let Old Man Cullen . . . and that *stranger* . . . get away with what they done?"

Rhomer swallowed some whiskey and said, "The mayor and them others on that citizens committee? Rode out of town together, maybe an hour ago. Headin' out for a meetin' at the Cullen spread, I'd wager."

"Meetings," Gauge said with contempt. "They've

had plenty of those before. A handful of unarmed storekeepers, beatin' gums at each other."

"Yeah," Rhomer said, "but the way they scrambled to have a powwow, right after somebody made a move against us? That's somethin' different. That's new."

Gauge sat forward and spoke through his teeth. "Maybe so, but they won't have the occasion again." He grinned at Britt. "Jake, you ain't squeamish about a spot of bushwhackin', are you?"

Britt shrugged. "I take your pay, don't I? When?"

"Tonight. After dark, when the only thing awake on Main Street is the Victory. That's where our dude will likely land. He said something about playin' cards while he was in town."

Rhomer jerked a thumb in the Victory's direction. "I was just over there. The feller was doin' just that, playin' poker. Doin' pretty well takin' what little was left of cowpoke pay."

The sheriff frowned in thought. "Was Lola around?"

The deputy nodded. "Talked to her a bit. Says she spent some time with the stranger in friendly conversation, but ain't got a name out of him yet."

Gauge thought, *Maybe she didn't get friendly enough.* Then he said to Rhomer, "You stop by the hotel like I told you?"

The deputy nodded. "Our man ain't checked in yet. With the cowhands sobered up by now, some rooms'll free up, and he'll most likely check in tonight."

"No, he won't," Gauge said, and his grin had a sneer mixed in. "He'll be checkin' out *before* he ever checks in."

The sheriff, ever a gracious host, took the whiskey bottle and freshened the glasses of the two men he was designating for bushwhacking duty.

"Lars," he said, "head over to the Victory and keep an eye on the stranger. When he makes a move to leave, slip out the side door and meet up with wherever Britt is waiting. You know the rest."

"Have the horses ready," Manning said, nodding, "and back Britt up. You got it, boss." His grin was chaw-stained. "This dude may be fast, but he ain't faster than two guns in back of him."

Gauge frowned and shook his head. "No, can't have that. You boys position yourselves in the alley on the way from the Victory to the hotel. One on one side of the street, one on the other. When you see him comin', when he's in range, Jake, you step out shootin'. Lars, if by some miracle the dude gets his gun out, you come at him from the other side. Just watch out for a cross fire. Can't have my men killin' each other. Bad policy."

That made Britt smile, but Manning, frowning, asked, "And if somebody sees?"

Gauge jerked a thumb to his chest. "If there are any complaints, that's for the town sheriff to handle. You're both deputies and your orders are to stop trouble before it starts, right?"

The two men nodded.

Gauge said, "This dude's a known killer who was

gettin' ready to pull down on you. Do I need be any plainer than that?"

"Plain enough," Britt said, then shrugged and got to his feet. "Not like we ain't done it before."

Manning was on his feet, too, but he seemed a trifle jumpy. "You think this feller really *is* Banion, Harry?"

Gauge smirked at his flunky. "What's the difference, Lars, when it's an ambush?"

Britt chuckled deep in his chest. "What's the big fuss about Banion, anyway?"

"Are you kiddin'?" Manning said, wide-eyed. "He's the man that killed Caleb York!"

"Yeah," Britt said derisively. "*Bushwhacked* him!"

They went out, the taller man shaking his head.

Gauge leaned back in his chair, tenting his fingers, glancing at the remaining deputy. "And after the dude? Cullen goes."

Rhomer nodded, sipped some whiskey. "Damn troublemaker. Blind ol' buzzard. He's the leader. Get rid of him, rest'll tuck tail and run. But what about that daughter of his?"

"What about her?"

The deputy risked a small smile. "She even *suspects* you're responsible for her old man's death, you won't have a chance in hell with that one."

Gauge gave an easy shrug. "We'll just have to be more careful about how we handle Mr. Cullen. An elderly feller like that, blind in both eyes? He can go out a whole bunch of 'accidental' ways."

The door came open with considerable force and

Gil Willart, the foreman at Gauge's main spread—
a medium-sized man with an oversized mustache—
burst in. He was still in his chaps with the dust of
his work powdering them, as well as his blue-striped
silk shirt with weave designed to keep the wind
out. His olive-shaped, olive-color eyes were bloodshot in a leathery face.

"Boss," he said, his deep voice gruff, "we got real
trouble."

"No kidding."

The new arrival swept off his battered hat. "I'm
not talkin' about *town* trouble. I ain't interested in
them kind of problems, that's your business. Cattle
is mine."

Gauge gestured to an open chair. "Sit down. Sit
down. Pour yourself one."

"I'll sit, but I won't drink." The foreman sat down
heavily where Britt had been. "Dee and me just
came in off Swenson's Running C."

"What about it?"

The foreman sighed, shook his head, his upper
teeth bared in what wasn't exactly a smile. "Harry,
I *told* you not to pick up that mangy spread. . . ."

Gauge sat forward. "What the hell are you talking about, man?"

The dusty cowboy sighed again, shook his head
again. "Half of those hundred and fifty head? Dead
as hell. The others are in with our main herd, and
if they spread that crap around, as they surely will,
you won't have a steer to your name to sell."

Gauge was staring at the man as if he couldn't bring him into focus. "Spread *what* around?"

". . . The pox."

It felt like the world had dropped out from under Gauge.

What the hell calamity next?

The sheriff was halfway out of his chair. "Damn it all to hell! How did this *happen?*"

"Just does sometimes," the foreman said with a resigned shrug. "Happens *every* time you mix infected cows in with healthy ones."

"You didn't just discover it?"

He shook his head. "Been gradual, over the past three days. We just started spottin' them, scattered around, buzzard food. At first, I didn't think it was so bad. Just a kind of isolated thing. Few sick cows . . . *now?* It's a damn epidemic. And people catch it, too, you know."

Rhomer was sitting forward, squinting at Willart so hard, it was damn near comical. Gauge knew what that meant: his deputy was thinking.

"What is it, Vint?"

The deputy started to smile, but it was the way a man smiles who realizes he's just been taken by a sharpie. "So *that's* what Old Man Swenson was givin' me the horselaugh about. . . ."

Gauge slammed a fist on his desk and the whiskey bottle damn near spilled. "Explain!"

Rhomer said, "Old Swenson was over at the Victory a few nights ago. Liquored up to beat the band.

Fallin'-down drunk, gigglin' like a girl, laughin' and guffawin'. At Lola's request, I walk him out into the street and dump him in the alley, to sleep it off. He just looks up at me and says the joke is on you."

"On you, Rhomer?"

"No, not me—on *you*, Gauge."

Elbows on his desk, fists tight and going up and down, up and down, Gauge said, "That miserable, low-down chiseler. . . . He must've *known* they was infected when he sold 'em to me!"

Rhomer said, "He's been a holdout amongst the smaller ranchers for a good, long time, Harry. Explains why finally, after all this time, he was willin' to do business."

Upper lip curled back, Gauge said, "So he could stick me with a damn diseased herd. . . . If I could get my hands on him . . ."

Rhomer said, "Probably long gone now."

The foreman shook his head. "No, sir. One of the boys seen Swenson over by the stage relay station. Said he was just camped out near there with his horse . . . and a saddlebag full of bottles and bean cans."

Gauge, almost to himself, said, "He's waitin' for the stage with the buyers. They're due in, day after tomorrow."

Because of their proximity to Las Vegas—the biggest cattle railhead in New Mexico—buyers would come to Trinidad to make advance offers on herds. They would offer a price slightly under market, but would take entire herds and take a chance on any losses of stock that might occur on the brief cattle drive to the train.

Rhomer said, "Why the hell is *Swenson* out waitin' for the buyers? He don't have anything to sell 'em! And he's already got the money you give him, Harry. You'd think he'd light out."

"It's spite, Vint. Pure damn spite. He wants to get to those buyers and tell them my herd's got the pox before they even talk to me."

The foreman, an eyebrow arched, said, "Might be we still got time."

Gauge was thinking, nodding. "It'll be four days, anyway, before those other cows they're mixed in with show any signs. They'll be paid for by then. They'll be loaded up and on those trains and on their way before it shows."

Rhomer said, "Yeah, if Old Man Swenson don't warn them buyers first."

Gauge said, "Any suggestions, Vint?"

"Like maybe send somebody out to the Brentwood Junction relay station?" The deputy grinned. "You know, and just . . . discourage that old boy from talkin'."

"Who says you ain't smart?" He thought briefly, then asked Rhomer, "Was Maxwell over at the Victory?"

"He was. That was half an hour ago or more."

"Well, if he still is, tell him I said ride out there

tonight and see if Swenson has my money somewhere in those saddlebags, amongst the booze and
beans. Believe I'm due a refund."

Rhomer nodded, got to his feet, and was halfway out when the sheriff called to him.

"And, Vint? Tell Maxwell we want to make sure
Mr. Swenson don't misrepresent himself to no
other innocent parties in business transactions in
the future."

"Already figured that out, Harry," the deputy
said through a nasty smile, and was gone.

Gauge poured himself some more whiskey. This
was a problem, a real problem, one that made having a gunfighter in town pale by way of compari-
son. Cowpox making his herd unsalable was a
huge threat to everything he'd worked for, all that
he had planned.

But Harry Gauge prided himself on meeting
problems head-on.

And he was confident both would be solved,
and soon.

CHAPTER EIGHT

When Willa rode into town around eight, in plaid shirt and Levi's, Main Street was dark and deserted, the only light spilling from the windows and doors of the Victory. Moonlight helped, though, and she noticed a distinctive horse tied up in front of Harris Mercantile—dappled gray with a black mane.

She hitched her calico, Daisy, a ways down from it, then noticed a figure asleep under the boardwalk—that old drunk, Tulley, who'd made a mattress out of a long, plump feed sack he'd pilfered from somewhere.

She knelt by him, reached a hand in and shook him gently by a shoulder. "Tulley...wake up. Come on, Tulley—wake up!"

The rheumy eyes in the rummy's white-bearded face fluttered open and shut, open and shut, and finally, like a window shade yanked too hard, stayed open.

"Well, Miss Cullen . . . good evenin'. What brings you to town after sundown?"

Ignoring the question, she pointed toward the dappled gelding. "That's the stranger's horse, isn't it?"

Propping an elbow against the feed sack, Tulley grinned and said, "Shore is. Unusual-looking beast, don't you think? Handsome in its way."

She strove for patience, dealing with the chatty coot. "I thought he'd taken a stall for it down at the livery stable."

"Oh, he did, he did, and I helped him do it. But also, he asked me to bring the steed down here around seven and tie it up for him. Said he's goin' out for a ride a bit later."

"Where to?"

"Didn't say."

"When did you see him last?"

"Not in some while. Guess he's still down at the Victory. Been in there pretty much all afternoon and up to now."

"Sounds like you two have become real pals."

"He's a good man to know, Miss Cullen." His eyes came alive. "You saw him in action this mornin', better than just about anybody. I reckon that—"

"Is his name Banion?"

Tulley, eyelids getting heavy, said, "Banion?"

"Yes, Banion. Is that his name? Tulley!"

Tulley's eyes popped open and she repeated her question.

He chuckled, but this time spoke only to himself as he said, "Banion . . . that's rich . . . Banion . . ."

"Tulley!"

But the old desert rat was snoring now.

Shaking her head in frustration, Willa rose and began down the boardwalk, toward the Victory. She wasn't about to go in that den of iniquity, but she could wait outside for him. She'd barely started when she saw that dance-hall female Lola step through the batwing doors, in her satin-and-lace finery, her bosom hanging half-out, legs above her ankles showing through a slit at the front.

Trollop.

Right behind her, having held open a swinging door for her, was the stranger, a real gentleman in his dudish apparel, hat in hand and everything. For some reason, Willa felt anger flush her throat.

She tucked into the recessed doorway of the mercantile shop, just to get out of sight, not really to eavesdrop. But she couldn't avoid hearing, voices carrying on the clear, cool night. . . .

The stranger and the dance-hall female were walking slowly toward her up the boardwalk. Strolling, the dude's spurs jingling musically.

The fallen female said, "Would you like to walk me to the hotel, stranger? I keep a room."

"I need to seek lodging there myself."

Jingle jangle, creak of boards.

"You've made quite an impression around Trinidad, stranger."

"I guess I make friends everywhere I go."

"I'm glad I was able to provide a place for you to rest those weary bones of yours, this afternoon."

What did that *mean?*

"Very kind of you, ma'am. Very generous."

"I told you I prefer 'Lola' to 'ma'am.' Don't you think I've earned the right to get a name from you?"

"I like the way you call me 'stranger.' Kind of has a nice ring."

"Your name might have a nicer one."

"Maybe it would. . . ."

"So what is it?"

The jingle of spurs stopped.

The woman asked again, "What is it?"

But there was an urgency in the words that said the female was no longer asking about his name.

Willa froze, already plastered against the mercantile door, shadowed in darkness. She'd made no sound.

What might he have heard?

The spur jingle returned, making quicker music, and he walked right by her. Went over to his hitched-up horse and withdrew a shotgun from its scabbard, and a handful of shells from a saddlebag. He put three in a breast pocket, three more in the right pocket of his black cotton trousers.

The fancy woman was at his side now, concerned,

touching his sleeve. Eyeing the shotgun, she said, "What's *that* for?"

"I don't like sudden silences."

". . . It's a sleepy town after dark. You'll get used to it."

"You have to be dead to get used to it."

Finally they walked on.

This gave Willa the opportunity to slip out of her hiding place. She moved quietly to her horse, disgusted that these two were headed to the hotel together, disgusted with herself that she'd volunteered to come to Trinidad and find the stranger, and what? Bat her eyelashes at him till he gave her his name?

That Lola creature was ready to give him much more than that for revealing his identity. Maybe the woman already had done so, getting nowhere for her trouble. Served the trollop right.

Willa approached Daisy, who whinnied just a little, and the stranger and his female companion turned immediately toward her, just one store down from where she stood. She hoped the red burning her face did not show in the moonlight.

The female smiled big and said, "Well! Good *evening*, Miss Cullen. Aren't you afraid to be out in this chilly night air?"

"I am of the people out walking around in it," she said, even chillier.

The dance-hall queen had the temerity to walk nearer. "Then maybe it would be better if you stayed out on that ranch of yours. Where it's safe. Trinidad after dark is no place for a sweet young girl like yourself to be."

Willa glared at her, but said nothing.

With a tiny, sneering smile, the female returned to her escort, offering her crooked elbow for his arm, and said, "Coming, stranger?"

He gave her a mild smile. "Do you mind walking the rest of the way yourself? I have to meet someone tonight, before I check into the hotel."

"Anyone I know?"

"Nothing to do with you . . . ma'am."

He tipped his Stetson.

The female shrugged and said, "Good night, stranger. And thank you for this afternoon. Thank you very much." She reached her face up and gave him a quick kiss, then crossed the street, hips swaying—*Disgusting!* Willa thought—heading toward the hotel.

The stranger walked over to Willa, taking his time, glancing toward the retreating female, who was entering the hotel now.

"Well, you choose sides quick enough," she said to him. "What kind of offer did she make?"

"Does it make any difference?"

Burning, she said, "Not to me."

She started for Daisy and he stopped her by the arm.

"Let go of me!" she blurted.

"Try shutting up for a change."

The surprising harshness of that made her draw in breath, but he held up a hand, palm out.

He said, in a near whisper, "I don't like the smell of this."

"Smell of what?"

"It's hanging in the air like smoke."

"What?"

He put his hands on the sides of her arms, facing her. "Listen to me now. Step back into that doorway. Stay in the shadows. Something's going to happen and I don't want you to be part of it."

"Stop this," she said through tight teeth, shaking free. "Do you think I scare that easily? Because I don't."

"Good for you," he said. "Because I do."

Lola unlocked the door of her room at the hotel and flinched, startled by the sight of Sheriff Harry Gauge, seated in a hardback chair arranged to face her upon her arrival.

"What's the idea?" she said irritably, shutting the door behind her. "Want me to jump out of my skin?"

He didn't look at all friendly. He leaned forward, hands clasped and dropped between spread knees, his holstered .45 hanging loose, too, its tie-down strap dangling. He was at once casual and deadly.

"Well?" he said.

"Well . . . what?"

"What did you get out of that S.O.B.?"

She sat on the edge of the nearby bed, a bed big enough for two; its springs whined. "Nothing. Not a damn thing."

He frowned. "You mean, no name? No nothing? Damn, woman, do you have any idea how long you were in there with him?"

She shrugged. "He was dog-tired. Been riding all night, and probably exerted himself killing your stupid underlings. No hotel rooms available, so I let him nap all afternoon in one of the girls' cribs."

Gauge scowled. "You mean, you had him *alone* in a room, asleep, and didn't tell me?"

She curled her upper lip at him. "Why, so you could stage *another* killing in my saloon? And the answer is, yes—what I got out of him is exactly what I said. *Nothing.*"

His smile was terrible. "You aren't *that* stupid. You got two little fingers you can wrap men around, and I've seen you do it."

She shrugged, shook her head. "He doesn't talk much. Plays his cards close to the vest. . . . Speaking of which, he won several hundred this afternoon. Man knows his poker."

"Tell me you picked up *something.*"

She thought about it. "Well . . . whoever he is, he doesn't want it known. Very cagey about that. I think he really may be passing through. Could be wanted."

"A dude like that?"

She let out a little laugh. "A dude that shot down two of your boys who already had the drop on him. You can see that this one's got all the instincts of a gunfighter. I wouldn't pay any nevermind to the way he dresses. Hell, look how Bill Hickok used to dude up."

"He ain't no Hickok."

"But he's *somebody*. He's got a style about him that I just can't put my finger on."

Gauge got up suddenly, standing as straight as he'd been slumped before. "Maybe you'd like to lay more than just a finger on him, huh?"

She bared her teeth. "And what if I do? What if I *did*? Didn't you say you wanted me to use my talents?"

"I don't care about that. Once a whore, always a whore. Just don't go takin' a shine to that dude or anything." He started toward her, a fist raised like a rock. "Or I'll . . ."

"Or you'll *nothing*," she said, and she showed him the derringer she'd had up her sleeve. "You're not to hit me no more, Harry. Remember?"

"Not bad," he said, grinning appreciatively, nodding at the little gun. "Maybe I should've sent *you* to kill that stranger, not Britt and Manning."

She frowned. "You wouldn't send saddle tramps like those two to take *that* one down, would you?"

"Wouldn't I?"

She shook her head, rolled her eyes. "They aren't man enough for the job, Harry."

"We'll see."

She found his gaze and held it. "There's only one man in this town who could take that stranger, Harry . . . and I'm looking at him."

He came over and kissed her roughly.

But he didn't hit her.

Willa, in the recession of the barbershop doorway, watched as the stranger unhitched his horse with his left hand, the shotgun stock clutched in his right. He was looking everywhere, listening intently for any hint of sound over the muffled fun from the Victory.

Nothing.

She left the recession of the doorway and stepped across the boardwalk and down into the street, approaching him. He spun toward her, swinging the shotgun her way, making her jump back a little.

Then he let out so much air that he might have collapsed. "I *told* you stay back, woman."

She gestured to the quiet, dark street around them. "You're imagining things. Who are you meeting, anyway?"

He took a step closer to her. Softly he said, "You. I want to ride out to your father's ranch for a talk."

This news widened her eyes, threw her off balance. "Well . . . that's why *I* came to town. To talk to *you.*"

A tiny click froze them both.

Just the smallest little noise . . .

. . . a gun cocking?

Swiftly the stranger shoved her to the street, where she landed *whump* in a dust cloud of her making, and he ducked down to where that desert rat was napping, pulling out from under Tulley the seed bag that had been the old boy's mattress, and slinging the thing over the saddle of his horse, whose rump he slapped, sending the animal charging down the street, galloping in the direction of the hotel.

A dark-mustached man in a black vest emerged fast from the alley across the way, to aim a pistol at what he must have figured was the stranger on horseback, trying to get away.

But the stranger was in the midst of the street now and the shooter turned in surprise and got a bellyful of buckshot for his trouble. Blown onto his backside, the openmouthed ambusher stared at the sky, but wasn't seeing it.

From the alley off to her right came another attacker, a smaller man but burly, on the move, firing a pistol at the stranger, three shots cracking the night, but his target had hit the street in a roll and came up in a crouch, letting loose the other barrel of the shotgun with a boom that sounded like dynamite exploding.

The smaller man was lifted off his feet, then fell back and splashed onto his own spilled blood and innards.

Now she could smell it.

Gunsmoke in the air like gray-blue drifting fog, the stranger was getting to his feet, slowly, looking all around him.

She stayed down, trembling, wondering what might come next, and from her vantage point she could see men pouring out of the Victory down one way and people coming out more tentatively from the hotel down the other. The glow of lights came to windows of second-floor living quarters here and there, folks leaning out for a look, as the stranger calmly, almost casually walked first to one corpse, kicking it, then to the other, and doing the same.

A cowboy, who'd come out of the Victory, close enough to see, called out, "My gosh, he got Jake *Britt*! And Lars *Manning*!"

Townspeople, men mostly, tucking nightshirts into trousers they quickly stepped into, some in bare feet, were emerging from this place and that one for a look. Pushing through this assembling wall of gawkers, came the sheriff.

"*All right!*" Gauge yelled. "All right, get back, back, all of you!"

The stranger was standing near the second of the dead bodies he'd made, the shotgun cradled in his arms.

The sheriff faced the stranger, putting perhaps three feet between them. He almost snarled as he said, "What *is* this? What *happened* here?"

"I'd call it an ambush," the stranger said offhandedly, breaking the shotgun, snapping out shells, reloading but leaving the gun open. "Or I guess in more official terms? An attempted ambush."

Gauge backed away a few steps, hands on hips, and called around to those gathered at this latest shooting scene, *"Anybody see what happened here?"*

Around them were the faces belonging to what must have been a third of the town, anyway . . . and all were shaking their heads.

The sheriff wheeled back to the man with the shotgun and pointed a finger at him like a pistol. "Who ambushed *who*, stranger? What I see is two of my deputies shot down like dogs in the street, and nobody but you to say how it happened."

Willa was already heading over, dusting herself off from the fall. "*I* saw it, Sheriff."

Gauge turned toward her and his smile was witheringly sarcastic, as was his tone as he said, "Now, ain't that just nice. Ain't that convenient and all. The little lady comes up with a story just in the nick of time to clear her father's hired gun."

"He's not my father's hired gun," she said, almost spitting the words. "But I saw those two men try to bushwhack him. That one shot first, then the stranger defended himself, and after that, this one came out shooting and got what he asked for. Self-defense in anybody's book. Any questions, Sheriff?"

Before Gauge could respond, the desert rat scrambled out from under the boardwalk, saying, "Wait just a minute, Sheriff! Hold your horses."

Gauge looked with contempt at the ragged figure shambling toward him. "What is it, Tulley?"

The desert rat patted his chest, raising dust. "Maybe you better count me as a witness, too, Sheriff. I saw the whole blasted thing myself. Came about just like Miss Cullen said. Couple of back-shooters got shot front-ways. Better than they merited."

The sheriff scowled at this second witness. "Are you drunk, old man?"

"Not presently." Tulley pointed to the boardwalk. "That's what I was *doin'* under there—sleepin' it off!"

Gauge gave first Tulley, and then Willa, a lingering look at his disgusted sneer.

Then he turned to the stranger and said, "Fine pair of witnesses you got here, mister. Town drunk and the daughter of a man who hates my guts. Maybe I ought to take you in, anyway."

The stranger snapped the shotgun shut and grinned, though his eyes weren't friendly at all. "Guess you could try, Sheriff."

The two men faced each other for five seconds that must have seemed, to one and all, a very long time.

Deputy Rhomer stepped from the crowd—"Out of the way, out of the way!"—and took the sheriff's arm, jerking his head to one side, indicating they should move away from their potential prisoner.

Willa could hear what Rhomer whispered: "Take

it easy, Harry. Suppose he *is* Banion. He'll cut you to pieces with that shotgun!"

"If he ain't Banion," Gauge said, "he's a fool."

The sheriff stepped away from his deputy, sighed deep, hitched his gun belt, and returned to the stranger, saying, "I'm not going to waste time or taxpayer money arrestin' you. Thanks to these two witnesses, you're free to go."

The stranger smiled, nodded. "Right kind of you, Sheriff."

Gauge gave him a hard look, a hand on the butt of his holstered .44. "You still claim to just be passin' through, mister?"

"That's my intention."

The sheriff's chin raised, as if begging the stranger to take a swing. "You could stand to pick up the pace a mite."

Then the lawman went back to the milling citizens, perhaps half of whom had lost interest and gone back home and to bed already, and got somebody to go after Doc Miller. Not that pronouncing either of these two dead would take much effort. Nobody had to seek out undertaker Perkins, who always showed up, no matter what time of day, whenever there were gunshots. Just trying to serve his community.

Willa went to the stranger, who said to her, "Sorry about the rough treatment."

"I won't fault you," she said. "I believe you may have saved my life."

He nodded toward the sheriff, presently conferring with the undertaker. "You may have already returned the favor."

"*Mister!*"

They turned and Tulley was walking the dappled gelding toward them. "Here's your horse! Didn't get far."

"Thanks, Tulley." He took the reins from the old man. "Sorry about borrowing your bed."

The feed bag was no longer on the animal.

"Oh, it fell off back there a ways," Tulley said with a good-natured grin shy a few teeth. "Broke apart where it hit. Maybe somethin' will grow!"

"Maybe," the stranger said, and patted the old man's shoulder, "you can sleep at the stable tonight."

"Didn't earn enough of my keep over there today for that, mister."

"You tell Hitchens I'll pay your freight tomorrow."

Tulley beamed. "You're a fine human man, mister. Fine human man."

The desert rat headed toward the livery stable with some spring in his step.

Smiling, Willa said, "I guess you do make friends everywhere you go. Where are you going tonight? You staying here, at the hotel maybe?"

"I told you," he reminded her. "The intention was to ride out to your ranch and have a talk with your father. Wanted to wait till after dark so as not to advertise."

"Your intention, huh? Like your intention to just pass through Trinidad?"

"Sometimes I get sidetracked."

"I'll lead the way, then," she said. "Let's ride out to the Bar-O together."

He chuckled. "You sure you know which side I'm on in this fracas?"

"Not really," she said. "But I'm starting to get a hunch."

"Based on what?"

"Let's just say that anybody who guns down four of Harry Gauge's deputies in one day is at the very least not on the sheriff's side."

"How about your good side?"

"We'll see."

They rode out together, past Gauge and Deputy Rhomer, who grinned at her lasciviously as they went by.

She did not hear what Rhomer said to his boss: "You might have to pay a big price, Harry, if you ever want to own that one."

Nor did she hear Gauge's inelegant response: "Shut up," plus a nasty name she'd never heard, even growing up on a ranch.

CHAPTER NINE

They kept the pace brisk, if not hard, on the twenty-minute ride out to the Bar-O.

They didn't speak, the stranger lagging just behind Willa, who after all knew the way. They brought their animals to an easy trot as they headed down the hard-packed lane under the overhang displaying the ranch's brand. The stranger, she noted, was taking it all in with what seemed to her an almost childlike sense of wonder.

She couldn't blame him.

In the ivory moonlight, the ranch buildings had an austere beauty that nearly brought tears to Willa's eyes, in the midst of this struggle to hold on to what her father had carved out of the wilderness.

The stranger dismounted and tied up his dappled gelding at the post in front of the main house, where the front-room windows glowed with the muted light of kerosene lamps. She was tying up Daisy when her father came out quickly with foreman Whit Murphy tagging after.

Papa, as he stood on the porch staring out sightlessly, obviously having heard two horses arrive, called tentatively, "Willa . . . do we have a guest?"

"We do, Papa," she said, approaching the stairs up to the porch. The stranger fell in behind her at a respectful distance. "I brought him with me."

Her father walked to the edge of the stairs and rested a hand on a rough beam. "I'm guessing there's a story to be told here, daughter. You don't have this man at gunpoint by any chance . . . ?"

The stranger stepped forward, came up alongside her. "No, Mr. Cullen," he said pleasantly. "And she's not at gunpoint, either."

"Relieved to hear that."

"I'm here of my own free will. I presume . . . as a guest."

"You are indeed my guest."

"Thank you. And there *is* a story to be told. But I'm going to let Miss Cullen here tell it. She saw all of the action firsthand."

The old man's face, despite the easygoing manner of the stranger's speech, was taut with concern. "Willa dear, are you all right?"

"I'm fine," she said, adding lightly, "Except for being a target."

Perhaps to head off any worry her flippant remark may have caused, the stranger said, "*I* was the target, sir. But we're both without a scratch."

There, in the moonlight, she gave her father—and Whit, too—a succinct account of the ambush attempt and how their guest had saved her by pushing her to the street, and how he had gunned down his two attackers. She related, too, the way the old desert rat Tulley had made a second witness, leaving Sheriff Gauge helpless to arrest a man who had shot two more of his deputies. Especially there in front of half the town, attracted by the commotion.

Relieved now, even pleased, her father gestured toward the front door, his eyes seeking the stranger but not quite sure where to look. "Well, I owe you, friend, for my daughter's safety if nothing else. Come in, come in, both of you. We have much to talk about."

The stranger said, his voice absent of inflection, "Do we?"

She put a hand on his arm. "You're committed now. I think you'd better."

He looked at her, expressionless. But something in his eyes . . .

"I could use some coffee," he said with a shy smile, as if that were an admission of guilt.

Papa beamed and gestured again, rather grandly, to where a somewhat disgruntled-looking Whit held open the door. "We already got some going," her father said.

The fire was going, too—the night was that chilly. Willa ushered the stranger to one of the two big rustic, Indian-blanketed chairs angled toward the fire, and Whit got chairs for himself and her, positioning them on either side of the larger ones.

Willa took their guest's curl-brimmed hat with its cavalry crease and hung it on a hook near the door. Whit, to his credit, was taking care of getting coffee for everyone. A rough-hewn table, fashioned decades ago by her father, sat between the two bigger chairs, providing a resting place for the china coffee cups.

They sat washed in the orange flickering glow, with Whit seating himself next to the raw-boned dude as she nestled in near her father.

Bluntly, Whit said, "Just who the hell are you, mister?"

He turned toward Whit with the faintest smile. "Just who the hell are *you*?"

"Whit Murphy," he said, pounding his chest with the underside of a fist. "Bar-O foreman. See, that ain't a hard question to answer at all. No more beatin' around the bush. No more shilly-shallying."

The stranger's smile broadened. "You'd be surprised how rarely I shilly-shally."

Whit seemed at the boiling point and her father must have sensed it, because he said, "Why keep your name to yourself, mister?"

With no challenge in the words at all, the stranger said, "That's kind of my business, isn't it?"

Papa drew a breath in, let it out slow. Flames reflected on the milky eyes. "I may not know your name, but I know who sent you. Raymond Parker, of Denver . . . isn't that right?"

The stranger seemed mildly confused. "Why should he?"

Sitting forward, Willa said, "Mr. Parker and my father were partners years ago. They started this ranch together, and Mr. Parker sold his share to Papa and went on to make his own fortune in Colorado."

"Quite interesting, I'm sure," the stranger said.

Willa said, "Mr. Parker is who my father sent the wire to, seeking Wes Banion. To get rid of Harry Gauge."

Their guest said nothing, then nodded slowly. In the wavering glow of the fire, the sharp angles of his face were heightened, taking on a carved look.

She pressed on: "We think you *know* Mr. Parker. That he passed my father's offer along to you. And this means that you already have in your possession five thousand dollars of our money. *Cullen* money."

The stranger's eyebrows lifted and another faint smile formed as they came down. "Well, now."

Her father clutched the arms of the chair as if he were holding on to a bucking bronc. "Mr. Banion . . . if that's who you are . . . I can understand that you might like to keep a certain distance between yourself and those who hired you. Might serve as a protection to all concerned. After all, what we're asking of you isn't strictly . . . legal."

Willa, with a humorless smirk, said, "You mean *murder*, Papa?"

Her father frowned, but his tone was conciliatory as he spoke to his daughter. "Perhaps our friend here will face the sheriff down in a fair fight. He's demonstrated today that he has skills . . . including speed, I'm told . . . known to few shootists."

"However," Willa said, addressing the stranger with an openly sarcastic smile, "should that approach not appeal to you, you can feel free to shoot Harry Gauge in the back."

"Daughter! Let me speak my piece to our guest." Sitting forward, lowering his voice, her father said, "Maybe you can pull this thing off, comin' straight at it. . . . On the other hand, maybe you can't. Honor aside, it might not be worth the risk."

The stranger, listening without expression, said, "Why is that?"

Her father shrugged elaborately. In the fire's reflection, every year of his life showed. "Harry Gauge has too damn many men."

The stranger's upper lip twitched the tiniest smile. "He has six less now."

Her father nodded. "True, thanks to your efforts, and ours. But Gauge can afford to lose that many, and more. We can't. And not even Caleb York could have gone up against this bunch alone."

The stranger sipped coffee, put the cup back on the table. "What kind of help do I get?"

Her father didn't answer that directly, saying, "Gauge is in the middle of a power play right now. You've been a distraction to him—a welcome one from our vantage point—but wanting you out of the way is just a small goal for a grasping man like this."

"And the big goal?"

Her father gestured with both hands, palms up. "You're sitting in the middle of it—the Bar-O. We're the last and the biggest of the spreads that greedy, ambitious killer hasn't swallowed up. He's made offers and I've turned him down flat, but he's cut into us bad, even if he hasn't really made any major inroads. Soon he will, though. He'll *have* to."

"Why?"

Whit Murphy answered for his boss: "Because shipment season is comin' up. We don't have to drive cattle to Dodge City no more, not with the railroad so close. Ranches around here often sell to speculative buyers before makin' the day-or-two drive."

"Times *have* changed," the stranger granted. "But what pressure does that put on Gauge?"

Her father was smiling now. "The sheriff extended himself badly to stock the range he grabbed, and his grass is bad and his water's pretty much dried up. When those buyers come in, they won't pay him enough for his beef to keep him goin', no matter how much land he's got."

The stranger shrugged. "Then why not wait him out?"

Papa shook his head. "We can't. Ain't in a position to. He's been scattering our stock into the hills, makin' roundup on my reduced crew one hell of a hardship, if not downright impossible."

Whit put in, "And he's been rustlin' what he can get away with."

Papa said, "Comes down to this—we don't get paid for what we don't deliver."

"That's a fact," the stranger said with a nod.

Her father's sigh seemed to start down at his toes. "Except for the loyal handful I've got left, Gauge has run our men off. If we take any real losses in cattle, the Bar-O is finished. That leaves our ambitious sheriff a wide-open market. Then he'll buy up our banknotes on the cheap, and force us out."

The stranger was frowning. "You have no money in reserve?"

Not bothering to mask her bitterness, Willa said, "We *did* have. Now it's being paid to you—ten thousand dollars."

He lifted an eyebrow. Sipped more coffee. Said, "That could have paid off a pile of banknotes."

Cullen shook his head morosely. "Not when you're dead, my friend. Harry Gauge is responsible for the killings of seven of my people. Do

I have to tell *you* that there's nothing he won't stop at?"

"No," the stranger said.

Willa said, coldly, "So, in case you're wondering? That money you took from us is *blood* money."

He met her hard gaze. "You sound like you have a bad taste in your mouth, Miss Cullen."

She met his. "Hired killers affect me that way."

"Willa!" her father said. "This man is our guest. And he's one of us now."

With a bitter, little smile, she said, "I'm sure our new friend doesn't mind my frankness. Do you, Mr. . . . *Banion*, is it?"

"Strong-minded females affect *me*," the stranger said, letting her second question pass. He had a last sip of coffee, and got to his feet. "You might be surprised how. . . . Good evening, Miss Cullen. Mr. Cullen. Mr. Murphy."

Willa, surprised by his suddenness, said, "You're going?"

He walked slowly for the door, spurs jangling. "Yes. Been an interestin' visit. Thanks for the java. And the food for thought."

Her father was on his feet now as well. "Just a moment, please! . . . Sir, where are you going?"

"Back to town. See if I can find a room. Been a busy day."

"And tomorrow . . . ?"

"I'll be around." He was at the door. "I intend to satisfy my curiosity about a few things."

He took his hat off the hook, snugging it on as her father approached him, moving quickly through a world he knew well. "Wait! . . . Wait a minute."

The stranger turned to him. "Yes?"

"So, *are* you Banion? Or are you . . . ? Which . . . which one *are* you?"

"The other one," the stranger said, then tipped his hat to Willa and went out.

The remaining three exchanged exasperated expressions.

Then she followed him out to their horses, her footsteps echoing off the plank porch. Glancing back at the house, she saw Whit stepping out, but she shook her head at him. Glumly, Whit stepped back in, closing the door.

"You're just . . . *riding* off?" she said, at the hitching post where he was untying.

He wasn't looking at her. "You need to make up your mind."

"About what?"

Now his eyes were on her. "Do you or don't you want me to help your father?"

"Well, I . . . of course, I . . ."

An edge came into his voice. "You come to town to find me, bring me out here, then you needle me like . . ." Then he grunted something, not quite a laugh.

She turned her back to him, folded her arms; it was chilly, after all, and a bit of a shiver got into her words: "Maybe . . . maybe I don't *know* what I want."

He placed a gentle hand on her shoulder. "You want your father's ranch preserved. I understand. Anybody would." His hand left her shoulder. "But . . . you're awful damn picky about how."

She shook her head, keeping her back to him. "Paying a hired killer . . . it makes us as bad as the people we're trying to fight. Worse, because we *know* better. I want to hold on to this land. I want that more than anything. But doesn't *how* we do it matter?"

"Ask the Indians."

She whipped around to face him, eyes flashing, nostrils flaring. "You low-down, nasty . . . I ought to . . ."

"Let me."

He put an arm around her waist and drew her to him and kissed her, long and a little rough, yet something about it struck her as very . . . sweet.

Then he was up on his horse, tipping his hat to her again, before riding off.

And she was standing there with her fingers on her lips, still not knowing what to think, thoughts and emotions fighting for control of her, neither winning.

Just as the stranger was riding into town—heading for the livery stable and the stall that awaited the dappled gelding—he noticed a shopkeeper, claw hammer in hand, out after dark taking down the boards from his store windows.

"For the sheriff keeping such a quiet town," he said to the shopkeeper with a grin, "you folks have to go to a whole lot of trouble."

"Sure do, mister," the shopkeeper said, a small, skinny man with a trim mustache. He gave up a defeated, little smile. "Every payday, it gets good and rowdy in this town."

The man was in a half-unbuttoned threadbare shirt tucked into his paint-stained pants, obviously his fix-'er-up clothes. He added another board to the pile flush against the outer wall of his establishment.

The stranger asked, "Is it worth the trouble?"

"Too much invested to move," he said, pausing between yanking nails. He heaved a disgusted sigh. "Once a month, same darn thing—payday and hooraw. Harry Gauge waits till the cowboys' money is gone, and the town's half-wrecked, before quieting it down again."

A churn of wheels, rattle of reins, and clopping of hooves announced a wagon rolling into town. An older rancher at the reins, it pulled up alongside where the shopkeeper was at work and just behind the mounted stranger. Something in the open back of his wagon was covered with a tarp— from the shape, might be a body.

The rancher said, "Hey, Warren—remind me where the doc's office is, would you?"

The shopkeeper shook his head. "Why bother, Burl? He's out with the Haywood baby, or least he was."

The rancher sighed and shrugged. He had a full, well-trimmed gray beard and had seen more in his time than most had forgot. "Well, hell . . . not that Doc Miller could've done *this* feller any good, anyways."

The shopkeeper came closer, tapping his palm lightly with the hammerhead. "Who you got back there?"

"Old Swenson. Dead as they come."

"Shame! What the hell happened?"

The rancher shrugged again. "Found him out near the relay station. Looks like he was drunk. Anyways, smells like he was drunk. Fell off his horse, maybe. Hit his head on a rock, likely."

The stranger was climbing down off his horse. "You mind if I take a look?"

The rancher frowned. "Don't know as it's your business, mister."

"Do you know that it isn't?"

The rancher thought about that, and—perhaps realizing that this was the man who'd shot down four of Harry Gauge's roughneck deputies today—said, "Have at, mister."

"Thanks."

The stranger got up into the wagon and flipped back the tarp. He knelt near the body. Warren, the shopkeeper, folded his fingers over the far-side edge of the wagon and peeked in, like a kid over a fence.

The corpse was on its belly, slack face to one side, mouth open as if seeking the air it could no longer inhale; the wound was well-exposed. This was a man in his fifties or older, weathered and wrinkled and gray. And out of his misery.

The stranger said, "If it was a rock, sure had a funny damn shape to it."

The rancher, still seated on the buckboard, glanced back and said, with just a hint of impatience, "How's that?"

"Looks more like a gun butt."

The rancher made a dismissive face. "Naw! Who'd want to kill Old Swenson? Ever since he sold out the Running C to the sheriff, he's been a real drunkard. Bigger even than ol' Tulley."

"That so?"

"Sure as hell is. Once he fell in the Purgatory and nearly drowned hisself." He spit chaw. "Nice old feller, though."

Scratching his head, Warren said, "Well, he did have *some* money, Burl—maybe not a lot, 'cause he wound up sellin' out cheap to Harry Gauge, they say. But a grubstake, anyway. *Somebody* mighta pistol-whipped and robbed him."

"Possible," the rancher said, clearly not caring. "People been killed for fifty cents. Less."

The stranger asked, "What about his horse? The one you think might have thrown him?"

Rancher Burl gestured vaguely. "I left it tied up out at the relay station. I didn't check his saddlebags for money or nothin'. I'll leave that to the sheriff. Mind coverin' him up again?"

The stranger did so, hopped down.

The rancher said, "With the doc away, I'll go wake up the undertaker. Maybe stop and see if anybody's in at the sheriff's office, first. Damn, it's a pain in the butt bein' a Good Samaritan like this. . . ."

The wagon rolled off, and the shopkeeper shrugged. He and his hammer went back to work unboarding his windows.

The stranger stood in the street and watched the wagon go.

The storekeeper, noticing the dude's presence, asked over his shoulder, "Something on your mind, mister?"

"Just thinking that the sheriff might be easier to convince than I was," he said, "that Old Swenson fell off his horse."

Then he nodded good night to the shopkeeper and got back on the black-maned gelding and rode down to the livery stable.

Ten minutes later, he walked into the hotel, sweeping off his hat. The bell over the door woke the desk clerk, a weak-chinned character with pince-nez and scant hair, in a brown-and-gold vest with a white shirt and black bow tie. He'd been slumped, sleeping on an elbow over a copy of *Beadle's Dime Library*—*The Legend of Caleb York* by Ned Buntline.

The stranger chuckled at the sight of the cheap publication, and was amused as well by the startled blinking look the wakened clerk gave him. This was one of the faces from the crowd who'd gathered earlier—twice, actually. This morning after the shooting in front of the sheriff's office, and tonight after the bushwhackers had been dealt with.

"Pretty lively out there last night," the stranger said. "Like that every payday, I hear."

"Afraid so, mister. Couldn't have accommodated you then, but I'm pleased to say I'm able to now."

"Well, that's fine. Something on the Main Street side?"

"Certainly." The clerk reached for his register, opened it, and turned the book around for his customer. "It was, uh, a little lively out there *today* as well."

"Could call it that." He looked up from the register. "Does the sheriff check this book on a regular basis?"

"Yes, sir. He or one of his deputies. Likes to keep track of people staying in town."

The stranger cocked his head. "When does he do that? Check the register, I mean."

"Oh, sometime in the evening."

"Has the sheriff or any deputy of his done so yet tonight?"

The clerk shook his head. "No, sir. But somebody should be around, oh, most any time now. Why?"

"No reason. Just curious by nature." The stranger grinned at the clerk, leaned an elbow on the register. "Now, just for fun—what name do you suppose might shake our sheriff up the most?"

The clerk's eyebrows climbed his endless forehead. "Well, uh . . . of course, we'd prefer your *real* name, sir. Not that we stand on ceremony."

"No, really, be a sport—what name might spook him some?"

The clerk tugged at his collar. "Well, uh . . . I assume you've heard the, uh, talk around town . . . speculation that, uh, you are, uh . . . Mr. Wesley Banion. If you, uh, *are* Mr. Wesley Banion."

"And that name would sit the sheriff up straight, you think?"

"Well might," the clerk said with a sickly smile. Then he nodded at his dime novel. "But, of course, what would *really* get his attention . . . if I might say so, sir . . . is *that*."

The Legend of Caleb York.

"Of course," the clerk said, with a shrug, "Caleb York is *dead*."

The stranger chuckled again, reached for the pen. "Why don't we do what heretofore only the Almighty has managed?"

"What's that, sir?"

"Bring the dead back to life."

And he signed the register, *Caleb York*.

The clerk, somewhat confused and not yet seeing what the guest had written, handed across a room key. "Upper floor, sir. Top of the stairs, it's the last door on your left."

The stranger nodded at the clerk, catching a glimpse of the man reading the register, eyes popping as he covered his mouth with a nervous hand.

CHAPTER TEN

Lola entered the hotel and was headed for the stairs to the second floor, where she kept a room, when she noticed the stranger leaving the check-in desk, about to start up himself. He saw her, too, smiled, took off his hat, and waited for her.

"Well, my silent stranger," she said.

He leaned against the banister post. "Is that what I am?"

"I wouldn't call you talkative. Finally getting a roof over your head, I see."

"Finally."

He gestured in an after-you manner and she went up, putting a little extra sway into it. She was still in her elaborate, low-cut dance-hall gown— the walk to the hotel from the Victory was a short one, so she didn't bother changing before heading back.

Halfway up, she said, with an over-the-shoulder glance at him, "I'm a little surprised to see you back in town so soon."

"Why's that?"

"Oh, I suppose because Willa Cullen seems to hold a peculiar . . . fascination . . . for a certain kind of man."

At the top of the stairs, he let his eyes drop briefly down to her décolletage and back again. "And you don't?"

She gave him a coquettish look that didn't pretend to be anything but joshing. "It would be immodest of me to say."

"Walk you to your room?"

"Please."

She led the way, stopping at room 6.

"Believe I'm next door," he said, gesturing. "In number five."

She smiled and it was anything but coquettish. "Well, perhaps that will prove convenient. For example, should you need a cup of sugar."

He gave her another grin. "Very neighborly of you."

The man didn't seem to embarrass easily. She liked that.

She laid a lace-gloved hand on his cheek. "We might start with a nightcap. I have a bottle in my room? Bourbon. Straight from New Orleans."

"Mighty tempting. Another time?"

"Another time."

"Good night . . . ma'am."

She watched him walk down to his nearby door, use his key, pause to smile and nod at her, then go in.

For a moment, she just stood there, thinking, *Now this is a man.*

Despite the dudish clothes on the one hand and his frightening abilities with a gun on the other, something decent managed to come through.

But not so decent that they hadn't been able to enjoy an afternoon together. . . .

She went into her room, which was no bigger or nicer than any other in the hotel, down to the same drab wallpaper. But she had dressed the space up with a few nice pieces of Victorian furniture brought here from Denver—hand-carved mirrored maple dresser with a floral-pattern toilet set, baroque walnut plush-upholstered armchair, a carved rosewood bed, and a few other things. She lived here, after all, and had a right to be comfortable.

If Gauge came through for her as promised, a fancy two-story Victorian house, furnished like this throughout, on its own nice piece of property, would be hers one day soon. Or she should say, *theirs.* These were nice-enough quarters for a dance-hall queen.

But the wife of a cattle baron would have it so very much better. . . .

A sharp knock came at the door. She smiled proudly at herself in the mirror—*the stranger had changed his mind!* He'd gone to his lonely room and stared at the wall, driven mad by thoughts of the delights awaiting him on the other side. She laughed at herself, and him.

She was in her corset and silk stockings now, but found that perfectly acceptable apparel in which to greet him, to encourage her new friend to have that nightcap after all, and perhaps . . . ?

She opened the door just a crack, but the face there did not belong to the stranger or Harry Gauge, either.

"Hi, Lola."

Vint Rhomer pushed through, shutting the door behind him in a near slam. The red-haired, red-bearded deputy—in his usual gray shirt with sleeve garters, buckskin vest, dirty denims, and tied-down .44—reeked of liquor. Reeked, period.

She glared at him. "Vint! What the hell are you doing here?"

He gave her a hooded-eyed grin, teeth like a rabbit's poking through the red brush. "Just thought I'd stop by for a friendly little visit."

Her hands went to her hips. She didn't give a damn that he was seeing her like this; in her profession, modesty was not an issue.

With chin high, she said, "There are plenty of girls over at the Victory. Slow night like this, you'll have your pick. Go visit one of *them*."

He came over, stood close to her, arrogance and stupidity rising off him like two more foul smells. "Maybe I'd rather visit you, honey."

She gave him a defiant smile, hands still on her

hips. "You're takin' one hell of a risk . . . 'honey.' What if Harry Gauge came walking through that door?"

He shook his head. Tobacco was in there with all the other odors. "Harry's busy. Got called away on a matter. He's got way more to worry about than me makin' time with his . . . whatever it is you are to him."

She bared her teeth. "Lay one finger on me and I'll tell him you ravaged me."

The dark blue eyes narrowed and his upper lip curled back in its red nest. "You really think he'd give a damn?"

Her chin crinkled in anger, nostrils and eyes flaring like a rearing mare. "What the hell do you think you're *talking* about, Rhomer?"

He chuckled and went over and sat in the fancy chair. Crossed his legs.

Casual, he said, "You really shot yourself in the foot, Lola, when you brought Harry into the picture. Oh, I know the whole story. How this town was gonna run you and your tramps out when you sent for Harry and his big gun. Paid his damn stage fare, then just handed him a half-interest in the Victory."

She stood with her arms folded now, looking down at the seated intruder, but keeping a distance. "This is fascinating, hearing my life story told by an idiot."

"You made a bad partnership, honey. Harry

Gauge wants more from a woman than *you* could ever give him."

Her chin came up again. "Harry's got everything he ever wanted—the land, the cattle, the town . . . *and* he's got me."

Rhomer's shrug was slow and his sneering expression nasty. "Yeah, only he don't *want* you."

"Is that right?"

"Dead right, baby. What he wants is sweet, little Willa Cullen."

She scowled. "You're as crazy as you are stupid, Rhomer. All he wants is her *ranch*."

His eyes went huge. "And you call *me* stupid! She *goes* with the damn ranch. She *is* the damn ranch! You really think when Harry Gauge sets himself up as king of this part of the country, he's gonna do it with a shopworn soiled dove like *you* at his side?"

She was trembling now, with rage, and . . . something else. *Fear?* Not of Rhomer, but that . . . that he might be *right* . . . ?

She pointed at the door. "Get out! Get out of here *now*."

Rhomer got to his feet, in no hurry. He came toward her in an easy lope. "Don't cry, honey. No need to cry. Vint here still thinks you're sweet. Hell, I don't mind takin' Harry's sloppy seconds. He can *have* that sage hen Cullen gal."

He undid his gun belt and tossed it on the chair he'd vacated near the window on the street. As he turned back to her, grinning horribly, she was right there to slap him, hard, and it rang out like a gunshot.

Rhomer grunted and returned the slap, but twice as hard, and she cried out. Then he slapped her again, even harder, and started in clawing at her, trying to rip off what little she wore, but dealing with a corset was beyond his intelligence and she pummeled his chest with hard, tiny fists and bit him on the ear, hard, tearing at his flesh, spitting out a bloody lobe.

He screamed and let go of her, scarlet trailing down one cheek, and yelled, "You *witch!*"

He pushed her onto the bed and was coming at her with grimacing hatred and his right fist was high when the door splintered open and someone came in fast.

The stranger.

Bareheaded, no sidearm, he grabbed Rhomer from behind, by the shoulders, and flung him across into the dresser, where the deputy hit hard, the mirror shaking, drawers rattling, pitcher in its basin careening.

She sat up on the bed, breathing hard, her mouth bleeding—*the stranger must have heard the struggle!* And came to help his neighbor out.

Rhomer's right hand went to his side—forgetting for a moment that his gun in its belt was over on that chair—and then grabbed the pitcher from the dresser top and hurled it at the stranger, who ducked, and so did she, as it flew into the wall behind her and crashed into chunky fragments.

The deputy raised his fists and with a sneering smile came slowly toward the man who'd interrupted his fun.

"About time," Rhomer said, "somebody taught you to mind your own damn business."

The stranger, his own balled hands at the ready, was smiling, but his eyes weren't. "Please try."

In the cramped space of the hotel room, there was little for the two men to do but stand there and slug it out, though Rhomer landed few blows. The stranger kept rocking him back, taking only a handful of hits on his arms and his body, just glancing blows.

Then Rhomer brought around a looping right hand that could have done real damage, but the other man ducked it and brought up a right hand that caught the deputy on the chin, sending him, already bleeding from his ragged ear, stumbling back.

Not even breathing hard, the stranger said, "Maybe it's time I taught you not to burden a lady with unwanted attentions."

Lola felt tears come. The physical punishment Rhomer had dealt out to her hadn't made her cry. She was used to that kind of thing, much as she hated it. But her unlikely savior's oddly formal defense of her . . . her virtue . . . had sent tears streaming.

The stranger was delivering a flurry of punches to Rhomer's body, his chest, his belly, his sides, and the deputy seemed to be staying on his feet only by the force of those blows, bloody spittle flying.

Then in one last desperate move, Rhomer shoved the stranger away, and scrambled after the gun belt on the chair near the window. As the deputy bent over for it, the stranger came up behind him and kicked him in the backside and through the glass shatteringly, shards flying, wooden pane frames cracking.

From below came a loud *whump.*

Lola rushed to her rescuer's side as they both looked out the window.

Rhomer was plastered down there on the hotel's wooden awning, on his belly, breathing hard, but out.

"Little boy's had a busy day." The stranger turned to her, touched her face gently near where her mouth bled. "Are you all right?"

She nodded. Something shaky in her voice, she said, "You really think saving *my* virtue was worth the risk?"

He grinned. The only blood on him was Rhomer's. "Anytime. And I'm not about to stand by and see a woman get manhandled."

"But you *couldn't* see it."

He shrugged, nodding toward the wall they shared. "I could hear it. Anyway, how's a man to get any sleep with all that racket?"

"You joke." She nodded toward the window. "Rhomer will kill you for sure now."

"Well, he'll try. Are you going to the sheriff about this? That deputy isn't about to."

She shook her head. "I'll find Rhomer tomorrow, give him his gun, and tell him I'll keep my mouth shut if he does the same."

He jerked a thumb at the shattered window. "Why not let those two bums shoot it out?"

"I have my reasons. My secrets."

He gave her half a grin this time. "Don't we all? You better have that desk clerk give you another room for tonight."

She put a hand in his hair, then brought it back. "We could always share yours."

"Lovely thought. But this little man has had a busy day, too."

He broke away from her to take another glance out the window, and she came along. Rhomer was still down on the awning, sleeping off his drunk and his beating. A plump, little man on a horse came riding along Main Street, in no hurry, a Gladstone bag tucked on the saddle before him.

"Isn't that Doc Miller?" he asked her.

"That's him. Why? You want to get Rhomer a doctor?"

"Not hardly."

Then he kissed her on the forehead and left her there.

* * *

In the moonlight, the expanse of range looked like the aftermath of a terrible battle, the kind where there are few if any survivors, corpses strewn everywhere. Only this was a war where the casualties were cattle.

Harry Gauge and his grizzled foreman Gil Willart stood over one such victim, whose exposed fleshy underside bore telltale blisters.

"Cowpox, all right," Gauge said with a sigh and a shake of the head. His hat was in his hand as if out of respect for the dead steer.

Willart shot a stream of tobacco sideways into the night. "What now, boss?"

The moon was painting the grotesque landscape an unreal off-white. It was cool out, almost cold, and a breeze made a hoarse, spooky whisper.

Gauge pointed to the east. "Drag these damn carcasses over to the ravine and start a slide and cover 'em up."

"We can do that. But the men won't take to handlin' such dead critters as these."

He frowned at the foreman. "They're already wearin' gloves, ain't they? They'll be fine. Tell 'em I'll pay double wages."

Willart nodded. "That should do it. What about the main herd?"

Gauge gestured toward the landscape of death. "These were too far gone to follow the graze. The others should last long enough to get themselves sold."

The foreman nodded, then raised his eyebrows skeptically. "Even our survivors are pretty scrawny, up against the Bar-O herd. As it stands, boss, Cullen's likely to get the lion's share of buyer dollars."

The sheriff gave his man a surly grin. "Not after tonight. Get started cleanin' up this mess. . . . *Hey, Tenny!*"

The foreman went off, just as Joe Tenny, a cowboy who had run with Gauge in outlaw days, ambled over. He had shaggy eyebrows that met in the middle and a lazy smile with a droopy, thick mustache shaped like the smile's upside-down twin.

"Y'know," Tenny said, "I was thinkin' maybe we oughter have ourselves a bar-be-cue. Or maybe you got a better idea?"

"Funny feller." Gauge nodded vaguely north. "Listen, you know those foothills near the Sangre de Cristo?"

That was the mountain range that expanded northward to become the Rockies.

"Ought to," Tenny said with a nod. "We hid out there enough times."

Gauge put a hand on his old accomplice's shoulder. "I want the Bar-O cattle driven into those canyons. Every damn cow. Main herd's in the valley now, and you can get them over the foothills before daylight."

Tenny raised his shaggy eyebrows. "That'll take a heap of men."

"Not so many," Gauge said, shaking his head.

"Those Bar-O boys won't be expectin' us to hit their camp. Anyway, they're spread thin over there. Hell, you won't even have to waste bullets killin' 'em."

Tenny frowned. "You know, Harry, I ain't real big on leavin' witnesses. . . ."

Gauge patted the man's shoulder. "Joe, in this case it'll be better if you do. Wear masks or somethin'. But leave them breathe so they can spread word that the Bar-O is finished. What hands Cullen *does* have left'll leave like rats off a sinkin' ship."

Tenny was thinking that over, his battered hat pushed back on his head. "There's no water in them draws, y'know."

"Those cows'll get by till I need 'em."

"What do you need 'em for?"

Gauge gave his old friend a big, beautiful grin. "Why, Joe, we're gonna kill off the rest of our sickly beeves and restock with Bar-O cows."

Tenny gave up his lazy smile of approval. "I like it. Damn, if I don't like it a bunch. Always figured offerin' money to that blind old coot was a waste when we could just take what he had."

Gauge glanced again at the moon-swept, remains-strewn terrain, where cowhands were dragging dead cattle off through grass riffling with the breeze. "All right, Joe. Get the men you need and move out."

Tenny nodded and went off to do that while his boss stayed back to watch cowhands haul dead cattle by their hooves to the nearby ravine. It was a bizarre-looking process and it took a while. Gauge didn't supervise—he left that to foreman Willart.

They were just starting to get a slide going, to cover up the dead cows, when Gauge collected his horse and started back to town, as his underlings continued his dirty work. He felt very much a cattle baron in the making.

Never realizing that even after all he'd accomplished, he was still no more than the leader of an outlaw gang.

On the Cullen range, a camp of sleeping cowhands were kicked awake by armed, masked gunmen. Without a word, in the glow of a small fire, the invaders gestured with weapons toward the small remuda, and without having to be told, the cowhands walked to their horses and rode off into night, heads hanging, while behind them the herd that had been their responsibility was being driven off by more armed men on horseback.

Two of the Cullen cowhands paused atop a bluff, reins pulled back, and looked down as their herd disappeared off toward Gauge range.

"I guess that's the end of the Bar-O," one said.

"I guess so," the other said. "Never had a chance, did we?"

"Never a chance in hell."

And they rode away—away from the herd, away from Cullen land, on their way to somewhere else.

* * *

Dr. Miller had his latest patient—the corpse of Cyrus Swenson—on his examination table in his simple surgery. His office and living quarters were on the second floor of the brick building that housed the bank.

The stubby, rotund physician—his rumpled suit looking as exhausted as he felt—had just gotten back to town after delivering the latest Haywood baby when rancher Burl Owen rolled up in a wagon with Swenson laid out in back of it.

Sometimes it seemed those were his only patients here in Trinidad—newborn babies and freshly-made corpses.

Burl had been irritable as hell, after being shuffled around from some deputies at the jailhouse who didn't want anything to do with the corpse, and undertaker Perkins who had insisted that the first stop for the deceased be the doctor's office for a death's certificate.

Luckily, somebody had come along to help the doctor cart the body up to his office by way of the outside wooden stairway in the alley. The volunteer was, of all people, the stranger who'd shot four of his other most recent patients.

Now the late Swenson was on the table, on his side, so that the doctor could get a look at what appeared to be the fatal wound.

"You figure this is a murder," the doc said to his new helper.

"That's how I figure it."

Everybody thought they knew better than their doctor.

"Mister," Doc Miller said, "nobody in this town or anywhere else would be bothered murdering Old Swenson."

"So I hear. But wasn't there bad blood between him and the sheriff?"

The doctor nodded. "Bad blood that got resolved by Swenson selling Harry Gauge that little spread of his, finally."

The doc leaned in for a closer look at the wound, black and clotted now. Deep. Oval-shaped. Hard damn blow.

The stranger said, "I imagine you've seen your share of wounds like that before."

"Quite often. Some were caused accidentally."

"Not most?"

The doc shrugged, raised both white eyebrows. "Most were from a gun-butt blow from behind."

"This could be that?"

"That, or he fell on some farm implement."

"Out by the relay station?"

"Or an odd-shaped rock. Still. That indentation does look like a gun butt. . . ."

"Enough for you to change your diagnosis?"

"This *could* be murder, yes . . . but . . . hell."

"What is it, Doctor?"

"Stand back a bit, would you, son?"

The corpse's shirt had got untucked near the

bottom, giving the doctor a troubling glimpse of something. He moved the body onto its back. Pulled up the shirt. Took a close look at the man's belly, where it was broken out in red pustules.

The doc said, "Help me with his trousers . . . but don't touch him."

The stranger did as he was told.

The doctor had a look at the man's legs, which bore the same red blisters. Quickly he took a sheet and covered up the body.

More to himself than his guest, the doc said, "This corpse needs to be buried immediately." Then meeting the stranger's eyes, he said, "Perhaps you might help. You'd be performing a service. You could help avoid a panic."

"What kind of panic?"

"You ever see these signs before, son?" The doctor lifted the sheet, indicated the stomach. "Step closer. Don't touch."

"Don't worry." The stranger's eyes widened. "My God—is that . . . cowpox?"

The doctor covered his patient up again. "Exactly right. And it can wipe out a town like this and leave nothing but the grass . . . and I'm guessing that's why Old Swenson here got himself killed. Somebody didn't want him spreading this foul thing."

But the stranger was shaking his head. "That's not why, Doc."

Almost amused, the doctor said, "You have your own diagnosis, do you?"

"Not exactly. And my suggested treatment is the same as yours—bury him."

"You're willing to help? Not afraid of infection?"

"I'll follow your lead, Doc, as to precautions." The stranger's expression was grave. "But the reason Old Swenson was killed is even worse than you think."

CHAPTER ELEVEN

It was going on three in the morning when Harry Gauge rode back into Trinidad.

He could have bedded down under cool sheets to rest his head on down-stuffed pillows at any of the ranch houses on the spreads he owned; but with what he had sent his bunch off doing right now, Gauge figured being seen—and thought of—as the sheriff made better sense.

Anyway, he could catch a few winks at his office and then, bright and early, go and deal with a certain town problem—that gunfighter, who he'd come to believe was almost surely Wes Banion. Time to show Trinidad that strangers couldn't just ride into town and start shooting down deputies. . . .

Gauge had figured to stretch out on a jail cell cot, but found Rhomer had beat him to it, sleeping it off in their nicest accommodations. His number two man looked disheveled and battered, his left ear bandaged, the white of it stained red.

The sheriff kicked the cot until the red-bearded deputy woke with a start, propping up on his elbows, dark blue, bloodshot eyes popping.

Gauge frowned at him. "What the hell happened to you? Horse throw you?"

Rhomer swallowed thickly, held one side of his head, then sat up, rattling the chains that held the cot to the wall. "Hell . . . really tore one on over at the Victory. Is it morning?"

"It's the A.M., but it ain't morning. Your ear's bleedin'."

"One of Lola's girls got rough and I got rough and . . ." He grinned stupidly. Touched his bandaged ear, grimaced. "Kind of got bit."

"Well, I hope you gave her as good as you got. Is our shootist still in town?"

Rhomer nodded. "I think he's over at the hotel. But that ain't the half of it."

Gauge sat next to him. "What is?"

The deputy swallowed, apparently not relishing the taste, and gathered his thoughts, such as they were.

"When I went over to the doc's," he began, "to get this flapper patched up? Doc and Banion . . . I mean, I *figure* it's Banion. . . ."

"So do I. Go on."

"Anyway, Doc and Banion come down the steps carryin' somethin'—somethin' all wrapped up in a sheet. Now, I figure right off it's a body . . ."

Wincing, Gauge thought, *I really do need to find a brighter second-in-command.*

". . . and then I was *sure* it was a body, when I saw this hand flop down, and the doc kind of picks it up and tucks it back under. The doc, he was wearin' work gloves, what's a doc wearin' work gloves for?"

"I don't know. Go on."

"Anyhow, the doc and Banion cart this body out back and walk past the houses to where it's nothin' but country, and just disappear off into the dark. Did I say that there was this shovel laid out on top of the body, on the sheet?"

"No. You didn't."

Rhomer nodded shrewdly, eyes narrowed. "I figure that was a body that they was goin' out to bury in the boonies."

"Seems at least a possibility."

"Anyways, I sat on the stairs in the alley there, by the bank, waitin' for the doc to get back. When he finally does, Banion ain't with him. Or the body, neither, of course. All he has is that shovel."

"Did you ask him what he'd been up to?"

"Well, yeah, in a way, but mostly I was hurtin' and wantin' him to tend to my ear. I lost a piece of it, and he done some stitchin'. So we was just jawin', while he was sewin', and I ask him where he'd been and such. I josh him—'You off diggin' for gold, Doc?' He laughs a bit and says, no, he just had this-here dead dog to bury."

"Bury a dog. Middle of the night. You just let that slide, did you, Vint?"

"I was lucky gettin' the doc to patch me up, middle of the night, is how I took it."

What body would the doc and the stranger feel the need to bury, right now, right this instant, under cover of night?

Troubled, the sheriff rose. "Catch yourself some more sleep, Vint. We may have a busy day tomorrow. Likely an early start."

Gauge decided to go over to the hotel to get a decent bed—maybe a few hours would help him think straighter, to cipher through this conundrum of bodies buried in the wee hours But as he passed his desk, he noticed something: an envelope with *Sheriff Gauge* written neatly there. He went around to sit and saw that it was a telegraph office envelope.

He tore it open and read:

TO SHERIFF HARRY GAUGE, TRINIDAD, N.M.
WESLEY C. BANION KILLED BY DEPUTIES THIS
CITY TWO MONTHS PRIOR. R. BISHOP,
MARSHAL, ELLIS, COLORADO

"When did this come?" he demanded of the deputy in the jail cell.

Rhomer, already half-asleep again, sat up like a man out of a bad dream. "Don't rightly know, Harry. Saw it on the desk when I come in. Door was open. Somebody dropped it off, I guess."

The telegraph clerk Parsons. Gauge had told him to deliver anything that came in, whenever it came in. . . .

"And Banion's over at the hotel?" Gauge asked.

"Far as I know," Rhomer said, touching his sore ear, then flopping back down on the cot, hurting side up, and turning to put his back to his boss.

A few minutes later, Gauge found Lola, in a dressing gown, standing at the check-in desk. She turned to him with surprise, maybe even alarm, showing in her features. The same could be said of the scrawny, near-hairless clerk, eyes wide and blinking behind spectacles that pinched his nose.

Lola, rather breathlessly, said, "*Harry!* . . . I was just coming to find you."

"What are you doin' up?"

Her smile seemed nervous to him, as she said, "Oh, some damn kid threw a rock through my window. Now there's a mess up there, and I was inquiring after another room for tonight."

The chinless clerk was nodding and smiling in a sickly fashion, backing her up.

Gauge frowned. This didn't sound right. But he had bigger things on his mind.

"Let me see that register," he said to the clerk, gesturing impatiently at the tall, narrow volume.

The clerk swallowed, making his bow tie bobble, and said, "Just so you know, I was going to send somebody over to your office first thing in the morning, Sheriff."

"Give it here."

The clerk turned the register around and pushed it across. "I mean, it's plain that this stranger was playing me for a fool. Just the same, I thought you should *see* this. . . . Like I said, I was going to bring it over first thing . . ."

Gauge was looking at the name that the stranger had signed into the book.

Caleb York.

Lola, at his side, was looking, too. "It's a joke. Has to be. Caleb York is long dead. A year or more. Wes Banion shot him."

"Two years ago," Gauge said.

She looked at him with wide eyes in a pretty face still wearing evening paint. "Then . . . he *is* Banion."

"No. Just some fool." His gaze bore into the clerk. "Is he here?"

"No!" The quavery man pointed to the upstairs. "He took a room"—and then to the entry doors—"but he went back out some time ago."

Gauge nodded, shut the register hard, shoved it back at the clerk, and turned to head out. Lola's hand at his arm stopped him.

"Harry . . . what now?"

"Now I'm gonna rouse Rhomer out of his dainty slumber and have him round up every man I got in this town. Then I'm gonna send them out lookin' for this would-be Caleb York, and have them—"

"*Kill* him?"

What did she care?

"No. Have them bring him to me." He stopped just before he went out to add, "I'm going to kill him myself."

Dawn was just a yellow-orange threat, like a distant fire hovering over distant buttes, as Willa brought more coffee to her father, their breakfast over, the dining table otherwise cleared. Both were in red plaid flannel shirts and denims, a blind man and his daughter, well-matched and ready for a working day.

Her blond hair ribboned back in a ponytail, Willa filled her own cup, then joined Papa at one end of the big table. There was so much to talk about . . . yet neither seemed able to find a word.

When a wall of stones is about to fall on you, she thought, *which rock do you discuss?*

Hoofbeats out in front of the ranch house caught the attention of both, and Willa got up and went to see who might be calling so early. Her father followed, moving every bit as quickly as his sighted daughter. She cracked the front door, saw who it was, then opened it wider.

Behind her, her father said hopefully, "Is it him? It's *him*, isn't it?"

The stranger in black was climbing down off his foam-flecked mount—both man and beast had been riding hard.

"It's him, Papa."

Their visitor was tying up the dark-maned dappled animal now. His expression she found unreadable.

She stepped out onto the porch and so did her father, moving around her to lean against the rough post there. The guilty hope in his voice was a terrible thing for her to hear. "Is it . . . *done,* then?"

The stranger walked over and stopped at the foot of the steps. "If you mean is Harry Gauge dead, no."

Softly, bitterly, she said, "Yet you took our money."

"Did I?"

Her chin came up. "Why are you here, then?"

He took off his hat. "I have other news. May I come in? Might there be coffee?"

Hesitating only a moment, she nodded assent to both, and soon the three were seated at one end of the big carved Spanish table.

Before even taking a sip of the steaming black liquid, the stranger asked, "How far is the Swenson spread from here?"

She said, perhaps a tad snippy, "There is no Swenson spread anymore. It's all Harry Gauge's land now."

Her father said, "About twelve miles."

The stranger asked, "Your herd—it's separated from his?"

Willa, frowning in curiosity now, said, "A draw divides the area. Why?"

He looked from father to daughter and back. "His cattle ever mix with yours?"

Papa shook his head. "We're barbwired in. Most of our herd stays on the north section, where the water is. The Swenson water is on the other side of what was his spread. What's this about, friend?"

Ignoring that, their guest asked, "What about the other spreads?"

Willa laughed hollowly. "*What* other spreads? Harry Gauge has most of them now. Only four independents left, counting us. As my father said—what's this all about . . . 'friend'?"

That he ignored, as well, asking, "Does Gauge mix his herds?"

"I understand so," her father said. "Tore out the wire, I'm told, to make a single spread out of all of those he latched onto."

The stranger's eyebrows went quickly up and down. "Then just maybe . . . maybe you're lucky."

Finally he took a sip of coffee while Willa, infuriated by his obtuse manner, sat forward and demanded, "What in blazes is this *about?*"

He met her eyes. "Somebody murdered old Swenson last night."

"No!" her father blurted.

She sucked in a breath. *"Murdered . . ."*

He nodded. "Pistol-whipped to death. Found out near the relay station. Been camped out there awhile."

Papa was shaking his head, dumbfounded.

"Murdered, *why?* He's long since sold out to Gauge."

"That old man dying like that," she said, squinting at their guest as if that might bring things into focus, "that's sad . . . awful . . . but if it's murder? Well, I guess we all know who likely did it, or at least had it done. But like Papa says . . . *why?*"

"To cover something up," the stranger said, and let them mull that while he drank more coffee.

"There's more," her father said, "isn't there?"

He nodded reluctantly. "Here's where it gets hard for you. Before he was killed, Old Swenson contracted cowpox."

Willa's hand flew to her mouth, stifling a gasp.

Papa took it more stoically, his milky eyes narrowing, tightening. "We should be fine. I'm sure we'll be fine. I'll have Whit check the main herd."

"Critical you do that, sir," the stranger said.

The old man reached over and found his daughter's hand and patted it. "We keep our cows nicely separate from the others, daughter. It's an awful thing, the pox, and I hate to say it . . . but maybe this is God raining down his judgment on Harry Gauge."

If so, she thought, *at least the Almighty hadn't charged them ten thousand dollars.*

Hoofbeats sounded again, moving fast, then abruptly ceasing. They all looked in that direction as, within seconds, Whit Murphy, not bothering to knock, stormed in, dusty and bedraggled.

The foreman whipped off his hat and rushed into the dining area, where he nodded to Willa, ignoring the stranger and going over to stand near her father.

"Sir . . . excuse me, but . . ." He gulped for air, panting; he had obviously been riding hard and fast.

"Whit," Papa said, sitting up straight, not waiting for his man to catch his breath, "there's an outbreak of cowpox at the Swenson spread, and it's probably contaminating all the cattle on Gauge land. You need to check our main herd. Get the men out and look for strays. Might find some near the fence line."

Still grabbing his breath, Whit managed, "There *ain't* no main herd, Mr. Cullen."

"*What?*" Her father gaped blindly at his foreman. "What the hell are you *talking* about, man?"

Hat in hands, with a shamed look as if what he were about to report were his fault, the foreman said, "They hit our line camp last night, Mr. Cullen, sir, and run 'em off. Every damn head."

Papa sat stunned for a moment, his mouth hanging open. Then he said, " '*They,*' you say . . . ? Who . . . who *did* this?"

The stranger got up, vacating the chair next to her father, motioning for Whit to sit there. Whit nodded thanks, came over, and took the chair as the stranger moved down one.

Then the foreman leaned in closer to the rancher.

"Mr. Cullen, I can't say who done it. I wasn't there. But my ramrod, Carl, filled me in. Said these marauders wore masks. Nobody got a good look at 'em. Came in heavy and took the guns off everybody and tossed 'em, then ran our boys off. Most of the line hands, but for Carl and two others, ain't been seen since. My guess is they ain't comin' back."

Willa said, "But what about the cattle . . . ?"

The hardened foreman looked across at her as if on the verge of tears. "Miss Cullen, Carl says this bunch was movin' 'em out toward the foothills. It'll take a week to round 'em up. Maybe more, without the boys of ours who scurried off, like frightened rabbits."

Papa slammed a fist into the table. "*Damn* that Harry Gauge!"

Then all the air seemed to go out of George Cullen, and he slumped back in the ornately carved chair. When his voice came back, it was soft and weak, a tone she'd never heard from him before.

"We'll *never* make market in time." He shook his head, squeezed shut his eyes. "This finishes us."

The stranger said, "You can try."

Willa let out a bitter laugh. "What do you suggest? You heard Whit—we don't have enough hands to fill a poker game. What, you think anybody in *Trinidad* is going to help us? They won't lift a finger as long as Harry Gauge and his scum can gun anybody down at will, and get away with it."

"That's a bad choice on their part."

She drew in a breath, let it out; her voice was trembling with frustration and rage. "Harry Gauge set out to own this territory, and now he's going to get away with it."

The stranger, betraying no shred of emotion, said, "There's a way to get the townspeople in this with you."

She arched a skeptical eyebrow. "Really? And what would that be?"

He shrugged. "Well, if they knew how close they were to dying? I believe they'd take an interest."

Whit frowned and said, "What are you on about, mister?"

The stranger's expression was impassive, but his eyes were hard. "Doc Miller says this is as virulent a strain of pox as is out there."

"What about it?" Whit snapped, clearly irritated.

"This old boy Swenson had the sores all over him. Belly, legs, arms." He gestured with an open hand. "By now, Swenson's herd has probably infected the rest of Gauge's cattle."

"Likely," Whit admitted.

"And," the stranger continued, "if our good sheriff wants to keep this quiet, he may well bury his dead cows and try to take to market what he has left."

Willa frowned. "That . . . that could spread an epidemic all across the country. Would he *do* such a thing?"

The stranger grunted a laugh. "What do you think?"

"But . . . could he get *away* with it?"

Again the stranger shrugged, giving her a disconcerting smile.

"Why not?" he asked. "Who could prove it? Once the buyers mix those cattle in the pens, they'll never be able to pin down where it started. Gauge will come away clean. Of course, you can bet he won't be eating beef for a while."

"We can't let this happen!" she said, distress pushing out all other emotions. "This is more than just our ranch, it's . . . it's . . ."

"This whole part of the country," the stranger said. "And maybe beyond."

They sat in silence for several endless seconds.

Then the stranger turned to the foreman. "Mr. Murphy . . . Whit . . . how many men do you have left?"

The foreman thought briefly, then said, "Eight, countin' myself."

The stranger nodded, his eyes slitted. "Then get those men out on the Swenson range looking for fresh-dug graves. And if you can get inside the herd itself, try to spot any sick steers. So we can show the buyers what Guage has pulled."

Whit's eyebrows went up. "Boys may spook at doin' work like this."

"Tell them they're fighting for their lives on this one."

Whit nodded.

Papa, whose spirit seemed back, said confidently, "Any man still with us will *stay* with us."

Willa asked, "What about our cattle?"

The stranger said, "If they're not infected, they'll keep. Better send somebody around to the other independent ranches, still fenced off, and quietly spread the word. We don't want a panic. But I wager you'll get some willing hands in a hurry."

Her father said, "You're sure this is the way to go about this?"

"You care to bet against it?"

"That's a lot of talk, mister," Whit said. "And it sounds good, I admit. So you probably deserve our thanks."

"You're welcome."

"I said 'probably.' But besides tellin' everybody else what to do . . . just what are *you* going to do in all this?"

"Take a real personal interest," he said.

Her father asked, "In what way?"

"By talking to a few people in town. I already know a few to approach. Sir, can you give me the names of citizens who you consider allies?"

Her father did so, beginning with the members of the Citizens Committee.

"Thanks," he said, rising. He hadn't written them down. "I'll start there."

Half-rising herself, Willa said, "Would you like

to catch a few hours of sleep first? We have plenty of room in our bunkhouse now, I'm afraid."

He gave her a smile. "No. Sleep is a luxury none of us can afford right now. Whit . . . I'm hoping to join you on the range with some volunteers. Can you give me directions to somewhere we might meet around . . . eleven, say?"

"I can do that," Whit said, just a touch grudging.

A few minutes later, Willa walked their guest out. The sun was climbing and the morning promised to be as beautiful as the problems they faced weren't. Still chilly, though. The sun would be working on that.

At the bottom of the porch steps, she stopped him with a hand on a sleeve and said with concern, "If this cowpox is a reality . . ."

"It is."

". . . and we *don't* make it to market, that means . . . well, it means the Bar-O will be wiped out, doesn't it?"

They were facing each other, perhaps two feet away. Morning sun was at his back and he was bathed in cool blue shadow.

"Possibly," he said. "Not for me to say, really. I don't know how exactly your business affairs stand."

She gave him a sharp look. "Well, that ten thousand dollars my father promised to pay you—"

He cut her off with a raised hand, then said, "It had a catch in it, as I recall. I had to kill Harry Gauge first, right?"

"Right." She let him see a smirk that stopped just short of insulting. "Of course, you got half that much just by showing up."

He smiled wearily, then said, "Miss Cullen, something you should know about me. . . ."

"Yes?"

"I don't take money for killing people."

She shaded her eyes with a hand. "Then . . . who *are* you, anyway?"

"Not some hired killer. Did it never occur to you that I might really just be somebody passing through, who got caught up in things?"

"No, it didn't. It still hasn't."

He sighed through his nose, a hint of disgust in it. "Well, your father can keep his money."

She kissed him.

It was sudden, and sweet, then grew forceful on both their parts, as he held her to him, her arms going around him as she stood on tiptoes to meet the big man. Then, looking at each other, noses almost touching, he brushed the side of her face and her hair, and gazed at her with a tenderness that did not fit a man who had gunned down four men yesterday.

She asked, "Why . . . why *do* you kill, then?"

"Not for pleasure."

He touched her face again, unhitched the gelding, and rode off toward town.

CHAPTER TWELVE

Stripes of mid-morning sun cut through barred windows, as Sheriff Harry Gauge entertained a guest in his office—Dr. Albert Miller, who right now looked like he could use a sawbones himself.

In the open area between Gauge's desk and an old, small deputy's table sat the lawman's distinguished guest. The doc's eyes were swollen, his nose trailing blood from its nostrils, skin along cheekbones ragged and red, lips puffy, discolored and bleeding. The plump little physician's brown suit was rumpled and torn in front from where it had been grabbed repeatedly to shake him or to hold him for a slap, his white shirt splotched with crimson. Thin white hair mussed, he looked dazed, barely awake.

But he was.

Painfully so.

At that small table, two deputies were seated in
hardback chairs, grinning, watching, smoking rolled
cigarettes, sharing some morning whiskey, and playing two-handed poker for matchsticks. To their
one side was a wood-burning stove, unlit, and looming over them was the wall of wanted posters from
which stared faces almost as unpleasant as theirs.
The presence of these deputies was not really necessary to this interrogation—the sheriff was plenty
good enough at this sort of thing on his own steam.

Brown-haired and shaggy-mustached, bug-eyed
Clovis Maxwell was the bigger of the two watchers,
a cowboy who'd been among those who shoveled
dirt over cattle carcasses last night, his filthy low-
crowned plainsman hat and heavy leather chaps
attesting his profession.

Across the small, scarred table was towheaded
Cole Colton, small, even skinny, with close-set brown
eyes, a trimmed gambler's mustache and a sugar-
loaf sombrero that seemed to dwarf him. He was no
cowboy, just another former outlaw turned deputy
in jeans and dark blue twill military shirt. He drank
too much and was rattlesnake mean, but as a con-
scienceless killer, he had value to the sheriff.

These were the two men who had handled the
dispatching of Old Man Swenson out near the
stage relay station—Colton swinging the gun butt.
They'd been invited to this questioning less to
back up their boss than because they had a stake in
what their guest had to say.

Both men carried .44's, the weapons on the table

as if serving as ante, though really to avoid falling out of their tied-down holsters.

They seemed to be enjoying the show.

Gauge slapped the doctor viciously on his right cheek and, when the man's face turned to one side with the blow, bloody spittle flying, the sheriff slapped him again on the other cheek, just as hard, returning it to the other side.

"You're a damn good Christian, Doc," the sheriff said with a grin. "Turnin' the other cheek like that."

Maxwell guffawed at that; Colton didn't get it.

Dr. Miller, breathing hard, did not seem to find any humor in the remark, either. How much he was seeing out of those swollen eyes was up for conjecture. His reddened ears had been cuffed enough to be ringing, so how well he was hearing was questionable, too.

"Maybe you'll notice, Doc," the sheriff said, eyes half-lidded, smile easygoing, "that I got a real touch for this kind of thing. Touch a medic like you might covet. See, I know just how far I can go without gettin' to where there ain't no comin' back."

He swung a sudden fist deep into the older man's stomach. Wind whooshed out, accompanied by an anguished cry that was a mix of pain and exhaustion.

And the sheriff had only been at this twenty or so minutes.

Gauge placed both hands on the round man's

shoulders and leaned in, his seeming good humor gone.

"No more lies, Doc . . . and don't hold out on me, no, sir. Good as I am at this, I can only hold back so long . . . and you're too damn old and weak to take much more."

His breath heavy and ragged, the doc said, "This . . . this is one thing . . . you won't . . . won't live down . . . *Sheriff.*"

That last word was uttered with unmistakable contempt.

Gauge let out some air, backed away, then began walking slowly around the seated man, like a stubborn loser at musical chairs.

"Touches my heart, Doc," Gauge said gently. "That you're so concerned about me, and my standin' in the community. But, hell—you don't need to worry yourself about Harry Gauge."

Right behind him now, Gauge looped an arm around the doctor's neck and pulled back, hard, as if flexing a muscle for an admiring female, forcing him back with the front chair feet off the floor, choking off the prisoner's air, summoning a terrible gargling sound.

Then Gauge let go, chair legs finding the wooden floor with a jostle, and the sheriff again began walking slowly around the seated man.

"Just worry about yourself, Doc," he advised.

When Gauge came around again, the doctor looked up at him, pleadingly. "I . . . I *told* you I didn't bury anybody last night. Your man . . . who says . . . says he saw me . . . must have been *drunk.*"

Gauge's eyebrows went up and down. "Well, good chance that he was. But that don't change what he saw. Simple question, Doc. *Who did you bury?*"

"No . . . nobody."

Gauge grabbed him by his suitcoat and shook him like the least obedient child on earth. Over at the table, Maxwell and Colton were smiling at each other, the smaller man giggling to himself.

"It was Old Swenson, wasn't it?" Gauge demanded. "Don't bother lying."

His breathing ragged, the doc managed, "If . . . if you *know* . . . why ask?"

Gauge backed off, nodded slowly, hands on hips, appraising his bloodied interview subject. "Then we agree. It was Old Swenson you buried."

The doctor's nod was barely discernible, but it was there. "Can I . . . can I *go* now? Why . . . why don't we . . . all agree that . . . that I'll forget about this little incident . . . and you won't tell anybody . . . what your man saw me do."

"Guess that's against medical ethics or some such, right, Doc? Not to worry—we don't tell tales out of school here at the sheriff's office. Though . . . we *are* about to move on to my next question."

Miller's swollen eyes closed in anticipation of what pain and indignities were yet to come.

But Gauge merely leaned back against the edge of his desk, arms folded, casual, friendly, implying that no more punishment was coming, as long as the doctor continued to cooperate.

"Tell me, Doc—why did you sneak off and bury Old Swenson?"

Miller shook his head, an effort that clearly had a cost.

Gauge lurched forward and slammed a fist into the side of the doctor's head. The doc's mouth went slack and pink saliva drooled from pulverized lips barely recognizable as lips at all.

The doctor began to cry.

To sob.

At the little table, Maxwell was grinning like a kid at the circus while Colton started in with a high-pitched laugh, saying, "He's bawlin' like a little *girl!* Like a damn *girl!*"

Gauge frowned over at his deputies, shaking his head a tad.

Then he resumed his questioning. "Doc, we got us a problem. Good as I am at this, when we get past a certain point? You're gonna be the next one buried out there in the brush somewheres. You do follow?"

The doc swallowed thickly. Nodded sluggishly.

"Okay, then. Why the fuss over Swenson's body?"

"I . . . I think you *know* why."

"Let's say I don't."

Again the doc swallowed, and he lifted his chin, as if inviting yet another blow. His speech became less halting as he summoned strength from somewhere.

"All right . . . I'll *tell* you why . . . though as I say . . . you likely . . . likely know already." He sighed, tremblingly. "Swenson came down with the pox not long before he died."

The deputies at the table weren't smiling now.

The doctor nodded his head back, indicating the two spectators. His mouth was trying to form something that might have been a smile.

"Your men handled the body, didn't they, Sheriff? Was it *these* two? . . . I hope all of you know that *you* can get this unforgiving thing, too. Maybe . . . maybe it's not such a good time to be murdering your town doctor."

Maxwell and Colton were on their feet, wild-eyed, the latter reaching for his pistol.

But Gauge waved at them to sit back down, giving them a few shakes of the head and a skeptical expression that seemed to tell them not to worry about what the doctor had said.

Bending over, hands on his knees, the sheriff stared into the grotesque mask he'd created where the doc's face used to be.

"Don't try to rattle us, Doc. We've been around cows too long. We've seen the pox before."

"Then . . . then you must've seen people *die* from it. And maybe . . . maybe this is *your* turn. At least, if that is the case? You fools won't spread the infection any further."

Gauge scowled and drew back his hand to slap the doc.

But their guest's chin had dropped to his chest,

the man finally unconscious. Not dead, still breathing. But out.

The door half-opened and Rhomer stuck his head in. "Harry . . . better step outside here a second."

Gauge told the two deputies to leave the doc be, then stepped out.

On the porch, hands on hips, Gauge asked, "What's going on?"

The deputy gestured all around. "See for yourself—not a damn *thing* is goin' on, and that's the point."

Main Street did look strangely deserted.

Rhomer went on: "We got a stage due through here this afternoon, right? Stage comin', every merchant in town is standin' outside of his place of business with a big welcomin' smile plastered on his puss, and the ladies're all dressed up and lined along the boardwalk rails to see who new's comin' into town. Now . . . what do you see *this mornin'*, boss?"

"Not a damn thing," Gauge admitted. "All we lack is tumbleweed rollin' down Main."

That stage would be carrying the first round of cattle buyers. Gauge had already decided to do business with them. With the clock ticking on the cowpox infestation, doing that was critical. No time for competitive bids.

"Stores all closed," Rhomer was saying, shaking his head, gazing down the street.

"Is the café open?"

The proprietor, Lucas Jones, used to ride with Gauge, who was co-owner.

"He is, and Luke says he sold more than a few cups of coffee, first thing. Right around when men started in just sort of driftin' out of town, not long after sunup. You know what else he says?"

"Why don't you tell me?"

The deputy's eyes narrowed meaningfully. "Thought he might've saw the stranger goin' into the hardware store, right after it opened . . . but ain't sure."

Gauge looked up and down the empty street.

Rhomer was saying, "Seems like all that's left in town is women and kids, and they're mostly keepin' inside. What the hell's goin' on, Harry?"

He shook his head, disgusted. "It's that stranger's work. Has to be. Somehow he convinced these lily livers to go out and help Cullen in his time of need."

The redheaded deputy tugged gently at his bandaged ear, making a sour face. "You should've killed that S.O.B. when you had the chance, Harry."

"Well, Vint," came a familiar female voice from behind them, "why didn't *you?*"

They turned to see Lola—ready for riding—in a blue-and-white shirt and navy split-skirt with matching gloves and boots—smirking at them sassily.

Gauge frowned. "What the hell's that supposed to mean?"

Lola shrugged. Her eyes met Rhomer's and he glanced away. "Nothing. Just an observation, posed as a question."

"Well, keep your damn observations to yourself," Gauge said irritably. "Questions too."

She tossed her head. Her hair was up as usual, but she wore only light face paint. "All right. If you think Deputy Rhomer here is the kind of . . . *advisor* you prefer."

Rhomer gave her a hard-eyed, nasty look, just before Gauge shoved his face at hers, taking her aback some.

He said, "How about you just keep that pretty mouth shut? I just about had it with you lipping off all the time."

"Harry, I was only . . ."

"Lola, I killed men for less than I put up with out of you lately. Bear that in mind."

Rhomer had a goofy smile going that Gauge picked up on. "What *you* grinning about, Vint?"

"Nothin', Harry! I . . ."

He nodded behind him. "Go in and get that doctor out of sight."

Rhomer frowned, cocked his head like a dog trying to understand its master's words. "You mean . . . six feet *under,* out of sight?"

Gauge touched his chin, thought momentarily. "No. Not yet, anyway. If there's trouble, we may *need* that quack."

"Then . . . what . . . ?"

The sheriff jerked a thumb toward the office.

"Stick the doc in the back cell and keep somebody on guard. When this thing is over, if nobody needs patchin' up . . . or, anyway, after they been patched up sufficient . . . then we'll dig Miller a new surgery out on Boot Hill. About time this town had a new doctor, anyway."

Rhomer, liking the sound of that, was just about to head back inside when Lola asked, "Say, Vint, what happened to your ear? Cut yourself shaving?"

The smile in his nest of beard oozed menace, but the deputy was turned away from Gauge, who didn't tumble to it.

Rhomer said, "Naw, thought you knew, Lola— one of your girls did this to me. I got a little . . . rambunctious, I guess."

"Boys will be boys," she said.

"Well, she better look out. Might get what she deserves."

He went in.

Then Lola was at Gauge's side, saying, "So you've got the elderly doctor handled. Congratulations. Now, what about Banion? What are you going to do about him?"

Gauge chuckled, stepping away from her. "Banion? Why, I'm not going to do a damn thing about Banion."

Relishing his secret joke, he got the wire out, reading it to himself yet another time, savoring the words that spoke of Banion's death two months before. Then he wadded up the slip of paper and tossed it into the street.

After watching this curious conduct with some confusion, Lola reared her head back and smiled at him . . . but her eyes were hateful, and this he caught.

"Why not go after him, Harry? Or has Banion got you scared?"

He backhanded her and she went down on the porch like a bundle of kindling, the plank flooring groaning though she herself made not a sound. She stayed down there awhile, her back arching like an animal about to strike.

Then she had that derringer in her hand, courtesy of the gambler's holdout rig up her sleeve.

As she started up, Gauge kicked the little gun out of her gloved fingers, as easy as swatting a fly. The toe of his boot caught her hand enough to make her yowl.

She was still down there, a wounded, cornered animal, breathing hard, looking up at him with eyes showing white all around, nostrils flared, teeth showing, leaning one hand against the planking, the other touching the redness of her cheek.

Her breath regular now, her voice seemed surprisingly soft and almost uninflected—no anger apparent, only hurt, and not the hurt of flesh, but something deeper.

"Why do you keep doing that, Harry? How many times have I told you never to hit me? How can you treat me like this after all we've been to each other?"

He grabbed her by an arm and hauled her up,

and it took her a while to get her footing, brushing off her split-skirt as she did.

"You're right, Lola. We have . . . *been* . . . something to each other. 'Been,' as in 'we ain't anymore.'"

She stared at him as if he were a stranger now. "What are you . . . ?"

He took her by both arms and squeezed, not enough to hurt, but to demonstrate control.

"I just don't need you anymore, kid. Oh, I'm not throwin' you out—not exactly. You do what I tell you to, and maybe I'll let you stay on in Trinidad. Misbehave, and maybe I won't."

She swallowed hard, her chin quivering, small, trembling fists held waist-high. "I brought you to Trinidad, Harry. Never forget that. I *made* you. You started with *my* money."

"That's right," he said. "You made me. But how many times did I make you?" He laughed lightly and shrugged. "It all worked out real nice, didn't it? Well, it'll work out even better now."

She stood very close to him, gazing up at him, and there was something fearless about it that impressed him some.

She said, "You really think that Cullen girl is woman enough for you? Not that she'd ever *have* you. She'd kill herself before letting you touch her."

"Maybe I don't mean to ask," he said, and he shoved her away and went back into his office, slamming the door on her.

Gauge didn't see Lola—going out in the street to retrieve the derringer—notice the wad of paper he had tossed there. And bend down in the street to pick it up. . . .

Nor did he see her come back up on the porch, intending to confront him again, but stopping as voices from inside came through the open shutters.

"Vint, that stage stops at the relay station to make its change of horses before comin' into town."

"That's right, Harry, same as always. And the passengers can have a drink or two while they's waitin'. So what?"

"So we'll meet those cattle buyers out there, before they even get to town. Old Man Cullen won't think of that, and even if he does . . . we'll be waiting."

Lola tucked the derringer back in its sleeve rig and the wrinkled slip of paper into a pocket, then walked quickly to the livery stable, where she got her horse and rode off to deliver her own message.

CHAPTER THIRTEEN

From her saddle atop Daisy, Willa—in red-and-black plaid shirt, red neck-knotted scarf, denims, and stirrup-friendly boots—shielded her eyes from the sun and let them roam over the endless, slightly rolling grassy expanse before her. She and a dozen other riders were paused at a slight rise in their search for dead cattle that didn't seem to want to be found.

They had been at it since shortly after dawn, and—after meeting up with the stranger and thirty-some other men on horseback whom he'd managed to enlist from Trinidad—they'd put in another two fruitless hours. The volunteers from town, shopkeepers and clerks, looked almost comically out of place on the range in their suits and ties and bowlers. They had split up into three groups, the men from town joining cowhands from the Cullen spread and the other independents, a rancher leading each contingent.

Willa's group consisted of foreman Whit Murphy, several Cullen hands, half-a-dozen Trinidad men, and herself. And, of course, the stranger, whose tenderfoot-worthy apparel was looking considerably less fancy after the dust, sweat, and riding of the morning.

Right now they were looking at a whole lot of nothing under a sun that was almost directly above them, and growing ever hotter.

Whit, his expression foul, said, "This is loco—we ain't found any sign of dead cows."

The foreman sat on horseback on one side of her and the stranger on the other.

The man in black on his dappled gelding said, "They're around."

"Really?" Whit snapped. He threw an open hand out. *"Where?"*

"That's the question."

A rider came up quickly—Matt Gerrity, the small, tough owner of another of the few remaining independent spreads. In his forties, with sharp cheekbones, untrimmed reddish brown mustache, and cleft chin, the grizzled Gerrity was otherwise indistinguishable from any of the hard-riding cowhands who worked for him, half a dozen of whom—supplanted by the fish-out-of-water townsmen—arrived moments after their boss.

The rancher pointed and said, "We covered all

that end, Miss Cullen, Whit. No sign of nothin' be-in' buried there."

The stranger asked, "No sick cattle?"

Gerrity shook his head. "We swung all through that herd Gauge's got staked out for delivery. Checked all around." He shrugged, shook his head again. "No sign of the pox."

The third group of riders came up and their leader—Charley Mathis, another independent rancher—drew up beside Gerrity. Nobody looked happy.

Whit said, "How about it, Charley? Find any-thing?"

Mathis was in his fifties, weathered, white-haired with matching handlebar mustache and small, shrewd eyes that crowded a hooked nose.

He said, "Not a damn thing, Whit. The south range looks clean as a whistle."

Whit said nothing, or at least he spoke no words—his darkening expression was eloquent enough with-out them.

With a weight-of-the-world sigh, the foreman climbed down off his horse, and when he came around in front, he had his .45 in hand, aimed the stranger's way.

"Keep away from those guns, mister," Whit said. "Sidearm and shotgun both. Hands up, shoulder-high."

"*Whit!*" Willa said, stunned.

The man under the gun followed instructions.

"Well, Whit. You seem to have somethin' on your mind."

The menacing figure was sneering up at the stranger. "You could say that. Like thinkin' how things are startin' to make sense, about now."

Her forehead tense, Willa said, "Whit, what in God's name do you think you're—"

"All due respect, Miss Cullen," he said, cutting her off, "this is between one man and another one."

"You work for me!"

"No. I work for your father."

The others on horseback were watching, some with interest, others in confusion. Perhaps half the men wore a glowering cast and appeared to share Whit's sentiment.

"We're on the same side," the stranger observed. "Squabbling gets us nowhere."

Gun thrust up at the man, Whit said, "Really? Well, you never even said *which* side you was on, stranger! Hell, you never even gave us a name. Could be you're workin' for Harry Gauge."

Willa, head spinning, said, "Why would you *say* such a thing, Whit?"

With his free hand, the foreman gestured to the vastness of range around them. "Gauge rustled our herd, all right, and moved 'em toward the foothills. No question about that. And what with all these men we put together for this dead-cow hunt, we damn well might've located them beeves by now."

"Possibly," the stranger allowed.

Now Whit spoke to the other men on horseback who were looking on, while never taking his eyes—much less his .45—off the stranger. The one thing they all knew about this man in a pearl-buttoned black shirt was that he was dangerous, and deadly with a gun.

Whit continued, "Only, we didn't go lookin' for Mr. Cullen's herd, no. Instead, we spend all our time lookin' for dead cattle that ain't here—that ain't *nowhere*."

"Whit," the stranger said quietly, with the tiniest nod, "you're going to want to put that gun away."

The foreman just grinned up at him. "You and Gauge hatched yourselves one hell of a scheme. Put on quite a show. But when we send you back to him, across your saddle? He's gonna know things ain't worked out exactly as planned."

Willa said, "Whit—are you listening to yourself? He killed four of Gauge's *deputies*."

"Small sacrifice for Gauge to make out of his numbers," Whit said, with a downturned smile, "if him and his helper here could put this over."

"Whit Murphy," Willa said, pointedly, "you're not making *sense.* . . ."

"Miss Cullen, you need to stay quiet now."

A faint smile traced the stranger's lips. "Not very smart, are you, Whit? A good man and loyal. Just not too smart."

"Keep 'em up!" Whit blinked away the insult. "Now, we can hang you or shoot you. Any preference, stranger? We're civilized people, around these parts. . . ."

But the stranger seemed not to be paying attention to Whit and the threat he posed. Instead, he was looking up and beyond his Colt-waving accuser.

Quietly he said, "Before you make me kill you, Whit, you might want to look yonder."

And the stranger, with one already upraised hand, pointed to the sky, above and behind Whit.

The foreman grunted a laugh. "You really *do* think I'm stupid."

"I do," the stranger admitted. "But that's not why you should look. Over by that draw . . ."

Willa already had looked and seen, in the distance, ominous dark birds with widespread wings, circling.

She said, and it was a suggestion not an order, "Put that gun away, Whit."

Everybody else was looking in that direction, too, and finally so did he.

"Buzzards!" Whit said.

"Well," the stranger said. "Now you're smart."

Frowning, Whit holstered his gun and got back on his horse, to join the rest as they rode in the direction of the swooping predators who'd sensed carrion.

Soon the riders on horseback were gathered at the edge of the draw, looking down to see the partially exposed remains of a steer under a landslide that had been created to form a mass grave. A buzzard was perched, pulling an eyeball from a socket, snapping a last stubborn string of flesh like a rubber band. Then, sensing the presence of other creatures—living ones—the buzzard flapped away.

"No wonder we couldn't see them," the stranger said.

Whit, now riding alongside his adversary of minutes ago, said, "I want to get a look at those carcasses."

"You want help?"

"No. No need to put anybody else at risk."

The foreman dismounted, withdrew a folded-up shovel from a saddlebag, and stepped down into the draw, navigating the steepness of the slope with some difficulty, but managing.

Reaching the new, uneven pile of earth that filled the floor of the draw, Whit used the unfolded shovel to stroke away dirt from several suspicious lumps and expose more dead cows. He bent to each one, making an inspection, using gloved hands to help him see what he needed to. Then he stood, surveyed the grim scene, and made his way back up the steep, treacherous slope.

The foreman lifted his eyebrows and said to Willa, "Infected, all right. And they all wear Gauge's Circle G brand."

Rancher Gerrity said to no one in particular, "You know what that means—we gotta destroy every damn head of the sheriff's herd."

Whit, refolding and putting his shovel away, glanced back and said, "There's hardly a cowhand on that spread of his who ain't also a gunfighter, mind. He'll be ready to fight."

"So will we," Gerrity said.

"If there's time," the stranger said.

Everyone looked at him.

"Gauge might be driving them into Las Vegas right now," the stranger explained. "He can meet with the buyers today and give them his numbers and make a deal."

Whit, frowning, said, "And once he's sold 'em and they're in pens mixed with cows from other herds, Gauge is in the clear."

Willa wiped sweat from her brow and said, "The first batch of buyers is due into Trinidad on the stage this afternoon."

The stranger asked, "How soon?"

She shrugged. "Three, four hours."

He thought about that. "But first they change horses at the Brentwood Junction relay station, right?"

"That's right."

Eyes narrowed, he said, "If I can reach those buyers there, before they hit town, I can pass the word about the infected stock. Those businessmen won't take a chance on paying for infected steers."

Gerrity spat chaw and said, "You don't have much time, mister."

"No. And I better not waste it here." He nodded to Whit, who nodded respectfully back.

Then the stranger swung his horse around, and as he passed by Willa, she raised a hand for him to stop.

He pulled up on the reins.

"Thank you," she said simply, "and good luck."

Her back to the others, with only him seeing, she kissed her palm and held her hand out to him. He took the hand, held it briefly, his eyes holding hers for several long moments.

Then he rode off.

They watered their horses at a nearby stream in a stand of cottonwood and made their plans.

With everyone circled around, Whit said, "We'd better get to riding, too. If Gauge's bunch makes it through the pass with that herd of theirs, they'll post a handful of men and hold us off long enough to have those beeves well on their way to the railhead."

His hat off, scratching at his white temple, Mathis said, "Leave us handle that, Whit."

Whit frowned. "What?"

The rancher put a hand on the Cullen foreman's shoulder. "Son, you and Willa got other fish to fry."

"No . . . we're all in this together."

Gerrity came up and put a hand on the foreman's other shoulder. "We already had a powwow and you been outvoted. You take half these men and see if you can find them Bar-O cattle."

"Listen," Willa said, shaking her head, "this is bigger than just the Bar-O—"

"No," Mathis said, shaking his head back at her, "you listen, young lady. In a way, all this whole damn mess is our doin', smaller ranchers and townsfolk alike, for lettin' Gauge get as far as he got. Independence-minded sorts sometimes don't remember that when their neighbor is in trouble, trouble's about to show up on your own doorstep, too."

"I know," she said, "but—"

"'But' nothin'," Gerrity said. "If we succeed, we're about to go off and destroy Gauge's cattle. And if our stock turns out to be infected, too, we'll have to get rid of all them. That means we may be needin' starter cattle for next year. It's George Cullen we'll turn to. So you'll be doin' us a favor, gettin' that healthy herd back in the right hands."

The other rancher said, "Miss Cullen, best you go home and stay at your father's side. Take a few men with you."

Gerrity was nodding. "No tellin' what Gauge might pull at this point."

"No," she insisted, shaking her head, ponytail swinging. "Papa's not alone there, and you can use another experienced hand."

"I just hope," Mathis sighed, "that we ain't too late."

Frowning, Willa asked, "What do you mean?"

"I mean, Gauge may be ahead of us. He may've figured that we'd try meetin' up with the buyers at the relay station, and's already sent somebody out there to stop us."

Gerrity said, "And here we sit, with all our hopes pinned on one duded-up stranger."

Whit said, "It's a safe-enough bet."

All heads turned his way.

"I was dead wrong about him," the foreman said. "He'll do right by us or die tryin'. Meantime, the rest of us need to help you destroy that infected herd."

Shaking his head firmly, Mathis said, "Face it, Whit—you're outnumbered. You're gonna do it our way. Half these men are going with you and get back those healthy cows."

There was no more arguing it. Whit did as he'd been told, and soon they were watching half of the men ride off in a dust cloud, hooves pounding.

Then Willa, Whit, and the rest rode off in the other direction, just as hard.

Tulley's morning had been eventful.

He had spent several hours of it under the boardwalk, curled up in its coolness with the bottle of rotgut he'd bought at the Victory. It had cost him a whole dollar out of the five he'd been given, highway robbery, but seemed worth it at the time.

Only thing was, damn it, that fool conscience of his had come kicking him in the hindquarters like a mule.

And speaking of mules, early this morning, the

stranger had give him all that money on the condition that Tulley buy back his mule Gert from Hitchens at the livery stable. That was what come of running at the mouth around a new acquaintance. Drunks had a terrible bad habit of telling people their life stories.

When he first come to town, Tulley was sober for a spell, and got to thinking that the life of a prospector hadn't been so bad. That had been his vocation before taking on the job of (as the stranger put it) town character. It beat sweeping out stables and doing odd jobs and sleeping in alleyways, didn't it?

Tulley had prospected for two whole days in the foothills before he remembered why he'd stopped doing it in the first place. Back in town, he resold Gert to Hitchens for three dollars, drank it up in two days, and Gert became just another female (well, sort of female) memory in the pages of an increasingly hazy past history.

Trouble with Gert was, she wasn't so hazy a memory, living in the stable as she did, where Tulley bedded down much of the time. Having that damn mule around served as a nagging reminder of his failings.

This morning, not that long after dawn, the stranger had given him that five dollars to buy Gert back and ride out to the Cullen spread to offer his services as a sort of guide. Nobody around Trinidad knew those foothills better than old Tulley.

The desert rat had agreed, shaking hands with

the stranger, who had ridden off, after which Tulley waited till the saloon opened at ten and bought his bottle. Crazy part was, he never uncapped the thing. He lay in the coolness under the boardwalk with the bottle in one hand and the rest of them dollars in the other.

Finally, around noon, he opened that damn bottle, chugged down several slugs of it, enjoying the burning in his belly, then capped it and went over to the livery stable and talked Hitchens into selling Gert back to him for three dollars.

When Tulley was riding out of town on Gert— no saddle, just an Injun blanket—Ralph from the telegraph office started in, yelling at him.

Tulley pulled back on Gert's reins (Hitchens threw them in).

"You want to make half a buck, Tulley?"

"Sure."

The clerk delivered the coin and also a slip of paper. "Run this wire out to the Cullen place. I think it may be real important. Can I trust you to do that?"

"Well, sure you can." Wasn't he already headed out there, anyway?

"If you drink it up, I won't be pleased."

"I ain't just on this mule, friend. I'm on the wagon."

So he had delivered the wire to old Mr. Cullen, who give him two bits more for his trouble. Actually, a ranch hand took the wire because the old man was blind and needed someone to read it to him. Tulley stood there while the man rattled it off to his boss, but the thing was just some business nonsense that Tulley couldn't follow.

"Mr. Cullen," Tulley said, on the porch of the ranch house as its owner and his man were about to go in, "you know that stranger? He wanted me to offer to help you look for your cows in them foothills."

"What?" The old boy seemed kind of out of sorts since he heard what was in that wire. "Oh, uh . . . they left hours ago, Tulley. I doubt you could find them. But I thank you for the offer."

Then Tulley remembered something he'd overheard back in town that might be of interest to the rancher, and he shared it, the news upsetting the blind man even more than that wire, though Tulley didn't really understand why.

Things in and around Trinidad had been happening so fast, since the stranger come to town, that an old sot like him could barely keep track or make sense of it.

After that, part of him wanted to head back to town with his bottle and sell the mule to Hitchens again. But Tulley liked the stranger, looked up to him like he hadn't anybody for as long as he could remember, and for no reason he could understand, Tulley just didn't want to let the man down.

So he left the road into Trinidad and started out overland, toward the foothills. After a while, he saw the dust of horses not too far off and headed that way.

Before long, he intersected with those riders, who turned out to be Willa Cullen, Whit Murphy, and a mess of Bar-O boys and some men from town, too. A regular posse.

"*Whoa* there, Gert! . . . Howdy, Miss Cullen, Mr. Murphy."

Whit Murphy, yanking back on his reins, frowning curiously, said, "What are you doin' out this way, Tulley?"

"Well, sir, that stranger asked me to throw in with you, if I was lucky enough to run into you."

This seemed to amuse Whit. "Why would we want you to join us?"

"Well, you might. See, I done a good share of prospectin' in them foothills in my day, Mr. Murphy, and there ain't nobody nowhere who knows every draw and gulley out there like this old bird does." He patted his chest, raising some dust. "Thought maybe I might help you look for them cows you folks misplaced."

Whit still seemed uncertain. "The stranger entrusted *you* with this?"

Tulley grinned, scratching Gert's right ear. "Well, I don't think he put *all* his money on this horse, or anyway mule. But he knows I see and hear things. I ain't always drunk and asleep in the street like some folk think."

Willa, smiling, said, "Listen to him, Whit. Tulley's a good man."

The desert rat beamed at her. "Thank you kindly, Miss Cullen. You warm an old feller's heart."

"Whit," she said to her foreman, "you take Tulley here and the rest of the men and follow his lead in those foothills. If Tulley can help locate the herd . . . well, we might be able to stall those buyers until we know we've actually got something to sell them."

Whit narrowed his gaze. "What about you?"

"I'll take Dave and Pete and head back to the Bar-O, and make sure Papa's safe from Gauge."

Tulley said, "That's a right good idea, Miss Cullen. I seen your daddy not long ago, maybe an hour? And he was pretty damn upset. Excuse the language."

She gave him a sharp look. "How so, Tulley?"

He told her about the telegram he'd brought her father from town, and apologized for not remembering what was in it.

Then he added, "And I also told your daddy how Gauge and his deputy got together some of their outlaw bunch and beat it on up the trail. They was headed toward the Brentwood Junction relay station."

"When was this?"

"Right when I was ridin' out of town."

Whit said, "How do you know where they were going?"

Tulley grinned. "Heard him talkin'. I hear all sorts of things. You be surprised."

Willa and her foreman exchanged troubled glances.

"Tulley," she said, "have you seen anything of the stranger? He might have cut across your path on his way to . . . well, any sign of him?"

"Not since this mornin' in Trinidad."

Whit said, "And you haven't seen Banion since?"

Tulley chortled. "Seen Banion since *when*? What, on angel wings? Though I doubt that's what he's wearin' right now, unless they's asbestos."

Whit snapped, "What the hell are you goin' on about, you old fool?"

Shaking his head, Tulley said, "You people keep talkin' 'Banion this, Banion that.' Wes Banion was shot down and killed dead over Ellis way, two month ago."

Whit frowned, saying, "You heard this where?"

"I didn't hear it. I *seen* it. Seen it happen, right in the street, afore these very eyes. You see a lot of things happen from under a boardwalk."

Willa said, "You sound sure it was Banion."

"Sure I'm sure. I'm one of the only ones who knew the man by sight back when he was still breathin'. Banion, he was a careful sort. Though, I guess, not careful enough."

"But the stranger," Willa said, frowning so hard it must have hurt. "Who *is* he, then?"

"Beats me, ma'am. I kinder think he was just passin' through, you know, and took an interest? Maybe an interest in *you*, Miss Cullen . . . if you'll tolerate my liberty sayin' so."

Willa swung her horse around, glancing back at Whit. "Get going. Locate that herd!"

Nodding to Tulley, he said, "And let *him* lead the way?"

"Yes."

Tulley said, "Sometimes a young fool can learn things from an old fool, sonny."

Whit sighed, but nodded dutifully at Willa, and Tulley fell in with them as they rode off.

Keeping up on the mule took some doing, but for the first time, in a long time, Jonathan R. Tulley felt like he was part of something.

Something that mattered.

Willa and the two Bar-O hands rode hard and fast, and soon she was rushing into the ranch house, calling out for her father.

No answer, just the sound of her own voice ringing off the walls.

Then she saw the telegram, discarded on the floor in the middle of the front room. She bent and picked it up, reading it before she'd even gotten to her feet:

> TO GEORGE CULLEN, TRINIDAD, N.M. MISTER
> PARKER IN CALIFORNIA ON EXTENDED
> BUSINESS. NOT AVAILABLE TO COMPLY WITH
> REQUEST. WILL HOLD MONEY AWAITING
> FURTHER INSTRUCTIONS. NELLIE PETERS,
> SECRETARY, PARKER COMPANY

She stood, and the house seemed terribly empty. And she knew why it was, as surely as if a note had been left for her spelling it out.

Then one of her men rushed in and came to her side, saying, "Nobody around. The buggy's gone. What's goin' on, Miss Cullen?"

"My father," she said, "has gone off to try to stop Harry Gauge himself."

CHAPTER FOURTEEN

His name was Caleb York.

He had come to Trinidad by happenstance, on his meandering way to California, where in San Diego the Pinkerton people were holding a position for him.

Well, "holding" was too strong a word—more like an open invitation, based upon his days as a Wells Fargo detective, during which time he'd made a certain reputation. As a sleuth, yes, but more so as a shootist.

That latter reputation had become a burden in some respects—particularly when crazy gunhands, young mostly, tried to make their own name by killing him. Pushing forty, he was getting old for the game, and when a shotgun-mangled body had been misidentified as him in Silver City, he had done nothing to correct the impression. He was fine with letting his "killer," Wes Banion—whom he'd never met other than by bad reputation— bask in the glory of being the man who gunned down Caleb York.

A few people he cared about—such as his highly placed pal with the Pinkertons, and a few relations—knew the story was false. Knew that Caleb York was alive and well, just not bragging about it. He had shaved his mustache, and taken to wearing nicer clothing than he'd ever allowed himself. Sure, people called him a "dude," but nobody bothered with drawing down on a dude.

At least not till Trinidad, New Mexico.

Before arriving in Sheriff Harry Gauge's town, he'd been enjoying his status as a "dead" man, despite an awareness that after his "death," his legend only grew. But ever since he'd ridden into this fear-choked town, he'd been dealing with people who either wanted to know more about him than he cared to share, or flat out wanted him *truly* dead.

He knew it didn't help that he never used some other name, something common like Smith or Jones. But to him an alias was something for bad men to hide behind.

And Caleb York, however many bad men he might have gunned down in his day, did not view himself as a bad man.

In part, that simple reluctance to admit who he was, and that Caleb York still breathed, had brought him to this fateful hilltop where he bent beside a dance-hall queen who'd decked herself out in riding clothes and come looking for him. Kneeling next to him, she looked down with him upon the Brentwood Junction relay station, a stop-over for stages to take on fresh horses and give thirsty passengers an opportunity for the wetting of whistles.

The woman he knew only as Lola—she had never given him a last name (but then he had never given her a name at all, so who was he to judge?). They'd had the kind of relations a man had with a woman who worked in a saloon. He'd paid her nothing but felt something—something for her as a woman who in a kinder world might have known a much better life.

She had caught up with him on the road—he'd come mostly overland, cutting over within two miles of the relay station—to warn him of what he was facing. She led him back over rough country to this hill where they had a good view of the small cluster of shabby weathered-gray structures—barn with stable wings, corral where half-a-dozen horses roamed, relay-station main building itself. Near the latter, two horses hitched to a buggy were tied up out front. On the ground between the corral and the relay station lay the crumpled form of a man, almost certainly dead.

York was using binoculars. "I count three on guard. One at the barn, another at the corral, another roaming. I think the dead man is one of Gauge's."

"Let me see."

He handed her the glasses and she looked. "Yes. His name is Watters. No great loss. But that buggy— it's Old Man Cullen's."

"I know."

She handed the glasses back. "You can bet Gauge is inside, and Rhomer, too, plus another three or four. That's six or seven men, stranger. Too many."

"It's always like that."

She touched his shoulder and he looked at her looking at him.

"You can't just ride into an armed camp," she said sternly. "And that's just what you would've done if I hadn't caught up with you first."

He gave her something close to a smile. "I know. Thanks. Tell me—why did you bother warning me?"

She rolled the dark, pretty eyes. "Let's say Harry Gauge and I fell out. See where it's red near my ear? And you saw firsthand how there's no love lost between Vint Rhomer and me."

"That the only reason?"

Her smile seemed sweet and wicked at once. "Maybe I'll tell you someday."

"Something to look forward to."

She nodded toward the relay station. "What's your plan?"

He gazed down there. "Take out those watch-dogs, one by one."

She frowned at him. "You start shooting and guns will come streaming out of that main build-ing, firing back. Or cut you down from the win-dows."

He shook his head. "No shooting. I have a Bowie knife in my saddlebag."

The lush lips worked up a smirk. "You don't hardly seem like the type to kill a man with a blade."

He grinned at her. "Yeah? And what was a nice girl like you doin' working in the Victory?"

She smiled wider, moving her beauty mark up. "Fair point. But you might still attract attention. I have a better idea. First I'll go down there. Ride in and see what they're up to."

He was already shaking his head. "That's a terri-ble notion. They might well figure you headed out this way to warn me or, worse, the Cullens. What about falling out with Gauge?"

"Oh, I can still talk my way in. I'll just say Harry made me mad when he hit me, and I rode off, like women in a tizzy are known to." Her tone was arch now. "And how now I'm rushing to his side to make it up to him."

"He won't buy it, Lola."

Now she looked away from him. "That isn't all I'm going to tell him. He doesn't know about

Rhomer the other night. How Vint tried to take me, and roughed me up trying."

"But if you and Gauge are really over . . ."

She shook her head. "Harry doesn't like *anybody* moving in on his property . . . even if it's 'property' he's grown tired of."

"And, you'll what? Get them to fighting?"

She shrugged. "Well, there isn't any other way, is there? If they're distracted inside, you can do what you need to outside. It won't be long before that stage arrives, and *then* where will you be?"

"No. Lola, no. . . ."

She got up and scurried toward the little nearby cluster of bushes where they'd left their two horses. He followed her, protesting, but she kept batting it away.

"When you see me go in there," she said, ready to place boot in stirrup and mount, "you can make your move."

"You don't need to do this."

A lovely smile blossomed. "What, and stay up here and watch you go to work with a knife? Don't you know I'm squeamish?"

She kissed him on the mouth lightly, turning toward her horse, and he swung her around by the arms and returned the kiss, only harder, with the kind of passion they'd briefly ignited the one afternoon they'd spent together.

Then they stood near each other, catching their breath.

Finally she said, "Thanks, stranger." Something melancholy swam in her eyes. "Even though I know who your kisses *really* are for. But maybe she won't miss just that one."

And she mounted and rode off.

Back on the rutted road to Brentwood Junction—as the juncture of this and the one to Las Vegas was called—Lola passed by a hill from behind which a figure on horseback rode out to fall in alongside her.

Gauge's man Cole Colton, in his oversized sugarloaf sombrero, gave her a sideways glance and a lazy, thin-mustached grin. "Afternoon, Lola."

"Somethin' I can do for you, Cole?"

"Nope." He nodded toward the relay station. "You're doin' fine. Just keep on ridin'."

Maybe she couldn't do anything for him, but Colton had done something for her—he'd left his post and made it easier for the stranger to work his way down to the relay station's buildings.

They rode in past the posted guards—barn and corral—as well as the fallen Gauge underling, Watters, who'd apparently been killed when Old Man Cullen's buggy rolled in and got waylaid. But she didn't ask. Another guard was walking the grounds, rifle over his arm. They had all been part of the outlaw bunch that Gauge headed up in the old days—"deputies" now.

She and Colton hitched their horses by the buggy outside the modest building with its saloon-style batwing doors. She'd been there before and knew what to expect—short bar to the left, open area straight ahead, dining tables at right. Tucked back behind the bar was an excuse for a kitchen. This low-ceilinged way station was unpainted and functional, and might be called "rustic," if you were generous of spirit.

What greeted her within, however, was an unexpected, unnerving tableau.

She was barely inside, Colton close behind her, when she froze at the sight of a slumped George Cullen on the floor, shoved up against a table and chairs, his legs out in front of him, upper right thigh soaked scarlet, his face battered and swollen, clothes badly mussed, the unseeing eyes puffed near shut, his thinning white hair a tangle. To one side of him a man appeared to be resting his head in Cullen's lap. But this was the shot-up corpse of a ranch hand, whose hair his employer stroked like a slumbering cat. Soothing the dead man, whose torso was riddled with bullets.

Leaning against the bar, with a bottle of whiskey between them on the counter, were a bug-eyed, shaggy-mustached Clovis Maxwell and a grinning, redheaded Rhomer, blood spattered on his buckskin vest and his gray shirt, too, where his deputy badge was pinned as if in defiance. Both were laughing and loose in that drunken way that led so easily to violence among this breed. Each had his hat pushed back on his head and his revolver tied down and slung low on his hip.

No sign of a bartender or whoever ran the way station. Was he or any helper dead in the kitchen? Tied up or huddled there? Or had they been run off? Who knew?

"Well, now!" Rhomer said, yellow teeth peeking out of bristly red. "The lovely Lola! What an honor! Such a fine lady. Might I tempt you with a libation?"

He said this while sloshing more whiskey into his own glass.

She stepped deeper into the grubby space, dirty floor whining under her boots. Pools of clotting blood were here and there, like some terrible dish had been spilled on its way to the dining tables.

She met Rhomer's sneering gaze with a blank one. Kept her tone business-like. "Where's Harry?"

The deputy gestured with his glass toward the outside, spilling a little. "He went on up the road to meet the stage. Y'see, when we seen you ridin' off, we figured maybe you heard us talkin' about comin' out here to greet the buyers. Well, Gauge didn't want to take no chances. . . . She come alone, Cole?"

Colton nodded. "Yep. All by her lonesome."

Drink still in his right hand, Rhomer curled the forefinger of his left, wiggling it, as if summoning a child. "Come here, lovely Lola. Have that drink."

She just looked at him.

"Come on, darlin'. I won't bite. Have a drink."

Not caring to rile him, she came over slowly. "No thanks. I'll wait for Harry and have one then."

"No. Have it now."

He splashed the drink in her face.

The whiskey burning her eyes, she barely saw the hand that came around to slap her, viciously. She went down on her knees, the flooring crying out when she didn't.

Eyes wild, he loomed over her. "What did you *do*, Lola? Ride out and try to find the others to warn 'em? But you *couldn't*, could you? They's all out on the range. You know, honey—'where the deer and the antelope play'?"

He slapped her again and her mouth filled with the coppery taste of blood.

Hovering over her, he said, "No, it's just you and me now, honey. Not even Harry's around to have an opinion."

"Keep . . . keep away from me."

"I don't think I will. See, if I see somethin' in the street that somebody tossed away, like it was garbage? Sometimes I think I can still see some *use* in that somethin'."

"Harry will kill you."

Rhomer shook his head. "I don't think so. I don't think he gives a diddle-doodle damn about you, no more, sweet thing. And, anyway, like I said—Harry ain't here."

She tried to kick him between the legs, but he blocked it, and came in and began to beat her with his fists. The blows and pain that followed seemed to come from everywhere. She began to reel from it, and soon was praying for unconsciousness.

"No, no, no . . . now don't you go to sleep, honey. Daddy's not through tucking you in yet."

Not far away, from where he slumped, Cullen cried out, "What are you *doing* to her? Leave her alone, you miserable bastard! If I could see, I'd . . . I'd . . ."

"Who knows?" Rhomer cackled, taking off his gun belt and tossing it on the bar. "You might just *enjoy* what you'd see, old man. Might bring back memories."

The old man's voice was a whisper, but a whisper with spine in it. "Leave her alone. If you are any kind of man, Rhomer . . . leave her alone."

"Sorry, no can do. But along them lines, Mr. Cullen, sir, I'm about to show this ravin' beauty what kind of man *I* am. But first I got to . . . kind of *pound* on her a mite more. You know, like when you're making a tough piece of beef more tender?"

He leaned down and hit her, again and again. She became groggy with pain, then began to grow numb from it and to it. Then he rose and began to unbutton his pants.

Colton was grinning wetly, eyes bright. "*Give* it to her, Rhomer!"

Maxwell was next to him, buggy eyes even bigger than usual. He said nothing, but was licking his lips.

Rhomer frowned at them, as if he'd forgotten they were there; maybe he had. "Get the hell out, you two. Nobody needs to be lookin' at me but that *blind* man, okay? Anyway, you birds go out there and get that body buried, before the stage rolls in. Plant it out back."

"Awww," they said as one, and went sullenly out through the swinging doors.

Then Rhomer grinned down at her. "Bet you wish you was dead about now."

"So . . . so much," she said.

"You know what they say—'if wishes was horses, beggars would ride.' "

And he began ripping at her clothes.

The guard on the barn was heavyset but sturdy, tall, clean-shaven, in a tan Stetson and a black shirt with denims tucked in tooled boots. He stood with his hand on the butt of a Colt dragoon revolver, alert, not missing a thing passing in front of him.

But he didn't see—or hear for that matter— Caleb York enter through the barn's rear doors and come up behind him, where the guard stood with his back to the front ones. York pulled him quickly inside, nudging the doors shut again with a foot, then he drew the Bowie blade across the man's throat, sending a stream of blood across barnwood.

From experience York knew the blood would spray forward, so it was no surprise that there wasn't a drop of the stuff on the tan Stetson that he borrowed from the dead man, tossing his own aside.

York had been lucky—the guard on the barn was the easiest to come up behind, and on top of that wore a black shirt and bore a superficial resemblance to the man who'd just killed him—clean-shaven, tall, a revolver low on his right hip. Everything but the pearl buttons and gray collar and cuff trim.

In the tan Stetson now—leaving his shotgun behind, too, since the guard hadn't been holding one—he eased over to the corral and the man posted there. This guard was short but burly, wearing typical cowhand garb down to the leather chaps, and cradling a double-barreled shotgun—a twelve-gauge, like York's own back in the barn.

That might prove lucky as well, since the cartridges in his pocket would work in that weapon as well.

Strolling over to the cowboy, York kept his head slightly lowered—the resemblance didn't carry *that* far—and the man asked, "What is it, Sam? Somethin' up?"

York raised a forefinger of his left hand as if to say, "Just a minute," and when he got close enough, put that left over the guard's mouth as with his right he shoved the Bowie deep into the man's belly.

Stepping slightly to one side, York made a circular motion with the inserted blade, opening him up, then let the dead man fall onto what had emptied out of him.

York started dragging the gutted figure on its belly by the elbows to hide him behind a nearby trough, leaving a snail-like trail.

When the final watchdog, the one who roamed, came around from in back of the relay station building, he saw York, who was only halfway to the trough with his cargo. With much of the relay station frontage between them, the man contorted his face as he raised his Winchester, taking aim.

But York's swift sideways throw of the Bowie caught the guard in the chest and rocked him back, rifle fumbling from his fingers and clunking to the ground. Still on his feet, the guard wavered, his mouth dropping open and his eyes popping wide, though he had nothing to say and nothing to see. He fell backward with the knife extended from him like a handle.

York moved quickly to him, not running, because the hard-packed earth of the apron where stages pulled up might give heavy footfall away. He removed the knife and dragged the body behind some barrels, leaving it there. Then—hearing conversation and something else . . . digging?—he crept around the near side of the weathered gray building, keeping low, knife in his fist.

Plastering his back to the sidewall, he peeked around and saw two men, each with a shovel, digging a grave. The ground appeared fairly hard and they were only two feet down or so. Nearby, on its back like a drunk after a very hard night, lay the corpse of one of their own—identified by Lola as Watters.

York considered: *Two at once with a knife? Both men with tied-down sidearms?*

How could he manage that?

Maybe he should go back for one of the shotguns, either his own in the barn or the dead guard's at the corral. While he tried to come up with something, they made the hole a little deeper and one of the men, a bug-eyed character in a low-crowned plainsman hat, threw his shovel down.

"*You* finish it, Colton. I'm headin' back inside. I am dry as this damn hole."

"Better stay put, Maxwell," the other one advised, his smallness emphasized by his absurdly wide-brimmed sugar-loaf sombrero. "The show in there might not be over yet, and Vint don't seem to want no audience."

York did not like the sound of that.

"That's his problem," Maxwell said, and threw down his shovel with a clang. "I need a drink."

York tensed, but Maxwell headed back around the other way. That meant, coming around front of the building, the ex-shoveler might notice that neither the barn nor the corral guard was at his post.

Well, York thought, *one knife per one man has been working just fine. . . .*

But the bug-eyed gunman didn't notice, moving quickly, heading through the batwing doors, single-minded in pursuit of that drink.

York went back to where the other shoveler, Colton, was still at work, his sombrero off now. The man was muttering to himself, pausing to wipe sweat from his brow with the back of a hand. Then he got back to digging.

Knife in hand, York slipped up behind the digger, who was still down in the hole—maybe three feet deep now—but Colton, pausing in his work, sensed something and whipped around, swinging the shovel. York jumped back, dirt flying, the shovel missing him but knocking into the blade and jarring the Bowie from his grasp. The big knife tumbled away and the man swung the shovel again.

But York caught it by the handle, jerked it from the man's grasp, and swung it himself, like a bat, with the back of the shovel smashing the man's face in, snapping teeth like brittle twigs and jamming the bones of the digger's nose up into his brain. The little man's close-set eyes rolled up with mostly white showing as two blood trails trickled out and curved left and right, making his mustache red, and he flopped backward into the hole he'd dug.

A perfect fit.

York leaned in to make sure the digger wasn't breathing—he wasn't—then dumped the shovel in with the more recent corpse before tossing the sombrero over the hideous crushed-in thing that had been a face.

Clovis Maxwell came in through the batwing doors and what he saw tightened his belly. He had seen much and laughed at things that sickened most men. Yet this turned his stomach.

The dance-hall woman, Lola, was on the floor, sobbing, her clothing torn, tattered, bloody. Her face was a mess, bruised and bleeding, eyes swollen, hair an awful witch's tangle.

Breathing hard, Rhomer was standing over her, tucking his shirt into his pants. She was crawling away from him, apparently trying to get to the end of the bar, maybe so she could get back behind there like the wounded animal she was and die in peace.

Rhomer, a cheek scratched and trickling red, grinned over at him. "You *did* miss a good show, Clovis boy."

Maxwell made a face. "I wasn't invited, remember? Hell, looks like you didn't leave much for me."

He barked a laugh. "That's more than what's gonna be left of Cullen here, if he don't come to his senses."

Rhomer stepped over the broken, crawling creature that Lola had become and approached Cullen, slumped on the floor, the dead ranch hand's head still in his lap. The old man looked dazed, his unseeing face masked in horror.

Rhomer said, "Too bad you can't see the lovely Lola, Cullen. Then you'd know for sure what'll happen to you unless you sign them cows over to us."

The blind man tried to talk, but it took several tries before he got out, "It . . . it wouldn't do you a damn bit of good, anyway."

Frowning, Maxwell asked, "What's the old man mean by that, Rhomer?"

"No idea," Rhomer admitted. The front of his gray shirt was splotched with the woman's blood.

From the floor, Cullen said in defiance, "Every one of my stock, every inch of my land, is in my daughter's name. You lousy, filthy piece of scum . . . you and Harry Gauge and the rest won't get one damn *head* of it."

"I wouldn't bet on that, old man."

From the batwing doors came: "What odds would you give me, Rhomer?"

York pushed through, shotgun barrels first— weapon on loan from the late corral guard.

Rhomer lurched toward his holstered gun where it, in its belt, lay on the bar. Maxwell, standing near York's end of the bar, had his hand on his gun, half-drawing it, when the man with the shotgun again spoke.

"Got a barrel for each of you fellas," he said, "and I won't even have to aim much."

Both men turned into statues, then each man's

eyes went to the other's, and instinctively both sent their gaze past York to the world outside.

York shook his head, letting them stare into the twin black eyes of the shotgun—eyes that stared right back at them. "Nobody out there to come to your rescue, boys. Just a whole lot of dead men. You're gonna want to put 'em up now."

Rhomer, scratched face still bleeding, let out a deep sigh and his eyelids went to half-mast as his hands went up all the way. Maxwell already had hands raised.

Keeping his eyes on both men, York angled over to Cullen sitting on the floor, cradling the head of a dead friend in his lap. The old man's upper leg was soaked red.

"How bad?" York asked him, half-kneeling.

"Not bad. Think the bleeding's stopped." The sightless man stroked the dead man's hair. "Lou caught a bad one, though." Then the milky eyes widened. "What about my daughter . . . ? Is Willa all right?"

"Should be fine," York said. "She's with your men out looking for the herd."

Cullen sighed in relief. Then he nodded toward something he couldn't see, but where his blind man's well-tuned hearing told him it was.

"You need to help her," the rancher said, pointing.

Back there, tucked between the end of the bar and the wall, lay what had once been a beautiful woman. She was breathing, heavy and irregular, but nothing else indicated she might be alive. Her clothing was torn, ripped to tatters, and her flesh was patched purple with bruising, her face a mass of welts and cuts and swollen tissue, her eyes all but disappearing into puffy bulges slitted only ever so slightly. Her right arm hung at an impossible angle, loose as a broken shutter.

He went to her.

In his concern, he did not see Rhomer and Maxwell exchange glances, getting ready to find their moment. . . .

He asked, "Rhomer do this to you?"

She managed a nod.

York stood, startling the two men, ending whatever impromptu move they might have been planning. He pointed the shotgun at Rhomer, who stood perhaps eight feet away. Maxwell was several feet beyond and to Rhomer's left. Not far from the doors.

Gesturing with the shotgun, York indicated the gun belt on the bar. Rhomer narrowed his eyes, as if to say, *You mean . . . get it? Put it on?*

And York nodded.

The deputy had to think about that for a moment, but then, very slowly, he did it. Right down to strapping down the holster to his leg.

"Back up a little," York said casually, still training the shotgun on him.

Rhomer did so, hand hovering over the holstered .44.

York bent at the knees, set the shotgun down,

and rose, his hand above the butt of his .44. He and Rhomer were now facing each other in classic showdown stance.

Drunk enough not to be afraid, Rhomer grinned and said, "Before we end this, mister . . . who the hell *are* you, anyway?"

"The man who's going to kill you," York said.

Rhomer's hand was on the butt of the .44, but the weapon was only an inch out of its holster when the sound of another .44 filled the small room like cannon fire, shaking glass, rattling chairs.

The deputy rocked on his feet, trying to maintain his balance, then glanced down and looked at the hole in his badge and the stream of red trickling out and down.

"Hell," he said.

Then he collapsed in a pile.

"And welcome to it," York said.

Maxwell had his hands up. "Don't shoot! I didn't touch her! I *swear*!"

"Toss the gun to one side—gentle. Don't want it going off."

Maxwell complied.

"Now get on the floor. Like you're taking a nap. Do it."

Maxwell did it.

"Stay right there."

Cowering, Maxwell nodded his head.

Gun in hand, York returned to Lola, knelt near her. "How bad is it?"

Her mouth made something awful that might be a smile. "Can't . . . can't you see?"

"What I see might could heal. How bad?"

Tiny head shake. "*All* bad, stranger. He's killed me. I'm torn up inside."

He started to rise. "I'll get the doctor."

She reached for his arm, gripped as best she could, bringing him back down. "Don't . . . don't bother. It's too late. I . . . I can feel it."

That was when Harry Gauge burst in, grinning big, the barrel of his .44 dimpling the neck of a terrified Willa Cullen.

CHAPTER FIFTEEN

York, kneeling at the side of the battered Lola, looked up at the crazed, grinning face of the big blond sheriff, who stood poised just inside the doors with a squirming Willa blocking much of him, his left hand holding on to a shoulder of hers, his right pressing the snout of that .44 into the side of her throat.

York's eyes went to Willa's.

She was terrified, breathing hard, but she did not look otherwise harmed—her straw-yellow hair, in a ponytail earlier, was disarrayed and down brushing her shoulders now, and there was a smudge or bruise on a cheek. So Gauge hadn't roughed her up much.

York would kill him, anyway.

The bug-eyed Maxwell was getting up, retrieving his gun, saying, "That's what I call the nick of time, Harry." Then he positioned himself near the end of the bar and trained his revolver on York, who was still bending down near the shattered dance-hall queen.

The blind old man on the floor had finally abandoned his dead helper, pushing the corpse off to one side; though with his shot-up leg, Cullen himself wasn't going anywhere.

Rather pitifully, the old man demanded, "What the hell is going on, Gauge? What the hell are you up to?"

York said, in a near-soothing voice, "He's got your daughter, Mr. Cullen. She's his prisoner. Try to stay calm. I'll handle it."

That made Gauge laugh. "*Will* you now? Big words."

"Papa," Willa called, "I'm all right!"

Of course, she sounded anything but.

Moving her a few steps into the dreary space, Gauge glanced at his dead deputy and said, "I see you took care of Rhomer for me, stranger. Well, poor Vint was what you call a weak link—probably best I'm rid of the fool."

"You're welcome," York said.

Gauge grunted a laugh. "All right, stranger . . . just toss that gun away from you—easy does it. If it hits the floor and fires, I'll fire, too."

York did as he was told, the weapon skittering past chairs under a table, well out of reach now.

Gauge nodded toward the twelve-gauge on the

floor. "Now that shotgun? Kick it over that way, too, gentle. Where nobody can get hurt with it. No tricks, now."

This York also did, though the bigger weapon went a shorter distance, maybe four feet.

Then he began to get to his feet.

But Gauge shook his head and said, "No, no, no, stay right down there. You're just *fine* right where you are." He gave Maxwell a quick look. "Go over and search him. Careful—he's got a knife on him. Slit a bunch of throats outside." He laughed again. "Didn't know you had it in you, dude."

"I'd rather it was in you," York said pleasantly.

Maxwell went over and patted York down, finding the Bowie knife in a sheath stuck into his pants in back. The big-bladed weapon got tossed off under the tables, as well. Gauge's man found shotgun shells in York's pockets, and these Maxwell also tossed.

The flunky glanced back to Gauge for further orders.

Gauge—holding on to the girl, who was squirming even more now, or, anyway, as much as she dared with the cold nose of a gun in her neck—said, "Good job, Maxwell. Now soften him up some. Just for fun. Maybe start by showin' him how you took care of ol' Swenson."

Maxwell grinned and pistol-whipped York, who fell onto his side, the inside of his head exploding with pain, eyes squeezed shut so as not to miss any of the Fourth of July fireworks in his skull.

But he wasn't unconscious, and was all too aware that Willa was pulling forward and screaming, "*No!* . . . Please *don't!* Leave him *alone!*"

Above him, Maxwell was saying, "This S.O.B.'s got a harder head than old Swenson."

York's eyes made themselves open and he saw Willa really fighting now, much more than squirming, really pulling away from Gauge, who finally just shoved her off him.

"Shut up!" Gauge growled at her. "Get over there!"

She fell, sliding on the floor and almost bumping into her father, who sensed her presence, reaching for her, taking her in his arms.

But she was looking toward the groggy York, hair at the back of his head damp with blood, and started scrambling toward him.

"Willa," her father said, grabbing her by an arm, stopping her with considerable force for his age and condition, saying, "stay away from him!"

"Let me go, Papa! Let me *go!*"

But he didn't, and York lifted his head—a feat no harder than clearing a boulder from a mountain path—and managed to raise a hand and weakly gesture for her to stay back. Stay back.

She did, chin crinkling, trembling all over, but not crying. Not letting herself do it. Warmth for her spread through York, part of it pride, part something else.

With another awful grin splitting his face, Gauge said to Cullen, "You are showin' some damn good sense, old man. Might be that we can do some business, after all."

Maxwell was working York over, fists to the body, occasional kicks to the side and legs—more of that "softening up" his boss had requested.

York's head would not stop spinning. He was fighting to retain consciousness.

"That's *enough!*" Gauge yelled. "Hell, man! Leave somethin' for me."

His head throbbing with pain, his breath ragged and heavy, York sat on the floor, in loose Indian style, Lola behind him a ways and to his right. He could hear her harsh, irregular breathing, whimpering mixed in.

Maxwell, spurs jangling, grinned cockily as he went over to Gauge's side. Then his expression turned curious. "Boss, what about that stage? I thought you went off to catch up with it."

Gauge waved that off. "It'll be here in half an hour or so. Gives us time to get things ready."

"Get ready how, boss?"

Gauge ignored the question, instead nodding over to where the old man and his daughter sat side by side on the floor, the corpse of their fallen ranch hand just behind them now.

"Before I could get to the stage," Gauge said, gesturing, "I ran into this little lady. Figured bringin' her back here was the thing to do."

"It surely was, Harry. And are you damn lucky you did!"

"Yeah?"

Maxwell nodded vigorously. "Turns out her old man over there signed the herd, hell, the whole damn *spread* over to this little girl of his. *That's* why." He pointed toward Willa. "She's the only one you can get a signed paper from. All the old man's good for is convincin' her to sign."

Gauge was grinning down at the Cullens. "Maxwell, where brains is concerned, you are a real step up from our late compadre Vint."

Pleased with himself, Maxwell stroked his droopy, dark mustache. "Mighty nice of you to say, boss. Think maybe with Rhomer gone, you might consider takin' on a new partner . . . ?"

"Well, you're my number two man today."

That put a big smile on Maxwell's face, the man not putting together that only the two of them were still standing.

Gun in hand, Gauge ambled nearer to Willa and her father, who remained huddled on the floor against the shoved-askew table and chairs. He loomed over them.

"Of course, when it comes to partners," Gauge said, with a little smile, "I think Miss Cullen here knows who I *really* have in mind."

Chin up, eyes cold, she said, "I won't sign a thing over to you. Not a damned thing."

"Such foul language from so sweet a girl. Sure about that, sugar?" He aimed his .44 past her, at her papa's head. "I suppose, in a way, it's kind of a blessin' that your daddy won't be able to see it comin'. . . ."

She hugged her father protectively, trying to shield his body with hers.

Gauge chuckled, then sat down at the table that father and daughter were leaned against. He set down his .44 close to him and, from an inside pocket of his vest, brought out a paper and a pencil.

"I'd prefer ink," Gauge said, slightly disappointed. "And eventually we'll go to the bank and put together some real pretty documents. For now, though, this'll just have to do. . . . Come on, honey. Sit with me."

He gestured to the chair beside him.

Willa scowled up at him, but her father nodded to her and, her face ashen, she rose and took the chair at the table. Gauge pushed the document and the writing implement toward her.

"Go ahead," he said, friendly, reasonable. "Read it over. You'll see I've arranged for you to keep the house. I won't move in there till you ask me to."

She looked at him, agape. "And you really think I *will*?"

"That blind old man on the floor? He was a *real* man, once upon a time. The kind of hard, ruthless frontier sort that can carve something out of nothing." Gauge shrugged. "Not too many of 'em left these days, and, well, hell, he's well past it."

Her eyes were wild. "If you think after forcing me to sign this, I would ever—"

"I think when this husk of a man that your father has turned into finally dies . . . and I won't harm a white hair on his head, if you sign this . . . you'll look around and see what *I've* done. What I've accomplished. You'll want your land back. Your life back. And I will be waitin', Willa . . . to give it to you."

She shook her head, astounded by him. "You really think anybody would believe I signed this of my own free will?"

"Well, first of all, you won't say otherwise. Because if you do, this old man will die hard and long and slow. I would imagine, in his time, he's done things to deserve that kind of death. So I won't feel too bad about it."

Her eyebrows climbed. "Can you really believe what you're saying?"

His manner became matter-of-fact. "*Everyone's* gonna believe what I'm sayin'. Look around, Miss Willa. See poor old Deputy Rhomer over there? He's gonna take the blame for all the bad things that happened today. He done me a favor, really, 'cause it's gonna look better this way."

"Better."

"Oh yes. See, he tried to take it *all*, take your herd and everything . . . even Lola over there. Look at her. She used to be a real beauty. An animal, that Rhomer."

Maxwell said, "I can be a witness, boss. I'll say it any way you want it."

The mustached gunhand was over by the bar, where he was training a revolver on the groggy man down at the other end. York remained slumped and reeling on the floor with Lola's barely conscious form not far away.

Gauge said, "I appreciate that, Maxwell. May come in handy. You could say how I arrived just in time to save the necks of our good friends, the Cullens here. I mean, after all—I *am* the sheriff."

Willa was shaking her head, amazed at Gauge's audacity. "And you think *I* will back up *your* story?"

"I would prefer it that you did." He picked up the .44 and aimed it down at her father on the floor. "But if need be, I will tell a sadder story— how I didn't get here till after Rhomer killed your daddy, *and* you."

"You . . . you wouldn't have your signature."

"Well, that's right. You'd both be dead. I'd have to go ridin' over to your ranch and find some examples of how you sign your name, and put somethin' like it on this document. You think I can't convince the Trinidad bank to back me up?"

She sat, frowned, mulling it.

Then she said, "And you'll let us go? You'll leave my father and me be? We'll have our house?"

He was nodding. "You got Harry Gauge's word on that. All I want is that herd. And I need it now. *Right* now."

She grabbed the pencil and signed the paper, and pushed them both back at him.

York was sitting up.

He said, "You shouldn't have done that, Willa."

Gauge, still seated, swung the .44 and its long barrel his prisoner's way.

Over by the bar, Maxwell, eyes glittering, said, "Go on and *kill* him, Harry! Blow his brains and then it'll be just you and me."

Gauge thought about that, then glanced at his new number two. "You know, I don't think so. I think I have all the partners I need right now."

The bug eyes widened even more. "Well, I just thought . . ."

"See, really, that's what I liked about Rhomer. He didn't think. He left me to do the thinkin'. And what I think right now is, you and Rhomer and all these other former outlaws scattered around these premises, dead, mostly thanks to our friend over here, well . . . With where I plan to go in my life, havin' such unsavory associates don't put me in an at all favorable light."

"Boss . . ."

"And I don't really need any witnesses to back me up, since who's to say somebody's story might not change, if it was to that witness's advantage? You follow me, Maxwell? Thinker that you are?"

"What are you sayin', Harry?"

"I'm sayin' goodbye, Maxwell."

And he shot him in the head.

The man was dead before his surprised expression could change. Gun tumbling from dead fingers, he slid down the side of the bar and sat on the floor, head hanging.

The room reverberated with the blast of the .44, gunsmoke drifting, leaving its scorched scent behind.

"You're out of your mind," Willa said to Gauge, horrified. "You said you'd let us go!"

"Hell, that didn't apply to *him.*" Gauge pushed back his chair and got to his feet. "*Mister!* Can you stand? I want you standing. Because I want to see you fall."

York struggled to his feet. When he got to them, he felt unsteady, and fought to maintain his balance, still woozy from the pistol-whipping.

"She's right, Gauge," York said.

"Is she? About what?"

"You *are* out of your mind."

Gauge ambled from the table to a position more directly facing the prisoner.

"Maybe I am," Gauge said. "Maybe not. Matter of opinion. But what are *you* besides mad, mister, comin' to Trinidad, tryin' to buck Harry Gauge?"

"I told you. I was just passing through."

"Sure you were." He used the gun for a pointing finger. "Listen, before I kill you, just answer me this. . . . I *know* you're not Banion. Banion's dead, that's a fact. So since you're *not* Banion . . . just who the hell *are* you?"

"Caleb York."

Willa's eyes widened, then immediately narrowed, as if she weren't sure she heard right. Just beside her on the floor, her father was straightening, saying, "What . . . what did he say?"

She whispered, "I don't know what he thinks he's doing, Papa."

"*You're* Caleb York," Gauge said.

"That's right."

"No, no—*you're* the crazy one. Banion killed Caleb York. It's well-known. Established."

York shook his head, just a little—more would have hurt too much. "Banion killed the wrong man," he said. "And he used a shotgun, and that . . . confused the issue."

Gauge thought about it. "All right . . . so you're Caleb York. Say I buy that. Why play dead?"

York sighed. "Because I got tired of shooting kids trying to take me. Trying to *be* me. Because . . ." He gestured to the carnage. "Because I wanted to be finished with this kind of thing."

Gauge grinned and laughed. "Oh, well, Caleb— mind I call you 'Caleb'? Caleb, you'll be gettin' your wish soon enough."

Cullen was muttering to himself, "Caleb York . . . all this time . . . Caleb York. . . ."

Willa spoke up, saying, "Gauge, you wouldn't have the *guts* to face Caleb York down if you *both* had guns."

Without looking at her, Gauge said, "It's not a question of guts, Miss Willa. It's a matter of brains. You don't want a stupid fool like Rhomer over there as your partner, do you?"

York said, "Sorry, Willa. He's just fine with shooting me down in cold blood."

Gauge nodded slowly. "You understand me, at least, Caleb. Killers under the skin that we are."

"Harry . . ."

The ragged, harsh, pain-racked voice belonged to Lola, from the floor where she looked almost as much a corpse as Rhomer and Maxwell. Worse than them, really, beaten and battered.

It was as if a ghost had spoken.

"Are *you* still alive?" he asked her coldly.

"We . . . we were something once, Harry," she said.

"Your opinion in this don't interest me, Lola. Stay out of it."

"Harry!" It was a desperate cry. "This man . . . this Caleb York . . . he was good to me. Like you *never* were."

Gauge grunted a laugh. Gun still pointed at York, he said, "You know, I'll give you this much, Caleb. You sure do make an impression on the ladies. They all go for you, in a big way . . . even when they're dyin'."

"Harry," she said. "Let me kiss him goodbye. . . . Would that kill you? . . . Let me die . . . with a kiss from somebody . . . who's a *real* man."

Gauge started to laugh. "Like anybody would want to kiss a face like that! Lips swelled like those! Go ahead, Caleb York. Have a ball!"

He gestured toward the broken woman, in an archly magnanimous fashion.

"You heard the lady, Caleb!" Gauge raved. "Give her a kiss goodbye. It'll be the last thing either of you do on this earth."

York looked at Gauge, cocked his head.

"I *mean* it! Go ahead, I said. My treat!"

York went to her, slowly, and knelt to her, putting his back to Gauge, who stood in the middle of the dingy room with the .44 waiting to fire in his hand.

Lola's eyes seized York's, then led him to her right wrist, and limp fingers that hung loose on her right arm, which itself hung loose, as it had been broken early in her humiliation. The cloth on her blouse was ripped, torn, and next to the flesh were exposed two narrow shafts of metal.

Parts of the gambler's trick sleeve rig that held the der-ringer that Lola, injured badly right away, had never been able to get to.

He leaned in to kiss her puffy lips, which he did ever so gently.

Then she smiled, life leaping in her eyes, as she whispered, "Hurry. I want to *see* it."

Impatient now, Gauge said, "That's enough! That's enough. You're makin' me sick."

York, the little gun palmed in his right hand, stood.

"Thanks for that, Harry," he said.

"My pleasure, Caleb."

York fired two .22 slugs into Gauge's chest.

The big man staggered, as if suddenly drunk, the .44 tumbling from his fingers.

"Those were for Lola," York said.

Then he went over and picked up the shotgun and aimed its barrels at Gauge.

"And these," he said, "are for me."

He emptied both into Gauge, who was blown back through the batwing doors and outside, his sudden exit leaving the doors swinging.

"Goodbye, Harry," Lola said.

York looked over at her. A mess of a woman. So beautiful.

"Goodbye, Caleb York."

Her eyes closed and breath left her.

Then Willa was there and they embraced.

In a few moments, York picked up the piece of paper Willa had signed, gave it to her, and they went out, his arm around her shoulders, her arm around his waist.

Harry Gauge was on his back with two overlapping bloody black steaming holes in his belly, as he stared up at the sky with an expression as stupid as anything Vint Rhomer ever mustered.

Willa tore up the signed paper and let the pieces drift like snow down onto the dead sheriff of Trinidad County.

"I told you I was just passing through," York said, smiling down at her.

"Are you sure?" she asked.

He had no answer. Just looked up at the sky.

Mid-afternoon now. Something drew his attention to a dust cloud in the distance.

He said, "Stage is coming. You'll be all right now."

Inside the drab way station, on a floor that had been squalid even before corpses cluttered it, sat an old man, no longer slouching, smiling now. He could see nothing, but he missed no sound—not the roll and rattle of an approaching stage, not the words exchanged between his daughter and a real man.

To nobody but himself, George Cullen said, "*Everything's* going to be all right now."

Don't miss the next exciting western
novel featuring Caleb York . . .

The Big Showdown

Coming soon from Kensington Publishing Corp.

Keep reading to enjoy a preview excerpt . . .

Caleb York was getting out of town on the noon stage.

Despite his reputation as a deadly gunfighter, York was not being run out of Trinidad, New Mexico, by the sheriff. After all, until very recently, York had been the sheriff here himself, a position he'd held down for six months until a replacement could be found for the previous holder of that office.

It was the least York could do for the dusty little community, considering he'd killed the man.

Not that Sheriff Harry Gauge hadn't needed killing—a petty tyrant seeking to become a cattle baron, a ruthless murderer that the West was well rid of. But removing Gauge from the Trinidad scene, on the heels of a cowpox epidemic, had left the town in something of a topsy-turvy mess. The

Trinidad Citizens Committee had asked York to pick up Gauge's badge, wipe the filth from it, and pin it on. At least for a while.

This York had done.

But now he'd found a suitable replacement in his old friend Ben Wade, who'd been a lawman in Kansas and Arizona, working alongside the likes of the Earp brothers and Bat Masterson. Even at fifty-some, Wade was twice the man of most anyone he was likely to come up against.

Right now York was walking down the boardwalk, its awning shading him from morning sun, mercilessly bright in a clear sky, though the temperature on this dry, lightly breezy September morning was around sixty degrees. He was on his way to the office that had been his till he turned it over to Wade last week.

Townspeople nodded at York, and he nodded back, casting smiles at the men, tipping his hat to the ladies. He was unaware that many of the latter turned to look at him as he passed, with wistful smiles and the occasional girlish giggle. Even from the older ones.

York indeed made a fine figure of a man, long of leg, broad of shoulder, firm of jaw, his hair reddish brown, his face clean-shaven, his features pleasant, rawboned, with washed-out blue eyes that peered out a permanent squint. He had settled easily into that vague space between thirty and forty when a man was at his best and, in the case of a Caleb York, his most dangerous. His Colt Single Action Army .44 rode his right thigh at pocket level, the holster tie loose and dangling; his spurs sang an easygoing, jingling song.

When he'd ridden into town last year, those who didn't know how to look at a man saw only a dude, and York still dressed in a manner unlike either the cowhands of the surrounding ranches that Trinidad served, or the shopkeepers who did the serving. York considered his somewhat citified attire professional, and it reflected the time he'd spent in big cities like Denver and Tucson.

But even Trinidad's few professional men—Doc Miller, the bankers, the lawyers—did not approach the sartorial flair of Caleb York, who wore black as did they, only with touches of style—gray trim on collars and cuffs, gray string tie, twin breast pockets, pearl buttons down his shirt, black cotton pants tucked into hand-tooled black boots, curl-brimmed black hat with cavalry pinch, gray kerchief knotted at the neck.

But ever since Caleb York had gunned down Gauge and half a dozen of his hardcase deputies, no one in Trinidad had called him "dude."

If pressed, he'd have admitted that he would miss this prospering little town of three hundred, and the surrounding ranchers and their families and hands who kept it thriving. Not that there was anything particularly special about the place.

One end of Main Street—the dust kept down by

a layer of sand brought in from the nearby Purgatory River—was home to a white wooden church, the other end a bare-wood livery stable, steeple and high-peaked hayloft mirroring each other. Between them was a typical collection of businesses—hardware store, apothecary, barber, hotel with restaurant, telegraph, saloon, café—false-fronted clapboards and now and then a brick building, like the bank.

As he neared the livery stable, York felt a twinge—his black-maned, dappled gray gelding was in a stall within that homely structure. The blacksmith, Clem Wiggins, would sell the steed and wire the proceeds to him in San Diego. It might take a while, because the animal was worth a small fortune—less than five hundred would be horse theft. But even twice that couldn't make up for the loss of a loyal steed like that.

He doubted he'd even need a horse in San Diego. That would likely be a city where you either walked or hopped an electric streetcar. Where the only horses you saw were attached to buggies or milk wagons. A different world, but a world he needed to learn to live in.

He was nearing the scarred, bullet-pocked adobe building that wore a high-up sign saying SHERIFF'S OFFICE AND JAIL. Across the way was a handful of smaller adobes, the homes and businesses of the town's modest Mexican population. He took the few steps up to the wooden porch, sheltered by an awning, and knocked at the rough-wood door, a solid thing that could help make the office a fortress when need be.

"It's open!" a deep voice boomed.

York went in and took off his hat.

The office was a plank-floored space with two barred windows onto the street, a wood-burning stove, and a rough-hewn table overseen by a wall of wanted posters and a rack of rifles. This was at left; at right was a big dark wooden desk with a chair behind it and a man in the chair.

Ben Wade was white-haired and white-mustached and wore his white flat-brim, Canadian-creased hat indoors as well as out, probably to hide where he was balding. Wade was a mite touchy about his age, since most gunfighters didn't live as long as he had. The lawman had a well-fed look that replaced the leanness York had first known in him, when Wade was a deputy marshal in Dodge City.

Wade, in a light blue shirt and tan cowhide vest, was making a cigarette. "Find a chair, Caleb," he said.

York pulled one up and sat down. "Nice to see a geezer like you with such a steady hand."

The sheriff licked the paper, finished making the smoke, and fired it up with a kitchen match. Waved it out. "You're not that young yourself, friend."

"No. I'm not. That's why I'm headed to the big town."

Wade shuddered. "Exactly where I don't want to be. Six years in Denver, working as a hotel house dick. You don't want to know the horrors I seen."

"Pay was good."

"Costs plenty living in a big town. You'll see. But your loss is my gain."

York gestured toward a window. "It's a decent little town, Ben. Your biggest worry is the handful of Gauge's men who're still out there. Gunnies pretendin' they're ranch hands."

He nodded. "You told me such enough times that I'm startin' to pay attention. But ex-gunnies have to make an honest living, too. Times have changed. Times are changing."

"Not that much, Ben, not in Trinidad. Maybe over in Las Vegas, since the train come in. But this little town—could be twenty years ago, and you'd never know it."

"Cowboys still get drunk on payday," Ben said, with a deep chuckle and nod of agreement, "and kids who read too many dime novels will always try to play gunfighter. And die young like those who went before them."

"Old gunfighters who hang on too long, they die, too. Don't forget that, Ben."

"Judas Priest, Caleb," the sheriff said, letting out blue smoke, leaning forward. "*You* got in touch with *me.* You got sudden second thoughts about leavin' this little slice of heaven? You tryin' to talk me out of this job? You want this badge, son, you'll have to rip it off my shirt. Because I am right where I want to be."

"How does Hazel feel about it?"

He flinched, took another deep draw on the smoke. "She's, uh . . . not happy. She likes her house in Denver. She likes her creature comforts. Our son and his daughters live there, you know."

"Hell. I didn't mean to bust up your happy home."

Wade shook his head. "She'll get over it. One of these days, the stage'll pull up and she'll step off. Mark my words. She was beautiful once, but now she's old and fat like me. She knows I'm the only man on God's good earth who looks at her with eyes that still see beauty. She'll show."

York twitched half a frown. "I hope you're right. I don't need *that* on my conscience."

Wade's laugh exhaled smoke. "Since when does Caleb York *have* a conscience? How many men you put down, anyways?"

"I don't rightly know."

Wade's mustached grin filled a bunch of his face. "Sure you do, son. Only the crazy ones don't keep track. You're hard, but you ain't crazy. How many?"

". . . Twenty-seven."

"Countin' the war?"

"Not counting the war, Ben. You never really know in war how many you put down."

"How do you sleep at night?"

"Fine."

"Bad dreams?"

"Only if I got a fever."

"Good. So I guess I can risk troubling your damn conscience. I got the job I want—this is how I want to spend my last working years. With a badge and a gun and a desk and a chair . . . and a hundred a month. More than that, with my cut of the taxes I collect."

"Much more. It's a good-paying job. I'm glad you're pleased. I hope Hazel comes around."

Wade was nodding. "She'll come around. She'll step off that stage. You'll see."

"Speaking of stages," York said, and stood. "I have one to catch, in about an hour."

Wade gave York another face-splitting grin. "I have a bottle in this desk, if it ain't too early for you. You can spend the rest of your time in Trinidad tellin' me how sorry you are you got me this job I so dearly wanted."

York grinned back, snugging on his hat. "No, I have an early lunch date."

"Certain pretty gal?"

"Certain pretty gal."

"And I reckon she's not real happy with you, is she, son?"

"No. Not happy at all."

"Well, then that's a knack we share."

"What is?"

"Disappointin' our womenfolk."

York gave his old friend a smile and a nod, then went back out into the pleasant morning. Last night, however, had not been so pleasant. That was when he'd told Willa Cullen that he would be leaving at noon today.

Both Willa and her father had been seated at the big carved Spanish-style dining-room table in the rustic ranch house of the Bar-O. They were having coffee in china cups.

Willa, typically, wore a red-plaid shirt and denims, her straw-yellow hair up and braided in back. Her mother had been Swedish and that came through in pretty features and an hourglass figure. Tall, sturdy of frame, Willa was feminine, but in a Viking kind of way. And right now she looked like she'd be pleased to send him to Valhalla.

Or maybe someplace more southern-ward.

Seated across from York, she met his news with cold eyes and flaming cheeks. At the head of the table sat her father, George Cullen, his white hair thin as desert grass, his eyes milky with blindness.

A big man made smaller by time, Cullen wore a white shirt and a black string tie, his strong, white-mustached face undercut by sunken cheeks, his flesh gray from too much time of late spent indoors. Blind men did not ride the range with their cow-hands, no matter how much they might want to.

The old man was first to respond. "I'm disappointed, my boy. I reckoned you and Willa here . . . I'd *hoped* . . ."

York said nothing, looking away from the man's milky gaze.

Cullen stuck out his hand, still rough from work, despite how little of it he'd been able to do these last few years. York shook the man's hand. Across from him, Willa was a pretty stick of dynamite trying not to explode.

"Won't be the same around here," Cullen said. "We've come to think of you as part of the family. Be that as it may, we remain in your debt. Without you, this ranch would be lost to us. That cur Harry Gauge might well be sitting here, where I am . . . and I would be under the ground."

"Hard to say," York said. "Your men were there, backing you. In a pinch, the townspeople came through. But I'm happy to have pitched in."

Willa's hands were clenched into small, trembling fists, held before her on the table like those of a child about to throw a tantrum. The red was fading from her cheeks, but her chin was crinkling and trembling and her eyes were tearing up.

Cullen was smiling, his blank eyes looking past York. "You know, my boy, I thought perhaps I might make a rancher out of you. With no son of my own . . ."

"You have Willa. She can run this ranch. She'd be better at it than most men. Maybe *any* man . . . because you raised her, Mr. Cullen."

Tears were rolling down the young woman's cheeks, but she made no effort to wipe them away, her hands still fists.

"You may be right," Cullen said. "But it's a hard road for a woman to travel alone. I won't be here forever. She'd be better with a man at her side. And perhaps one day she'll find herself one."

Willa got up, her chair scraping on the floor like a wheel coming off a wagon, startling her father, who bounced in his chair some.

Cullen said, *"Girl!"*

But she was already out of the room.

York said, "She's upset with me."

Cullen smiled. "Well, I don't need eyes to see that, son. Let her cool off some. Are you heading to San Diego? To that Pinkerton position you meant to fill, afore you got sidetracked in Trinidad?"

"That's right, sir. I'd be number two man in the office, but I won't be abandoned behind a desk. I'd be leading investigations. I'd be out on manhunts."

"I hope you know I wish you the best of luck. Should you get out there and it don't suit you, come back here to us. You'll always have a place at this table, and in our hearts."

York rose and rested a hand on the old man's shoulder and squeezed. Cullen put his hand on York's and squeezed back.

"Don't you go forgetting us now," the old man said.

"Not hardly."

She was on the porch in the moonlight. The ivory of it suited her. She'd wiped away the tears now, but her lush full lips were trembling.

"I'm sorry to just spring it on you," York said. "But you knew that I was just taking the sheriff post temporary."

She nodded. Swallowed. She either didn't want to speak to him or couldn't.

He risked a tiny smile. "Would you do a thoughtless lout a small favor?"

She glared at him.

"See me off tomorrow? The stage leaves at noon. Maybe we could have a late breakfast or early lunch—around eleven, there at the hotel?"

She said nothing.

"Would you do that for me, sweetheart?"

She turned toward him, eyes and nostrils flaring like a rearing horse. He might have slapped her, judging by the reaction.

But then she'd done something truly surprising: she nodded, and rushed back inside the ranch house.

When he exited the sheriff's office, York almost bumped into a familiar figure, standing there waiting like an eager puppy dog: that old desert rat Tulley, skinny and white-bearded, but that beard barbered now, and the baggy canvas pants washed in recent memory and under blue suspenders a clean BVD top. The bowlegged town character had dried out, at York's encouragement.

"I seen ya go in there," Tulley said in the good-natured rasp that was what was left of a voice ravaged by years of smoke and drink. "You don't think I'd let ya leave town without an *adios,* do you, Sheriff?"

The unlikely friendship between the two men had grown out of Tulley befriending the stranger who'd ridden into town and into the middle of nasty doings.

"I'm not the sheriff anymore," York reminded him.

"And a damn shame! Damn shame all around. You had a good thing goin' in this here hamlet, Sheriff. Good pay, respect, folks looked up to ye . . . and then there's that yellow-haired gal. You *know* when ol' Cullen finally up and croaks, that ranch'll be hers. You *do* know what you're walkin' out on, don't you?"

"I know, Tulley."

"And friends like Jonathan R. Tulley don't grow on trees neither, you know."

"I suppose not."

Tulley's face clenched like a fist. "Then to hell with you, Caleb York. I may jus' go back to drinkin', jus' find me a bottle and crawl back in, and whose fault will it be?"

"Mine?"

"*Yours!* Your and yours alone. So to hell with you, you selfish son of a bitch."

Then Tulley gave York a big, startling hug, and almost ran back to the stable. He might have been crying.

York was laughing, gently. Who'd ever have thought that *that* old reprobate would be one of the things he'd miss most about Trinidad?

He walked back to the hotel where he checked out and left his packed carpetbag with Wilson, the weak-chinned, pince-nez-sporting clerk who'd given him a register to sign, all those months ago. The .44 in its holster with cartridge-laden gun belt was tucked in the bag, right on top. No need for a weapon on his hip, riding on a stage or a train, not in these times. Why not be comfortable?

At eleven A.M., the hotel dining room, with its dark wood, fancy chairs, and linen tablecloths, was all but empty. A pair of business types were having a late breakfast of bacon and eggs, and a young lovey-dovey couple just passing through were having an early lunch of oyster stew, a specialty of the Trinidad House Hotel.

Willa was seated by the window, a vision in a mote-floating shaft of soft sunlight, looking not at all the tomboy or cowgirl, but the lovely young woman she was. No plaid shirt or Levi's today—she was in that navy-and-white calico dress that he liked so well on her. Nothing fancy, just a simple, feminine frock. That yellow hair was piled high with little curls decorating her smooth forehead.

Nothing of last night's girl holding back tears and anger could be seen in today's self-composed young woman. She even smiled when she saw him enter the dining room. He left his hat on a hook near the entry and joined her.

"Thank you, Willa," he said.

"For. . . ?"

"For meeting me. For seeing me off. I wasn't sure you'd come."

Her smile was a pursed thing, like a kiss she was about to throw. "Neither was I. But I felt I should apologize for my behavior last night."

"Nothing to apologize about."

She shook her head and all that glorious hair moved a little. "You never lied to me. You made it clear you would be leaving one day. One day soon. I had no right to think otherwise."

"Willa, this frontier life . . . it's going to be over one of these days. And I want something else. I haven't asked you to come with me because I knew you wouldn't."

Her eyebrows rose. "That's a little presumptuous, isn't it?"

"No. I know you're going to stick by your father. As well you should. Long as he's alive, and the Bar-O is chugging along, you need to be at his side. Perhaps some day, after he's gone . . . perhaps you'll decide running a ranch isn't for you."

Her eyebrows were back down, but the eyes themselves were half-lidded. "What else might I do with my life, Caleb?"

"You could join me in San Diego."

"Why—is there another position open with the Pinkertons?"

She was teasing him, but in a way that said, behind her adult attitude, the angry child still lurked.

"There's an opening for you, all right. As my wife."

A tiny laugh. "You're proposing marriage, minutes before boarding the stage out of town?"

He nodded. "I'm not offering you a ring. I'm not asking for a commitment. You are free to live your life."

She flushed a little. "Well, that's very generous of you, Caleb."

He reached across the table and touched her hand. That she did not draw it away from his was a relief.

"Sweetheart," he said, "if your feeling for me cools, if someone comes along who fits better into your life . . . is the right kind of man to run the Bar-O with you . . . I would never stand in your way."

She laughed just a little. Her eyes were sad but not tearing. "You have a peculiar way of telling a girl you love her, Caleb York."

"Well, I do, Willa. But the time has to be right. And the situation has to suit us both. Or we'll just be another one of these unhappy couples, hitched to each other like mules to a buckboard."

"No one sweet-talks like you, Caleb."

He shook his head. "I just can't ask you to wait for me. I won't be coming back to Trinidad."

"Not even to visit?"

"Well . . . maybe then. And maybe you could take a trip to San Diego on occasion. Very beautiful. Lots of ocean. Will you write me, Willa?"

"Will you write me?"

"Sure. With my well-known line of sweet talk."

They were smiling at each other now.

So they ordered lunch, both having the oyster stew—amazing what the cook back there could do with tins of those things—and Willa took tea, York coffee. They chatted, mostly about Willa's plans for the ranch. The buyers had paid well for the herd last spring and things were looking up.

"I'm a bit surprised," she said, "that you're leaving before Zachary Gauge gets to town."

Zachary was Harry Gauge's cousin, from somewhere back East, and word around Trinidad was that he'd inherited the late sheriff's property. Much speculation had been bandied about as to the cousin's intentions, since the sheriff had bought over half-a-dozen spreads in his efforts to secure the area's cattle trade, and had owned half interests in many of the town businesses.

York said, "I thought it best he and I not meet."

"Because you're the man who killed his cousin? Maybe he'll shake your hand—you're *also* the man who made him rich."

"Not so rich," York said.

The meal was done, dishes cleared, and they were on their respective second cups of tea and coffee.

"But he owns all of those spreads," Willa said. "That Harry Gauge made a powerful big landgrab, after all."

"Yeah, but the new owner will be cattle poor. The beeves were all destroyed, remember, because of the pox. And the business owners have hired a lawyer from Albuquerque to represent them in getting back control of their shops."

"Could they do that?"

York sipped coffee, nodded. "Our late, unlamented sheriff was running an extortion scheme. The shopkeepers of Trinidad were coerced into partnerships and then bullied into repaying 'loans' for the money Harry Gauge put up. They have a good case."

Willa sipped her tea, shrugged. "Well, any way you look at it, Zachary Gauge is going to own a lot of land. Control more of the range than the Bar-O and the remaining smaller spreads put together."

"Let's hope Zachary is a better man than his cousin."

She sat forward. Nothing but earnestness colored her voice now. "Don't you think you should stay, and find out? Wouldn't it depress you terribly to learn everything you and I and Papa and everyone went through, last year, was for naught?"

He smiled. "Darn good argument, Willa. You'll know where to find me if things get out of hand."

She smiled back. "I'll know where to find you. And you'll know where to find me."

The stage would be rolling in soon. He asked her to walk him out and she did, slipping her arm in his. He grabbed his hat off the hook and put it on. Just outside the hotel, on the boardwalk, with no one around, she took his hands in hers and looked up at him with a heartbreaking smile. There, in the middle of town, they were all alone.

"You do *know*, Caleb, that you could have . . . *been with me*, if you wanted. You know I feel that deeply about you. About this. About us."

He gave her a gentle smile. "Well, we did get a little frisky at times."

She blushed. But she said, "You could have had me, Caleb. You still could. You still *can*."

He touched her smooth cheek. "That can wait for our wedding night."

"It doesn't have to."

"It does. And, anyway—"

The sharp report of a handgun, only slightly muffled, stopped him, from across the street.

First Bank of Trinidad.

He took her in his arms, but not to kiss her, rather to spirit her inside where he said, "Get down. On the floor, now!"

She did. She'd been around gunfire before.

Another muffled gunshot. Yelling.

He flew to the check-in desk and the clerk was gone. Getting back around behind it, he found the little chinless buzzard cowering. But the carpetbag was right there, and York got into it, and yanked the Colt from its holster and ran out.

He hurtled the boardwalk railing and landed solid on the sand, .44 in hand, angled slightly up. Directly across the way, the three-story brick bank building sat imposingly on the corner. Out front at the hitching rail waited three black mustangs, looking calm as a millpond, unruffled by the sound of gunfire.

Not a good sign.

He'd barely landed when the first man blew out of the bank, running for his tethered horse; he wore jeans, a work shirt, the V of a red-and-black bandana kerchief covering his face from mid-nose down. On his heels came a second man, similarly garbed with a dark blue mask covering his lower face, dashing for his horse as well. The third man, also in work shirt, jeans, bandana kerchief mask (blue and white), came charging out, a six-gun in one hand and saddlebags stuffed with bank bags slung over his other arm.

The first one out never made it to his horse. York's .44 took the top of his head off, which flew away with the dead man's hat still on it. The robber fell near his horse, the animal so well-trained, so used to guns blazing, that a yawnlike whinny was its only reaction.

The second man got to his horse and on it and the animal was just about to gallop when its burden lessened, as two blasts from York's .44 caught him in the back, and he let go of the reins and fell off the saddle on the bank side of the street, but got dragged a ways before the horse, getting up a good head of steam now, broke free.

The last man, the saddlebags turned money-bags slung in front of his saddle's duck horn, was mounted already, York too busy killing his confederates to stop him from taking off. And while that shooting was going on, York was blocked from the third man by the two he was busy sending to hell.

Now the surviving robber was heading toward the livery, the horse already working some speed up.

That was when Sheriff Ben Wade barreled out of his office and down the steps to plant himself in the street in front of the oncoming man on horseback, the lawman taking aim with his Peacemaker. The rider swung around him but, as he did, fired once at the sheriff, with the ease of a marksman knocking a tin can off a fence post.

Then the rider was gone, cutting to the left, past the livery, where Tulley had come out with a shotgun in his hands but too late to do anything, hoofbeats receding.

The sheriff was just standing there, like he was thinking about what just happened, trying to make sense of it, weaving just a little. Then he went down all at once, like a house of twigs a child was building.

York went to the first one he'd shot, glanced down at the dead man, who was on his back with a soup of brains and blood emptied out of his ragged skull top, and kicked the weapon from limp fingers. He jogged to the other rider, the one the horse had dragged some, on his back with arms and legs going strange directions, and found the man at least as dead as his compadre, his six-gun lost in the shuffle.

Then York sprinted to Ben Wade, though he knew there was no hurry. The heavyset older man had wound up on his side, like a man sleeping who finally found a comfortable position, hat under him like an insufficient pillow. Some red had leaked from the hole in his chest across his vest and shirt and was soaking the sand, but no blood was flowing now. Dead men don't bleed.

Caleb York, the black he wore making him an instant mourner, knelt over the man he'd brought to town, to take his place, and he said a prayer for him. But at the end of it he didn't say, "Amen."

He said, "Goddamn."

Goddamn those who did this.

Townspeople were moving gingerly into the street, but Willa was moving quickly past the dead thieves, the bank president, and a clerk emerging with guns in hand—too little, too late—and over to York, who still knelt at his dead friend's side. She crouched near the man she loved, put a hand on his shoulder.

"Caleb, are you all right?"

"No."

"Lord! Were you hit?"

"No. But I'm not all right. I won't be till I bring in Ben Wade's killer."

York unpinned the badge from Wade's chest. Ben had said York would have to tear it off, if he wanted to take it back. But that wasn't necessary.

He stood, and Willa rose with him.

She asked, "Does that mean . . . you're staying?"

"For as long as it takes, I am."

She pinned the badge on him.